ME
AFTER

"Mind-blowing! *Find Me After* is a sharply ambitious, rip-roaring adventure through a haunting liminal space."

Brianna Bourne,
author of *You & Me at the End of the World*

"A gripping and imaginative story with an important message about epilepsy, as well as an irresistible romance – this had me hooked!"

Lauren James,
author of *The Loneliest Girl in the Universe*

Also by A. Connors

The Girl Who Broke The Sea

A. CONNORS

FIND
ME
AFTER

■SCHOLASTIC

Published in the UK by Scholastic, 2024
1 London Bridge, London, SE1 9BG
Scholastic Ireland, 89E Lagan Road, Dublin Industrial Estate,
Glasnevin, Dublin, D11 HP5F

SCHOLASTIC and associated logos are trademarks and/or
registered trademarks of Scholastic Inc.

ISBN 978 07023 3136 7

A CIP catalogue record for this book
is available from the British Library.

Printed and bound in Great Britain by
Clays Ltd, Elcograf S.p.A.
Paper made from wood grown in sustainable forests
and other controlled sources.

1 3 5 7 9 10 8 6 4 2

www.scholastic.co.uk

*For Meg, Gil and Evan – lodged in my
brain, as well as my heart.*

I wondered whether the Stillness on the face of the immensity looking at us was meant as an appeal or as a menace. What were we who had strayed in here? Could we handle that dumb thing, or would it handle us?

Heart of Darkness, Joseph Conrad

AUTHOR'S NOTE

While *Find Me After* explores all sorts of cool themes like the nature of reality, the fragility of life and the uniquely rubbish experience of waking up after an epileptic seizure, its primary purpose is to entertain. For that reason, I want to make sure that readers are aware of potentially upsetting content that might be triggering or disturbing to some.

This story explores the experiences of young people in an altered state of consciousness where unsettling transformations occur. It includes scenes of body horror, murder, threat and violence. There are depictions of seizures and their aftermath, as well as the physical and emotional toll of illness. This story also touches on questions of faith and religion in ways that might not resonate with all readers. And, finally, there are a handful of swear words where the intensity of the situation warrants it.

If that doesn't sound like your bag of eyeballs (oops, spoiler), this might not be the book for you. If you think you might enjoy exploring the darker corners of a liminal, eerie otherworld on the brink of life and death, where reality is not quite rooted in the physical world, and the not-quite-dead fight for survival … then come on in!

ONE

You know it's going to be a bad day when you wake and feel pavement against your face.

My first thought: *Oh, no, not again.*

Then, context: Hi, I'm Kyle. I'm seventeen. I have epilepsy. This happens to me a lot.

I'm lying face down, twisted like a fifty-storey splat, the pavement wet and cold and gritty beneath me, the dampness of this morning's rain shower spreading through the leg of my jeans. There's a moment when I think I must have fallen asleep, because why else would I be lying down with my eyes closed? But then the world settles into place around me and I realize it's happened again.

I'm on the high street in town. Grey concrete, leaden sky. Shoes and legs crossing indifferently across my field of vision. In the spaces behind them, I catch glimpses of familiar shop fronts, built like nuclear fallout shelters: Poundland, Specsavers, Boots, Timpson.

I hate this bit.

Coming back from a seizure makes you feel a special kind of rubbish. Hot and cold at the same time; my throat tastes like burnt pennies; my eyes feel like somebody took them out and put them in the wrong way round. I wait for the rest of my memory to come back. It always takes a few minutes, it's the familiarity of the routine that keeps me from panicking. They call it postictal confusion. I call it sulky-brain-syndrome. Epilepsy is like a loose wire fritzing in your skull. You get a spark and that spark sets off other sparks and then the whole thing blows a fuse. All I can do now is sit tight and wait for the BIOS to reboot.

I roll on to my back and haul myself up until I'm sitting against the wall of the WHSmith. Pins and needles start up immediately in the arm that's been crushed beneath me so I know I was out for a few minutes at least. I feel a tiny pinch of indignation that nobody checked in on me in all that time. They just went right on with their shopping.

I groan, maybe a little theatrically, maybe for effect. Is it wrong that I pretend I'm the action hero in an old war movie when I'm coming back from a seizure?

Go on without me. I'll hold them off as long as I can.

It's been a couple of months since my last seizure and I'd

started to think I might actually have things under control this time. But I guess not.

I do my checks.

Have I wet myself?

No.

Have I messed myself?

Er ... no.

Have I vomited?

No. Not yet anyway.

Hey, maybe today's not going to be such a bad day after all!

You have to take the little wins with epilepsy. I had a fit in a public toilet once and woke up to find the whole world and my mother bundled into the gents, my trousers around my ankles and the remains of somebody's damp cigarette lodged under my tongue.

That was a bad day. This is nothing.

But still ... no context.

The first fingers of panic flicker in my chest. Usually it's come back by now, the memory of what I was doing right before my brain decided this would be a perfect time for a lie down. But not this time. There's just a hole. No, not even a hole: an absence, like somebody forgot to hit the record button and whatever I was doing before didn't get saved.

I try to push the thought away. My brain is in brownout, bits of it are offline. The memories always come back in the end.

But what if they don't?

This sort of thing bothers me sometimes. If I forget everything I ever was does that mean I'm still me?

Let's not go there.

Epilepsy does weird things to your brain. It makes you feel like your thoughts aren't entirely your own. My post-seizure brain is like an overeager puppy trying to sniff every urine stain in the park at the same time. Images flicker against the inside of my eyes: a storm that will swallow me whole if I'm not careful.

I look outwards instead. The street, the shops.

This is my town and I hate it; I remember that much.

It's one of those grey little ex-mining towns in the Midlands. A kind of cross between an open prison and a theme park, where all the rides are rubbish but you can't find the exit so you queue up anyway to pass the time. It's the kind of town where anyone in their right mind packs their bags and gets out as soon as they can.

I'm working on that.

I try to think through the journey that would have brought me here, hoping it'll jog some memories. Over the bypass, under the railway bridge. There's a jacket potato truck just round the corner where I used to go for lunch when I was still at school. It's only twenty minutes from home. I could have walked here or Mum could have dropped me off before work.

There's just one problem with that theory.

I haven't left the house on my own for over a year.

Not since my GCSEs went so horribly wrong and I gave up on … life. Being outside, like this, is a big deal. It's not something I'd have forgotten.

I groan again. This is more of a lost-my-keys-down-the-drain kind of groan than a war-hero groan. The nausea has kicked in. The thing about epilepsy that everyone knows about – the seizures – aren't so bad because you're not there for that bit. It's the way it feels before and the way it feels after that really sucks. It's like I'm about to throw up and fall asleep and dismantle myself all at the same time. I'm guessing it's about mid-morning, which means I may as well write off the rest of the day.

I can't get over the fact that no one has stopped to help.

The last time I passed out in this part of town, I woke up to find an off-duty nurse moments away from giving me mouth-to-mouth resuscitation.

If I'd only pretended to be unconscious a moment longer…

Don't judge, I was fifteen – what did you expect?

Anyway, I threw up all over her instead.

But today: nothing. I suppose that was two years ago; I was a kid and nobody likes to see a kid passed out on the street. It's different now. I don't exactly look like an adult but maybe I look old enough for everyone to assume I've passed out from too much drink or drugs. That would explain why everyone's walking right past me like I don't exist.

I'm not sure whether I'm relieved or offended.

Then someone does stop and I wish instantly they hadn't. I don't see him coming; I notice him suddenly, standing right in front of me, staring at me. He looks a little surprised and a little worried and a little pleased all at the same time, like he's staring at an Amazon package on his front step that he wasn't expecting.

He's a small, grey, rusty rake of a man. The scar on his head cuts a knotted track from temporal lobe to frontal lobe: a gruesome, twisted stretch of pinkish scalp where the hair will never grow back. *It must be an injury*, I think. I reach up and touch the small ridge of bone on my own scalp where the surgeon corkscrewed a hole in my head and cut out the epileptogenic lesion in my temporal lobe.

"Keep moving," the man says, sounding kindlier than I'd expected.

"Wha—?"

"Keep moving or he'll sniff you out."

Fear rumbles inside me. His voice is so quiet I really shouldn't be able to hear him but somehow I do. The sound and the colour of the rest of the world pales.

"You're not where you think you are," the man continues, urgent now. "When you figure that out, all you'll want to do is close your eyes and wait it out. But you *can't*, do you hear me? You've got to *keep moving*."

Keep moving? I'm about to ask him what in seven-shades-of-hell he's talking about when a woman comes up behind him.

Thirties, quite well-dressed, a bit school-teachery. She doesn't see me, or she ignores me if she does. "Dad," she says, taking his arm. "Come on, we need to get going."

I watch them leave. For some reason I'm thinking about the time I was clearing out the garage with Grandad before he died. I upended an old armchair and a dead mouse hit the floor. I remember the shock, the cold drench. It wasn't a mouse anymore, not exactly. Its insides had turned to dust decades ago. It was a dried up, furry husk with milky, unseeing eyes fixed on mine.

That's what the man reminded me of: a husk, with nothing but dust and spiders inside him.

I pull myself up to standing and the world rocks around me like it's trying to shrug me off. I fish in my back pocket and I'm relieved to find my phone. I've never been robbed while I'm unconscious – I guess all the arm waving puts people off – but it's something I think about. Anything can happen while you're out. It's like leaving your front door wide open. Except it's not your house you leave unattended, it's *you*.

My phone is dead, the screen dark. I press the power button again anyway. Nothing. Maybe it broke when I fell.

I let my head fall back and stare hopelessly at the cloudless sky.

Nothing is easy after a seizure. My eyes don't work right, my fingers don't work right. I'm only a twenty-minute walk from home but I might as well be on Mars.

The smart move would be to beg a passer-by to borrow their phone and call Mum. She'll be working her shift at the local Waitrose right now and if I call her she'll be in the car and down here in about three minutes flat, Liquorice Allsorts in hand.

Mum's great in a crisis, I guess she's had a lot of practice.

Or I could just walk?

It sounds simple, but trust me, it's not. I might pass out again, or step into traffic. I'm scared. But I can't shake the old man's words.

Keep moving.

Something is off. Something about the weird old head-wound guy and the fact that nobody is even looking at me.

Keep moving.

I'm probably not thinking straight. I never make good decisions when I'm post-seizure, but all the same...

I need to *go*.

My blood feels like it's boiling, my arms and legs twitch with the urge to start walking. I slip my phone into my pocket and point myself towards home. *This is brave*, I think. *The first brave thing I've done in a long time.*

I used to have this idea that epilepsy was just one thing about me. It didn't have to define me; I could still have a life. I convinced myself it all came down to my GCSEs. They were the first great hurdle, I thought, the doorway to the rest of my life. I was going to nail my GCSEs and crush my A-levels and then I was going to get the hell out of this place. London. New York. Tokyo. Somewhere *alive*. Somewhere where the universe was actually paying attention.

But then my GCSEs came around, epilepsy took its chance to give me the biggest kick in the teeth it could and all my grand plans got scrubbed.

TWO

Most people with epilepsy get auras before they have a seizure. Visual disturbances, vertigo, distorted sensations. When I was little, my aura used to look like a person. I'd catch sight of something in the corner of my eye and turn to see a willowy man standing in the doorway next to me. Long and taut, with muscles on his arms and legs that stood out like twisted rope. I could never see his face, even when it was clear daylight, but I could tell, somehow, that he was watching me. He'd tilt his head to the side like he didn't quite understand me. I'd freeze, my breath like a marble in my throat, until—

I'd open my eyes and Mum would be leaning over me, shouting, looking petrified. I didn't know about epilepsy then. I used to think I passed out through sheer terror. But then Mum took me to the doctor and after a bunch of tests I got my diagnosis.

I stopped seeing the man after I started medication, but I still feel him. Now, my aura starts with a blue-grey tinge at the edges of my vision, followed by a rushing sensation, a sense of falling but not moving, as if the world is rearing up around me. And then there it is: the fear. Unreasoning and inhuman. The unshakable belief that somebody — *something* — is standing just outside my line of sight.

I walk on. The air is damp, the sky is a flat sheet of grey that looks like it's welded to the grey of the roads and the poxy grey pebble-dashed houses. My vision is still messed up, blurry in some places and not in others, like one of those tilt-shift photos that make real-sized houses look like perfect doll-sized toys.

Home is twenty minutes away.

Home. My room. My emergency pack of Liquorice Allsorts.

I reach the roundabout at the edge of the town centre. There aren't many people. The one or two I can see are on the opposite side of the road, so far ahead or behind they look like blurry smudges of oil in a Lowry painting.

Cars whip round the roundabout and hit the dual carriageway at a hundred miles an hour. I feel them more than I see them, a kind of *whhmm* as they go past, shaking the fence that divides the lanes and sending blasts of cold, gritty air right through me.

According to quantum mechanics, objects aren't really there until you observe them. I learned this from YouTube, not my physics GCSE, by the way. What we call reality is just one way of looking at the world. If you listen to Heisenberg, objects only exist *in relation* to other objects. When they're not interacting, they're not really there.

Epilepsy brain. Sorry.

Thinking about physics keeps me calm and calm is good because anxiety is a major trigger for my seizures. Although, to be fair, so is hunger, lack of sleep, norovirus, physical discomfort in any form and the weather forecast in Paraguay. That last one is a joke ... as far as I know.

Oh, and exams.

The irony is that I wasn't even that anxious about my GCSEs. It's just that two weeks of limited bathroom access, loss of sleep and long periods of time in a confined space with lots of anxious people turned out to be pretty triggering as well. By the time the day of my maths exam finally came, I'd taken so many extra meds that my brain felt like it was floating in custard. I was probably going to fail anyway but I would have liked not to have ended my school career by throwing up all over my paper and chipping a tooth on the sports hall floor.

One–nil to epilepsy.

I don't see the kids coming the other way until it's too late to cross over without it looking too obvious. There's three of them, or is it four? Their blurry outlines blend and separate, blend and separate, indistinct wave functions in superposition. I narrow my eyes, trying and failing to make sense of them.

The only thing that's clear is their sense of threat.

These kids are going to beat the living crap out of me.

That's the worst thing about this town, it's such a hole that pretty much everyone is looking for trouble if they can find it. And they'll see "victim" written all over me.

Side by side, deliberately taking up the whole pavement. They might be my age … or a little older … or maybe a little younger. It doesn't matter. Violence is inevitable. It's usually a shove or some verbal. But I've been punched plenty of times as well. Getting punched isn't the worst. The worst is when they kind of half swing but stop and you know they're not really going to hit you but you flinch anyway. I hate that.

Walking home was a mistake.

Suddenly I remember my rizatriptan. I keep a blister pack of melties in my coat pocket and sometimes they help to clear my head. I find the packet and try to pop the foil but I fumble it and the pill pings on to the floor instead. I crouch to pick it up and then realize that I'm pretty much crouching at the perfect height for a kick in the face.

I grab the ejected rizatriptan and pop it quickly into my mouth, ignoring the gritty pavement coating stuck to it. Then I kind of crab walk until I'm inside the bus shelter that I just spotted nearby.

Nice going, Kyle. Super dignified.

I collapse with my back against the far wall like I'm a soldier diving into a foxhole.

Captain Cower at your service, sir!

I hope the kids didn't see.

I close my eyes and try to focus on the rizatriptan as it dissolves against my gum. It tastes like a mouth ulcer, like when you keep a paracetamol on your tongue for too long.

But I feel safer here. I stare hard at the timetable on the opposite wall and try to distract myself from the stale, gritty diesel and urine smells of the bus shelter. My chest feels like a wicker basket that somebody's pounding on with a hammer.

I'm not usually this bad, not even after a seizure, I think. *Maybe I hit my head when I fell? Maybe I have a bleed, or a clot, or maybe I'm in some kind of neurological shock?*

You're not where you think you are.

I'm terrified that the kids are going to be waiting outside, ready to jump me. I hold my breath and listen. Silence. I twist and peer round the wall of the bus shelter. Nothing.

The street is empty in both directions.

But there's nowhere for them to have gone?

I press my hands against my temples and squeeze hard. *I hate this.* I hate that I'm seventeen and I should be out having fun but instead I'm hiding in a bloody bus shelter. I hate that I can't even trust my own *brain*.

Then I realize that it's not just the kids who have vanished.

There are no people at all. No traffic.

I can't even hear the bypass.

It's not me, I think. *It's everything else.*

The thought is strange and terrifying.

I remember the old guy who stopped earlier. I can't shake the sense that *he* was real, but no one else was. "*Keep moving*," he said.

But where? Any minute now the storm in my brain is going to turn into a hurricane and I'll fry myself from the inside out. I won't make it home.

Hospital, I think.

I let the thought settle for a moment. I don't love the idea. I've spent far too much time in hospitals to ever go there voluntarily.

But I don't have a choice. Something is wrong. Very wrong.

I pull myself to my feet and swipe at the tears and snot smeared over my face. Hospital is another fifteen minutes away: left after the bridge, past the industrial estate.

I can do it … Probably.

THREE

I cross the bypass by an arching concrete bridge that everyone calls the Banana Bridge. The light is messed up. The sky is flat, the sun invisible. The road is empty, but it shouldn't be at this time of day. Wrongness crawls through every vein and artery in my body. My vision fills with scotomas: colourful shards of glass that scintillate across my vision and follow my eyeline wherever I look.

Below me, the deserted bypass leads down to the A5 and from the A5 to the M1 and then to London. How many times have I imagined myself getting the National Express that way? How many times have I studied the map of central London, the great knotted mass of A-roads that converge on the West End like arteries converging on the brain stem?

People only live in this town because they were born

here and they don't know how to get out. But people *go* to London. They go searching for … *something.*

I like that.

Whenever I come back from a seizure Mum says, "You're special, Kyle. God can keep you any time He likes, but He sends you back because He knows you have a reason to be here."

I'm not sure the logic follows. You don't throw a fish back into the ocean because you think they have a reason for being there. But the image is fitting today. It feels like God still has one hand holding on to my ankle.

Mum likes all that God stuff. She can't get enough of it. New churches, new ministers. She always wants *more* than any of them can offer.

More what? I wonder. More certainty. More conviction.

Mum "faith-dates". It's a desperate sort of hobby, like Tinder for God.

Swipe right on Seventh-Day Adventists.

Swipe left on the Baptists.

Swipe right for Methodists.

The Seventh-Day Adventists were my favourite. Tall men in pin-striped suits clutching leatherbound bibles to their chests. They were a quiet, tentative bunch, until they started singing and then all hell (or maybe heaven?) let loose. But then, one time, I had a seizure during a service and things got weird after that. Sideways looks, hands reaching out to touch my shoulder as I walked in, like they thought I was about to start speaking in tongues or something. We didn't last much longer.

I never believed. I don't disrespect people who do, I just knew I never could. At some point I stopped going with Mum on her church visits. I think it broke her heart a little, but I couldn't help it. The roll call of all those different churches, all those ministers, all utterly convinced that *they* had it right and no one else.

Her latest is God's Scholars. They're small, they don't even have a church. Just a prayer group run out of Father Michael's living room. He calls himself *Father* Michael anyway – I don't know what qualifications you need in order to call yourself "father", but I'm sure Michael Thorn doesn't have them.

God's Scholars feels different to the other churches and that worries me. There's a trembling, sing-song excitement in Mum's voice when she talks about Father Michael. A sense that here – here and *nowhere* else – is the truth she's been looking for.

Father Michael.

A memory flickers inside me, an uncomfortable twinge. I can't help feeling like Father Michael has something to do with why I'm out on my own for the first time in a year. But it makes no sense; I only met him once.

I follow the footbridge until it rejoins the main road

and then work my way across the big roundabout. *There should be traffic. Where is all the traffic?*

At last, there's the hospital. A grey slab of 1950s concrete and glass, the big blue sign like a beacon that proclaims: YOUR HOSPITAL. YOUR NHS.

My heart pounds as I stumble through the big concertina doors and into the casualty ward. I feel like I should be shouting, "Help me! I'm sick, I'm really sick." But I'm silent and desperate, like somebody looking up at the sky while they drown. The lights are off in the foyer, the place has a shadowed, disused kind of look.

Is it closed? Do hospitals actually close?

Then I step through the heavy fire doors and the clamour of the sick and injured kicks in like somebody flicked a switch.

Here, at least, there are people. Rows of them, side by side on plastic moulded seats: a white-haired woman hunched over and half asleep, an overweight middle-aged man with his leg grotesquely swollen and mottled, a toddler clinging to its mum, snot caked around its face.

The noise is unbearable. The stink of humans and sweat and dirt and disinfectant. *Is this where everybody is? Has there been some kind of major incident?*

No, I think, *just the regular Casualty crowd.*

I shuffle over to the little ticket machine. I've been here

19

enough times to know that the receptionist won't talk to you unless you have a ticket.

756.

Or is it 765? Or is it not really numbers at all?

I can't tell.

I shake my head and try to think clearly. Hospitals make me anxious. Nothing good ever happened in a hospital.

My gaze lands on a man on the opposite side of the room. There's a thick dressing wadded against his neck and he's staring straight ahead. Blood has soaked through his bandages and stained a continent of dried, crusty dark red on to his shirt. His head rests at a funny angle against the wall, his eyes glazed. *If anybody deserves to jump the queue, it's him*, I think.

His gaze shifts and lands on me. His eyes widen.

He's too vivid, too *there* compared to everyone else. He reminds me of the man in town earlier, and I can't shake the feeling that he's thinking the same thing about me.

You're not where you think you are.

I turn away.

New idea. The neurology clinic is round the corner. You're supposed to have an appointment, but if I wait there for my number to be called I might get lucky and snag a passing neurologist instead.

The noise from the waiting room turns hollow and disjointed as soon as I step away. I move towards the bank of seats where I've sat and waited for the neurologist a hundred times before and—

I freeze.

Someone else is already sitting there.

A girl about my age. Jeans, a peach-coloured T-shirt and a denim jacket. She has jet-black hair that's wiry and kind of unruly, and the same terrifying *thereness* of the man from the street and the man I just saw.

But worse, I *know* her.

I glance over my shoulder and seriously consider bolting. But she's already seen me and she's staring at me with a weird combination of relief and dismay.

"Farah?" I say.

"Kyle?" Farah replies.

Farah Rafiq is, quite literally, the last person I want to run into.

FOUR

Before I knew Farah, I only knew *of* her. She was just another face in the school crowd, one of the shy Asian kids. Then she got brain cancer in Year Eight and the head made her famous by dedicating an entire teary assembly to her, giving us a rousing speech about bravery and resilience, telling us how proud he was of little Farah, who was a *fighter* and who would battle her affliction and *win*!

Obviously he thought she was going to die.

It caused a frenzy. The whole year group signed a giant card, kids who'd never spoken to her kept bursting into tears in French class and having to go to the nurse. There was even a concert to raise money so Farah and her parents could go to Disneyland. I remember feeling a weird sense of kinship towards her, because the other kids whispered about her like they whispered about me. I even put some money in the pot on concert day.

Farah went into treatment; she was gone for ages and then she returned and part of me felt like asking for a refund. Because she wasn't just back – she was back with *attitude*. She became one of the *mouthy* kids, part of a group of four or five girls who showed up late to class and acted angry all the time. They talked through classes and when the teacher called them out on it, they acted like he had no right and carried right on. Farah got detention pretty much every day but she didn't care.

I'm a rule follower, I can't help it. I'm one of those people who actually prefers to be told what to do. I couldn't decide if I admired Farah for her rebel-yell bad attitude or resented her for making it look so easy.

Then in Year Nine we finally got our allocated term of swimming lessons, except for me and Farah. We were exempt, because … well … neurology. Every week for a whole term, we sat together by the side of the pool for an hour a week while the other kids splashed and dunked each other and supposedly learned how to swim.

At first, we ignored each other. Farah did her homework, which I hadn't expected. I stared dismally at the kids playing in the pool. The Asian kids and the white kids didn't mix much in my school and I wish I could tell you a story of our blossoming friendship at the poolside, our bond of mutual adversity, but … not so much. We had nothing to say to each other.

But that didn't stop my fourteen-year-old self

developing a raging crush on her.

Every week I got more and more obsessed. Every week, I imagined that we'd find our way into easy conversation. I'd make her laugh and everything else would follow. But every week my awkward hellos were met with a faintly bemused frown as she turned back to her books.

I don't know what finally made me do it. It wasn't like she'd given me the slightest indication that she might say yes if I asked her out. I had a feeling, that's all. Like I *ought* to.

OK, I was a complete idiot.

When the time finally came, I'd spent so long working myself up to it I don't even remember what I said. My heart was pounding and I was more worried about passing out than anything else. All I *do* remember is her slightly sad smile and the smallest shake of her head before she turned back to her work without even giving me the dignity of a straight "no".

I can hardly bring myself to look at her, even now. She sits very still next to me. I glance at her, at the sharp line of her jaw that I remember so well, her unruly black hair barely contained in a scrunchy.

"Hey," she says.

"Hey."

Her eyes meet mine for a second and then skate away. *Maybe she doesn't remember me?*

I take out my phone and then remember that it's

dead. "Do you have a charger?" I ask. "My phone's not working."

Farah shakes her head ever so slightly. The same way she used to shake her head when I tried to say hello at the pool. "Sorry. Mine too."

I kind of half turn in my seat, looking around like I'm searching for the official phone-charger guy. "Maybe we should ask someone, we could borrow—"

"I don't think it's that," Farah says.

"What do you mean?"

"I don't think a charger will help."

I open my mouth but no words come out. Something about the look in her eyes makes me anxious. I recognize that look: I see it in myself sometimes after a seizure. Stunned. I wonder why she's here. She was supposed to have been cured back when she was thirteen.

"What are you doing here?" I ask.

"Getting my nails done, how about you?" she replies without a pause.

I groan inwardly. I should have a witty response for this. "Tonsils," I should say. But that's the kind of snappy one-liner I only think of about an hour after the conversation is over.

She taps the side of her head. "Tumour," she explains.

"I thought they cured that," I say.

"So did I," she says. "But I didn't come here for the view, did I?"

What was it? I wonder. What clued her into the fact that something was wrong? An unexpected seizure? A sudden weakness on one side? Blind spots? Something had alerted her to the fact that it was still growing silently inside her. She was the school bad girl and nobody could tell her what to do, but when your brain sends you to see the head teacher, you go, even if you're Farah Rafiq.

"What about you?" she asks.

"Epilepsy," I reply.

"Yeah, I remember."

"I had a seizure. Earlier this morning, I mean."

I don't know why I still feel ashamed when I tell people I had a seizure, like it's *my* fault, like it means I'm *weak*.

"Do you always come to the hospital after a seizure?"

"No," I say. Defensive.

She's watching me. No, not watching me, *studying* me. She leans closer, like she's about to tell me a secret and I realize for the first time how pale she is.

"What was different this time?" she asks.

"I … nothing."

Her mouth pinches in that small, sad smile she has. She turns away.

"I don't see you in school anymore, do I?"

"I'm doing retakes online. At home," I explain.

"Oh yeah." She smirks. "It's your fault I got an eight instead of a nine in maths, you know that?"

My heart sinks.

"I'm sorry," I mumble. I haven't spoken to anyone who was in that maths exam since it happened but I have every reason to believe they all hate me. It's the last thing you want, isn't it? Someone causing a drama when you're trying to concentrate on geometry.

"Forget it," she says, softening. "I'm just winding you up. Anyway, we all applied for special consideration on account of the disruption you caused. You're a hero to a lot of people."

I half laugh and for an instant she gives me a surprisingly warm smile. "What's it like doing retakes at home?" she asks.

"It's OK. Convenient."

"Don't you miss people? Going out?"

I should lie and tell her I go out all the time. I should tell her that I've made older friends who're working and who play in a band and when they move to London I'm going to go with them.

"I don't really get out much," I say. "Um … at all."

"You're a shut-in?"

It's so abrupt I don't know how to respond.

"I'm sorry," she says. "I didn't mean… I got a bit like that after I was sick. I didn't want to leave the house. *Couldn't* leave the house. That's just what I called it."

"The Japanese call it *Hikikomori*," I say. "It means someone who avoids social contact. It's a real thing."

Farah doesn't say anything. I stare hard at the ticket in

my hand in order to hide my embarrassment.

756. Definitely 756.

Still, I feel better for having someone to talk to, even if it is Farah. I take a shaky breath. *Maybe it's OK*, I think. All that weirdness – the lack of people, the blurry vision, the strange man who spoke to me – maybe it was all in my head. Maybe I'm starting to feel better.

"What number are you?" I say.

"755," she says.

"How long have you been waiting?"

"About nine days."

FIVE

Nine days? She's joking, right? I mean, she *has* to be joking. But there's something about the way she looks at me that makes me horribly afraid she's not.

I stare at the salty streaks of dried tears on her cheeks. She's scared.

My brain fizzes. A woman in blue scrubs passes by. A moment later, a man in green scrubs passes the other way. They don't even glance at us.

I must be dreaming, I think.

I pinch my nose and force my ears to pop. Then I count my fingers: thumb to index, thumb to middle, thumb to ring, thumb to pinkie. I do it with both hands simultaneously, like I'm playing scales. It's a technique a doctor showed me once to calm myself down – to check I'm still here, the world is real, I'm not dreaming.

"What on earth are you doing?" Farah says, half laughing.

I put my hands down quickly and slide them under my knees, my face reddening. "Nothing."

Not dreaming, I think. But I already knew that. It's too physical for a dream. I can *feel* myself sweating, my shirt sticking to my back and beginning to itch. I can feel the saliva catching at the back of my throat, making me swallow compulsively. The air in my nose, the grit under my fingernails, the pressure of the chair against my backside.

Somebody else in blue scrubs walks by. I leap up and try to intercept them but somehow I miss. They breeze past.

"Don't bother," Farah says. "They can't see you."

I give her a cold stare. "What do you mean?"

Farah shrugs, turns away and chews her thumbnail, like she regrets saying it. Something hangs between us. I'm not sure I want to know what it is.

"What's going on?" I say.

"Have you noticed that there's no lights, no electricity?"

I frown. "I guess."

"But we can still see?"

I glance around and see immediately what she means. We're in the guts of the hospital, heavy doors block off every corridor that might even remotely connect to a window.

But there are no shadows. Just a sort of dull, flat, grainy reflected light that comes from nowhere.

"What does it mean?" I say.

"It means we're not in Kansas anymore, Toto."

A wave of nausea hits me.

"I'm going to speak to somebody," I say, thickly.

I stride back towards Casualty. Farah calls after me, "It's no use."

I peer round the corner and scan the waiting room.

Nothing. No snotty toddlers, no old people with leg ulcers.

I turn back to Farah. "Where have they all gone?"

Farah shrugs.

"This place was full."

"I don't think so."

I look again. I was wrong. The room isn't completely empty. The same guy from earlier is still there, the one with the dressing packed against his neck and the blood soaking into his shirt. He watches me without a word.

"What about that guy?" I call to Farah. "Have you tried talking to him?"

"Don't bother. You won't get any sense out of him."

The air in my throat feels too heavy.

I do my checks again, more urgently than before.

Index, middle, ring, pinkie; pinkie, ring, middle, index.

My mind fights to make sense of it. *That's what the brain does*, I think, a little wildly; it's a sense-making machine. Neurons stretch through the body and take in billions of impulses from everything we see and feel and do and our brains turn them into a world. The brain doesn't just *sense* reality, it *creates* it.

But what if the reality it's creating is … *different*?

"But I *saw* people," I say, my voice catching. "This place was *full*."

"You're just seeing what you expect to see. It'll pass."

"Was there a fire drill?" I say. "An evacuation?"

Farah lets out a cynical laugh. "You know it's not that."

"Is it a dream?"

Farah stands and sighs. "Come on. I want to show you something."

SIX

I follow reluctantly as she leads me deeper into the hospital. Past another set of doors, down another corridor with a glass panel set into the wall that looks on to wards filled with empty beds.

No light. No light, but I can still see.

"Shouldn't we stay where we were in case they call our numbers?" I say.

She keeps walking. "You still don't get it, do you?"

The nurses' station is abandoned, monitors blank, phones silent.

"Where did everybody go?"

"I don't think they're gone," Farah answers. "Not exactly."

I don't want to admit it, but I know she's right. The nurses' station doesn't *feel* empty. It still has the official, unwelcoming air of a nurses' station. The sense that the people who watch over it are out of sight for just a moment, as if they might appear from down the corridor, or from the door behind the counter any second.

More corridors, more abandoned wards. Everything is orderly: no sign of panic, no mess. I've seen enough zombie movies to know that when a hospital gets evacuated there are scattered notes all over the floor and up-ended medication trolleys in the corridors.

It still smells like a hospital: antiseptic and sweat and, distantly, vomit and faeces. We enter another ward, small and cramped and smelling more strongly of human waste. There aren't beds in this ward; it has cots instead. Spaniel sized, with high Perspex sides.

"Do you hear that?" I say.

Farah gives me a pensive nod.

"Is that … a *baby*?"

"Don't be scared," Farah says.

"Are you serious?" I respond. "A crying baby in an abandoned hospital? I've *seen* this movie."

She smiles. "It's OK, I've been here before." She quickens her pace, urging me to keep up. "Come on, he's still here."

"Who?"

"You'll see."

The sound is awful in the empty ward. A guttural dying sound. Farah moves quickly to the cot and leans over the Perspex, reaching in and placing her hand gently on the baby that lies inside.

Its *thereness* startles me. It's like us, like the man in the waiting area, like the man on the street. Farah makes a gentle, soothing noise. It's hard to connect the angry girl I used to see at school with this person.

The baby settles in her arms, its hands clenching and unclenching weakly.

"You're good at this," I say.

"He reminds me of my brothers," Farah replies.

The other cots are empty. "I don't understand why there's a baby here on its own."

"This is the neonatal ward," Farah says. She looks at the baby again. It's smiling now, its dark eyes wide and all-knowing. "I think we can see him because he's sick," she says. "Because he's dying."

Reality hits me, winds me, then hits me again. "You think we're dead, don't you?" The words come out like an accusation. I step back and sit heavily in a nearby chair, which is lucky because without it I'm sure I'd have just hit the floor.

"Not dead," Farah says. "Dying."

"No," I say. "You're wrong."

Farah looks up, her eyes hard and enquiring. "Pop quiz. What do Epilepsy Boy, Cancer Girl, Scary Neck-Wound guy and a terribly sick baby have in common?" She waits a beat. "We're not exactly a boy band, are we?"

An involuntary whimper escapes me. "This is ridiculous."

I stand and stumble against the cot behind me. I turn

35

and push it angrily to one side. *This is a hoax*, I think. *I've stumbled into some sort of sadistic reality TV show.*

"Come out! Out!" I shout. "I don't know how you did it but it's not funny anymore!"

"Kyle, please," Farah says. "Use your brain, what do you *think* is going on here?"

"I had a seizure, I'm confused."

"It's not that."

"How do you know?"

"You think I haven't had a few seizures myself?"

"This is an aura," I insist. "Postictal confusion. There's always an aura."

"You *know* this isn't an aura, Kyle."

"I don't know… I *don't*…"

But I *do* know. Even my sense-making brain can't make up stories any longer. Postictal auras are rubbish but they don't feel like this.

I lash out at the empty cot and push it over. The Perspex case falls from the frame and tumbles along the floor with a loud, hollow clatter that makes the baby start crying again.

"*I'm not going to die!*" I shout. My voice reverberates around the empty ward. "I'm going to London. I've got a plan, I'm going to get a job in finance and I'm going to make a *tonne* of money and I'm never, *ever* coming back to this place."

"Kyle—"

"I'm *not* dying in this place."

Farah comforts the baby, jogging it gently in her arms.

"Hey!" I shout, afraid, suddenly, for the baby. I head back towards the nurses' station. "Somebody! There's a baby here and it needs help *right now*!" I lean across the counter and bang the flat of my hand down. "Hey! Come out! We need help!"

"Kyle—"

I pick up the desk phone and place it briefly to my ear. It's dead, of course, like everything else here. I put it back, miss and slam it down two or three times before swiping it angrily off the counter instead.

"Kyle!"

An idea occurs to me. I pick up the chair I've been sitting on and rattle it against the floor. "Hey! Can you see this?" I strain my eyes, trying to find the people who are almost but not quite there. "I'm haunting you!" I shout, making the chair dance. "Whoo-oo! I'm *haunting* you."

I know they don't see me. I can feel them though, less than a breath away, sitting, waiting their turn with the consultant. If I could make them *see*—

"Kyle, stop it," Farah snaps. "They can't hear you."

I fall silent.

"You're upsetting the baby," Farah says.

"Sorry, I think I'm done now."

Is this really it? I think. After every seizure I've always known there was a chance of dying, but I never believed it would happen. Yet here I am: dead or dying and spending my last moments with Farah Rafiq. The irony burns inside me.

One of the good things about being an atheist is that you're not supposed to have to deal with this kind of shit. There's no heaven or hell for us, just: off.

This must be some kind of neurological reckoning. An elaborate hallucination in which my dying brain forces me to atone for failing to be the person I always wanted to be. *Farah isn't really here*, I think. My brain is just telling me she is. *But why Farah? Why has my brain come up with her of all people?*

She puts the baby down and comes and places her hand gently on my back. I can feel the warmth of her palm burning through my shirt. *It doesn't matter*, I think. Whatever this is, I just need to ride it out.

"How long do you think we'll be like this?" I say.

"I don't know."

I swipe at my face and sniff and turn to her. "Seeing as we're here ... what do you think we should do?"

SEVEN

We *ride the trolley beds.*

It's Farah's idea but later she insists it was mine. We start by finding the longest corridor we can, propping open the fire doors and taking it in turns to propel each other towards the far wall. We set up bins and cleaning equipment, arranged in a V, like ten-pin bowling. Farah wins every round. I decide to ride my trolley face first, like a luge, in the hope of taking out more bins along the way, but I crash into a wall and land heavily on my side instead. I writhe in agony, wondering if I've broken a rib, while Farah laughs so hard I think she's going to throw up.

"Are you OK?" she says, running over at last.

I nod and haul myself up against the wall, probing my injured side. "I think I discovered a new way to prove that we're not dreaming."

Farah snorts and sits cross-legged, waiting for me to recover. "No dizziness?"

I look up and catch a playful look in her eye that I don't fully understand.

"Head's not … *swimming*, or anything?" she says.

Seriously? My heart sinks. I don't want to think about the swimming pool; I definitely don't want *her* to think about the swimming pool.

"Sorry," she says. "Couldn't resist."

I raise my hand and wave her off. After all, I'm probably going to be dead soon, so why should I care if I'm also being mocked about the most painfully embarrassing moment of my life?

"I'm sorry about that," I say. "It was a long time ago."

Farah shrugs. "Don't be sorry. It was sweet."

Sweet? I decide to change the subject. "What happened to you?" I say. "How did you end up here?"

Farah looks away for a moment. "I don't know. I got a headache. I was writing an essay and I thought I could keep going but it got worse and worse. Then I started not being able to see properly, so I came to the hospital."

"It might have been a migraine?" I say.

"I've had migraines before," Farah says. "It wasn't that. I must have lost consciousness right after I got to Casualty, I don't remember anything else. Next thing I knew, I was on the floor and everyone else was gone."

"And you've really been here for nine days?"

"I might have lost count. I tried to leave a few times. I'd go to the door but then I kept bottling it and going back to the waiting area. Have you noticed that the sky never changes here? No sun. No clouds."

I nod.

"But it gets darker and lighter, so I counted that as best I could."

"What is this place?" I say.

Farah shuffles closer so she's knee to knee with me, our hands almost touching. A warm flush passes through me. "I have a theory about that," she says. "I reckon we're in some kind of messed-up brain state."

I give her a quizzical look. "A messed-up what?"

"It's something we studied in philosophy A-level. The thing that we call reality is just something our brains *construct*." I nod; I know that. "But because we're so sick, our brains are constructing a *different* version of reality—"

I nod. I've watched videos on YouTube about this stuff as well, but I don't like where all this is going. Messed-up brain state? Life rushing before your eyes? Long tunnels and bright lights? We all know what that means.

"It's a pretty wild theory," I say.

"You got a better one?"

"Not really," I concede.

"Anyway, this thing we studied, it's from Plato: the Allegory of the Cave. Do you know it?"

"No."

41

"There's a cave and a row of prisoners chained up facing a wall. They can only face the wall; they can't see anything else."

"That sounds cruel," I say.

"That's not the point. Anyway, they—"

"Do you know what they were in prison for?"

Farah cracks a begrudging smile. "Do you want to hear this story or not?"

"Of course."

I place my hands primly in my lap. Sitting knee to knee with Farah is a rush. I have to resist the smile that keeps forcing its way on to my face. Farah clears her throat and begins:

"They've been locked up this way for generations, they don't know anything else. All they can see are the shadows of the courtyard outside, cast on the wall by the light of a fire behind them. They watch the shadows and they mistake them for reality."

"It's cruel, that's all I'm saying."

"*Kyle!*"

I grin. I'm enjoying myself. Farah Rafiq is telling me a cool – OK, slightly weird – story and I'm cracking jokes. I fantasized about having this level of conversation with her a thousand times and now here I am.

"Sorry. Go on," I say.

"They begin to study the shadows, make up rules to predict what kind of shadow will appear next. When a prisoner gets it right they're praised by the others. They call them: *master*."

"OK, I get it," I say. "It's an analogy. The prisoners are doing what scientists do: looking for patterns, trying to guess at the nature of reality. And some of them guess right and so everyone looks up to them."

Farah smiles. "Not just a pretty face."

I like the way she smiles with her whole face, even her eyebrows.

"You don't need to sound so surprised," I say. "I want to do A-levels too. After my retakes."

Farah nods shortly. I appreciate that she doesn't feel the need to remind me that there probably won't be retakes, or A-levels, or anything else now.

"One day, one of the prisoners escapes," she continues. "They blunder out into the real world. Plato called it 'the ordinary world'. And instead of seeing shadows, they see physical three-dimensional people for the first time."

"That … would be scary," I say.

"What do you think happens next?"

"They go all Ironman on them for locking everyone up? Blast the place to hell."

Farah smiles thinly. "You're not taking this seriously."

"I am, I promise."

"They go back into the cave and try to explain what they've seen. But nobody believes them. They think they're a fool."

43

I take a minute. "I see what you're saying. Everything we've known until now, the thing we call reality, might not be *the* reality. It might just be shadows on the cave wall."

"Right," Farah says.

"But we're still not really *here*, are we? In this corridor." I gesture around us. "I'm still passed out on the street or in the back of an ambulance on the way to hospital. You're probably on a ward too by now."

Farah shakes her head. "You're being too literal. The idea of you lying on the pavement in town is no more *real* than the idea of you and me sitting here. They're both different *representations* of something else entirely."

I think it through. "The thing we call 'real' is only the 'real' we're most used to."

"Exactly," Farah says.

"You think we've stepped outside the cave, don't you?"

"Outside, or into another one."

We find a cupboard filled with bandages and dressings and we fashion elbow pads and helmets from them. We fight with mop handles, swinging wildly, making thick *whapp*ing sounds against each other's paddings. We giggle so hard we can hardly stand and we fall into each other and stagger around like we're drunk or delirious. I swing my mop back over my head and it catches a glass panel in the door behind me and the glass shatters, turning into an astonishing cloud of jagged light.

We fall silent, staring in disbelief at our destruction. Then Farah places her hand over her mouth and guffaws. My heart thuds in my ears and I can feel my pulse behind my eyes and I can't help but feel guilty in spite of everything.

"Are you sure people in the ordinary world can't see this?" I say.

"Pretty sure," Farah says.

"How?"

"Think about it. We can't be the only people this has happened to. There's the guy in Casualty, the baby. I've seen a few others."

"I guess."

"You think you're the first person to smash things up?"

"No."

"Well then. It must be that they can't see us. Or else the ordinary world would be full of poltergeists." Farah frowns thoughtfully. "Are you hungry?"

"Not particularly," I reply.

But we go in search of food anyway.

The canteen has a sad, deserted feel to it that probably isn't that different to how it feels in the ordinary world. Moulded plastic chairs like in the waiting areas, a station with a shelf for sandwiches and a salad bar, some kind of heated counter, a windowed fridge, a rack with crisps and chocolate bars. I hope briefly that I'll find a packet of Liquorice Allsorts … but no luck.

"No fresh food but they have sandwiches and chocolate bars," Farah says.

"No people but chairs and buildings and beds," I remark.

"It makes no sense."

"It makes sense," I say. "The rules are different, that's all."

We gather a stash of whatever food we can find and lay it out on the table between us.

I don't remember the last time I ate. I should be ravenous. But I stare at the food with a sense of dismay.

"I don't think our bodies need food here," Farah says.

"No," I agree.

She picks idly at a bag of crisps. "Have you had a dump since you got here?"

I'm caught off guard and I snort into my can of Coke. I collect myself. "Nope. I haven't urinated either."

Farah laughs now. "Oh, oh, right, you haven't *urinated*?" She speaks in a haughty voice, waving her crisp in the air as she talks. "Have you been to the *boudoir* to powder your nose?"

"Shut up," I mutter, smiling.

Farah turns more serious. "I think that might be another thing we don't need here."

"What?"

"Food. Drink. Anything."

I push my plate away. I've been enjoying hanging out

with Farah and I don't like being reminded how wrong things are.

Farah seems to have the same thought. "Some last meal, huh?"

We fall silent. In the ordinary world, people come and go, load their trays, make phone calls while they wait for their sick relatives. But they're not *here*. It's just the building and the chairs and tables that somehow inhabit both worlds.

"I'm sorry I was such a cow in swimming lessons," Farah says.

I swallow and look away. I'm surprised by how anxious she seems, the catch in her voice like there's something irritating the back of her throat.

"You're OK, Kyle," she continues. "That's all I was trying to say when I mentioned it earlier. I didn't mean to make a joke of it, I do that sometimes, it's stupid."

"Forget it," I say. "It's no big deal." I smile thinly and hope that she realizes what I say next is a joke. "I'd actually kind of forgotten until you mentioned it."

Farah smiles. "That's what I thought. I mean, I bet you ask girls out all the time, right?"

"All the time," I say, loftily.

"So how many girls have you asked out? That you can remember, I mean."

"Oh … hundreds."

"Have any of them ever said yes?"

"Not one of them," I reply, deadpan.

Farah laughs and I laugh with her. It feels so easy here I don't understand how it always used to feel so hard in the ordinary world.

"I do wish we'd got to know each other back then though," she says.

"Swimming lessons would have been less crap," I agree.

"I had a bit of a thing going on," Farah says. "It wasn't personal. I wasn't very nice to anybody." She looks pained. "Was I really horrible?"

"Only to teachers."

She rolls her eyes. "I don't like people who put themselves in positions of authority."

I laugh at this and Farah frowns quizzically.

"That was *literally* their job," I say.

"And your point is?" Farah replies.

She glances away, a moment of doubt. I never really spoke to girls at school; I never really spoke to *anyone*. I was always too worried about saying the wrong thing or having nothing to say or messing up my words and making a fool of myself. I wish I'd tried harder, but somehow I always thought there was more time.

"You know you're probably just a figment of my imagination," Farah says, forcing a crisp into her mouth and chewing it like she's chewing cotton wool.

I grin.

"What?" Farah says.

"You're dying and you're fantasizing about me," I say.

"In your dreams, weirdo!" She throws her crisp at me. "Besides, if that's right, then you're fantasizing about me as well."

I smile, and say breezily, "It wouldn't be the first time."

This is too much for her and she's lost in hilarity, thumping her chest and gasping for air. I can't quite believe my audacity. But then: why not? It's starting to look as if I really did waste my entire life like I was always afraid I might. I may as well try to enjoy whatever little bit I have left.

On the next ward along, we find an annex where people with private medical insurance go. It's almost identical to the regular wards but smaller and nicer. Farah hops on to the bed and lies primly, smoothing down her shirt so she looks neat and tidy, tucking a few loose strands of hair behind her ear. She shoots me a meaningful look.

"Is it bad news, doctor?" she says, in a mock innocent voice.

"I'm afraid there's good news and bad news, Ms Rafiq."

"The bad news?"

"I'm sorry to say we're going to have to amputate your right leg."

Farah holds her hand to her mouth. "Oh, my! And the good news?"

"The lady from bed six had her left leg amputated last week and she'd like to buy your spare slipper."

Farah snorts. "That's *old*... That's..."

Her words fade and she looks bleakly at me. I know what she's thinking: we're exhausted, but neither of us wants to mention sleep. I guess sleep is still something we need in this world, but I don't want to sleep because I don't know if the world will still be here when I wake up.

I think about the last electrical eddies and currents flying around my dying brain. A fractured, wounded brain state creating a broken half-finished world. It's not so different to regular life: we don't know how or when it's going to end. All we know is that it can't last.

I hope that it comes without warning, I think. *While we're laughing.*

"Another game of bed-bowls?" Farah says, recovering and offering me her hand.

"Why not?" I reply.

I take her hand, a dainty parody, *Downton Abbey*-style, parading towards the corridor.

And then we stop.

The blood drains from my legs. It feels as if the air has been drawn from the room, my throat clenching at vacuum.

A small boy stands in the doorway.

"Hello?" he says, tentatively.

I try to breathe but I can't, I can only gasp. Farah

and I are still holding hands but it's not for comic effect anymore. I feel her fingers tighten around my own. *So this is it*, I think. *Death is a little East Asian kid in a Spiderman T-shirt.*

"You're like me," he says.

"Like you how?" Farah replies cautiously.

"You're ghosts as well."

EIGHT

I feel sick but when I look at Farah I see she's grinning and shaking her head slowly. "I know you," she says. "You're Chiu Lin, from Year Eight."

Chiu nods mutely.

"But … you're not dead. You're not even dying."

Chiu blinks once or twice like he's thinking this over. "What do you mean?"

"What's the last thing you remember?" Farah says.

Chiu squirms like he'd rather not tell us but Farah frowns at him with such a teacherly intensity that he eventually relents.

"I accidentally kicked our football on to the sports hall roof," he says. "And Alexi Koch dared me to go fetch it."

Farah nods, like she knows this already. "Do you remember what happened after that?" she prompts.

"Not really…" Chiu gives us a baffled look. "Alexi

was calling up to me and then a teacher came and I don't remember anymore."

"You fell off, dumbnut," Farah says, her face splitting into a broad grin.

"What?" Chiu's eyes grow wide.

"You tripped and practically nosedived off the roof. You'd be dead except there was a shed that broke your fall."

"I sort of remember." Chiu nods.

Of course. Even I know about Chiu Lin falling off the sports hall roof. It was after I left but a friend who'd stayed on to do his A-levels messaged me to let me know. There's nothing a school likes more than a good catastrophe to gossip about.

"You've been in a coma for six months," Farah says. "You have your own special section in the school newsletter. But you're *not* dying. They reckon you'll be fine."

Farah and I glance at each other, a hopeful glimmer. If Chiu isn't dying, maybe we're not dying either?

Chiu looks impressed. "I'm in the newsletter?"

Farah rolls her eyes. "They talk about it *every* assembly. It's quite boring actually."

We exchange stories as we follow Chiu along a corridor and into the next wing.

"I woke up here," he says. "In the hospital. But alone

and everything silent. I lay in bed for a while – I thought the zombie apocalypse had come." I nod and Farah flashes me a withering look. "Then I thought I must be a ghost so I got up and started exploring. Then I found the library … so I moved."

He swings open the doors to reveal the medical library. It's not big: an L-shaped room with no windows, half a dozen low stacks, some desks, a counter and bookshelves lining the walls. Chiu has made a kind of sleeping area in the corner of the L. He's dragged in a mattress from one of the wards and torn pages out of medical textbooks and blue-tacked them up like posters. More books are stacked untidily around the mattress, some piles kicked over and scattered on the floor among food wrappers and half-eaten chocolate bars. There's something unbearably sad about the whole scene. I imagine him here alone, convinced that he's a ghost, quietly setting up for the world's loneliest sleepover.

"How long have you been like this?" I ask.

Chiu doesn't answer right away. "A long time. I don't know. Months?" He kneels down and sifts through his piles of books. After a moment he pulls one out and hands it to me. "Here. I tried to keep track, but…"

He trails off. The book is an exercise book with finely squared paper, the sort of thing a librarian would use for keeping track of their to-do list. I open it and find a tally that fills the page, four vertical lines and a fifth line through each one. I catch a worried look from Farah. I can see right away there's a lot more than six months' worth of days here. Six bundles of five per row. That's thirty days a row: roughly a month. Twenty or thirty lines on the page filling a whole page and half of the next one. That's ... three *years*?

But it wasn't possible. Chiu only fell off the roof six months ago.

"You haven't been in a coma for that long," Farah says.

I look at the pile of food wrappers and wonder how many times he tried to eat even though he wasn't hungry; how many times he sat, disappointed, with the tasteless chocolate in his mouth.

"I think time is different here," Chiu says. "I read something, look—" He gets up again, becoming animated, and sifts through more of his books and torn-out pages. He pulls out something that looks like a magazine but it's thicker and it has a serious, academic look to it. The cover says: JAMA Journal of Neurology. "This is a study that a team in London published recently," he says. "Here."

We study the page together.

In a small study of six coma patients, Brownstein's team found that the brains of two burst to life on a regular cadence that resembled an accelerated sleep-waking cycle. These patients displayed a surge in the specific type of brain waves that indicate conscious thought. Production of those brain waves – gamma waves – spiked up to three hundred times, reaching levels higher than those found in normal conscious brains.

"You see?" Chiu says.

"Not really," Farah answers.

"They recorded gamma waves which means the patient was *awake*. But not in the ordinary world. So ... maybe they were here?"

"So we might not be dying, just in a coma?" I say.

"Not even that," Chiu replies. "You said I've been in a coma for six months but I've counted nearly three years. You've only been here a few days so this might be a heartbeat in the ordinary world. You might still be having a seizure, Kyle. Farah might have passed out or be fitting or anaesthetized. Just unconscious in some way."

Farah shakes her head disbelievingly. "What are you? Some kind of child genius?"

"I like to read," Chiu says, looking bashful. "I always did. And there's not much else to do here."

"What do you think?" I say to Farah.

"It's possible," she says.

"Why is it only us here?" I say. "It's a hospital, there's got to be a bunch of people in comas or under anaesthesia."

"Maybe it only happens occasionally. A chance thing."

"Lucky us," I say.

Farah stands and strolls thoughtfully along the stacks of books, allowing her fingers to trail across them. I watch her and wonder what's going on inside her head. I should be celebrating, overcome with relief – not dead, not dying, just unconscious – but a part of me is anxious. The tight, safe little world we've been enjoying feels uncertain again. I liked it better when it was just the two of us, when we felt that we might die at any moment and so nothing mattered.

"Anyway, there's a more pressing question," Chiu continues.

"Shoot," Farah says, vaguely.

"How do I know you're real?"

Farah turns and raises an eyebrow. "Do I look real?"

"You know what I mean," Chiu says.

Farah touches each book in turn as if reassured by their feel. "There's something we studied in philosophy once," she says at last. "A Chinese poem." She quotes: "Once, Zhuang Zhou dreamed that he was a butterfly: a butterfly flitting and fluttering about, happy with himself and doing as he pleased. He didn't know that he was Zhuang Zhou.

"Suddenly he woke up and there he was, solid and unmistakably Zhuang Zhou. But he didn't know if he was Zhuang Zhou who had dreamed he was a butterfly, or a butterfly dreaming that he was Zhuang Zhou."

"What does that mean?" Chiu says.

"It means we have no way of knowing what's *real*," Farah answers. "But that's the same in the ordinary world too. So … maybe it doesn't matter." She smiles a little. "You're a weird kid, Kyle … and Chiu's a clumsy idiot. But I *choose* this world if that's OK with you. For as long as I'm here, I *choose* this."

NINE

We drag two more mattresses from the ward next to the library and set up camp. We could easily have each had a room to ourselves, but we agree, without the need for much discussion, that we'd prefer to stay close.

The mattresses are heavy, so it takes a long time to slide them along the corridor. We lift them one at a time at an angle so they fit through the door and then shuffle them on their ends between the stacks.

"How did you do this on your own?" Farah gasps.

"I had ... a lot of time," Chiu responds, groaning with strain as he struggles with the squishy material.

I'm bone-tired again but I won't sleep. The mission of setting up our camp and claiming our little corner of the hospital feels too important.

Farah evicts Chiu from his corner spot and strings up a blanket between two of the stacks, making a private section for herself. Chiu objects at first but he quickly realizes that he doesn't stand a chance against Farah. At least she has the decency to make amends by carefully taking down each of his makeshift posters and relocating them next to his mattress. I catch a glimpse of some of the posters as they come down: an intricate drawing of the brain and its connections into the central nervous system, a picture of the top of someone's head, a window cut into the skull and the pinkish brain tissue exposed.

A couple of Chiu's pages are different, I notice. Not brain tissue or medical drawings, but close-ups of … anatomy. Farah and I realize at the same moment what they are.

"Chiu?" Farah exclaims, holding a page at arm's length. "You dirty little—"

Chiu looks shame-faced and quickly whips the pages down and stuffs them in the back pocket of his jeans. "Like I said," he mutters. "I was alone for a long time."

After we're all set up, we sit in awkward silence on our mattresses.

Then Chiu says, "Tell me a story!"

"Farah is the one with stories," I say.

Farah casts me a doubtful look but Chiu continues to stare at her with such child-like urgency that at last she relents. "Um … I don't know… Wait, I got one." She settles herself more comfortably, sitting cross-legged, her hands draped loosely over her knees.

"There's a farmer," she says, "in ancient Greece. Renowned for owning a beautiful horse. But one day the horse escapes and his neighbours, seeing his misfortune, rush to comfort him. They say, 'Oh, man, that's really bad luck, we're so sorry.'"

"Was it them who stole it?" Chiu asks.

Farah looks irritated. "No. They're just trying to be nice. But the farmer shrugs and says: 'Perhaps.'"

"He doesn't mind that he lost his horse?" Chiu says.

"The following week, the horse that escaped finds its way back. And it brings with it four beautiful wild horses."

"Awesome!" Chiu says.

"The neighbours come over and they congratulate the farmer. 'Wow,' they say. 'That's really good fortune you got all those horses.'"

"I bet they're secretly jealous," Chiu says. "Are they going to steal them?"

"No," Farah responds dryly. "It's not that kind of a story."

"Go on," I say.

"The farmer shrugs and responds: 'Perhaps.' The next week, the farmer's son tries to tame one of the wild horses, but it throws him and he breaks his leg. The neighbours come over and they say—"

"I know! I know!" Chiu says. "They say, 'Sucks to be you!'"

"Close enough," Farah answers. "Anyway... The farmer shrugs and says only—"

61

"Perhaps," I chime in.

"But then a war breaks out," Farah continues, smiling inwardly. "And all the young men in the village are drafted to fight, except for the farmer's son who can't go to war on account of his broken leg. And the neighbours come over and they say: 'That's such good fortune that you won't lose your son to war.' And the farmer responds…"

"Perhaps," Chiu and I say obediently.

There's a silence, then Chiu says, "I don't get it."

Farah sighs. "The moral is: it's not about what happens to you, it's about how you respond to it. I guess we're here so we should make the most of it."

Farah reaches up and pulls the dividing sheet across and seals off the space between us. It's just me and Chiu on this side with the silent stacks of books and the little counter where, in another world, a librarian sits and takes care of the library.

"G'night, boys," Farah murmurs.

"Goodnight," Chiu says.

I lie down, trying not to listen too closely to the sound of Farah moving around on the far side of the curtain, trying not to let my imagination run wild.

"Hey, Kyle," Chiu asks. "How long have you been here?"

"I came today," I say.

"So you haven't slept here yet?" Chiu says.

There's a note in his voice that makes me instantly alert.

I hear Farah chuckling knowingly on the far side of her curtain.

"What?" I say. "What is it?"

"Oh, boy," Chiu says. "You'll see. Dreams are pretty wild in this place."

TEN

"Promise me, no prayer meetings."

"I promise," Mum replies.

Mum's only thirty-six but she looks much older as she slides into our little Fiat and adjusts the rear-view mirror. She has a frail bird-like quality. She chews her nails constantly, inspecting the frayed edges of each finger as she goes. I wonder sometimes if it's all my fault: if Mum would have been a different person if she hadn't found herself the single parent of a child who scared the life out of her on a regular basis.

"Just be yourself," she says. "He'll love you, I'm sure."

I watch the grubby pebble-dashed council houses slide past, anxiety crawling inside me. The streets feel darkened – laden with a sense of threat. I haven't left home in six months and somehow I hadn't noticed how big of a deal it had become. I don't want to be outside. I don't want to be anywhere except safe and cosy in the familiar fug of my bedroom. But Mum wanted me to go with her to visit Father Michael. She practically begged me and I didn't know how to say no.

We pull up outside a row of terraced houses on the old side of town. It's a busy through road and the three-storey Victorian houses on this block are an odd mixture of the recently renovated and the soon-to-be-condemned. The house we're parked opposite has recently received new double glazing and Nordic style fake wooden panelling. Father Michael's house is next door and it's on the shabbier end of the scale. Cracked pebble-dash clings weakly to the wall and it's fallen away entirely in places to reveal ulcerous cavities and disintegrating brickwork. The big bay window at the front is thick with years of grime and provides a glimpse into a sparsely decorated front room littered with cardboard boxes that overflow with paperwork.

"He's a very special man," Mum says.

She knocks on the door and after a few minutes it opens a crack. A sallow face appears, half shadowed from the hallway.

"Mary?" The voice is soft, delicate.

"Father Michael," Mum replies. "This is Kyle, my son. I've brought him to meet you like we discussed."

Father Michael hesitates, trying to hide his irritation. After a moment, he sighs wearily and says, "Well, I suppose you'd better come in then."

He leads us down an unlit hallway with yellowing wallpaper and a frayed brown carpet. I can't help noticing that the door to the front room is one of those heavy fire doors with its own Yale lock screwed into place.

"Can I get you anything?" Father Michael says. "Tea?"

"I'll make it," Mum volunteers. "I want you and Kyle to get to know each other."

Father Michael gestures for me to sit on one of the filthy sofas that seem to be dotted with cigarette burns and takes the dining chair in the opposite corner. He's quite a lot older than Mum: a slim, awkward-looking man. His light-blue shirt is yellowed around the collar and looks like it hasn't been washed in a good few days, his hair clings damply to his scalp. He glances behind him, towards the doorway that leads into the kitchen, like he's anxious for Mum to return.

"It's a pleasure to meet you, Kyle," he lies, turning back to me.

I give him a dogged smile. *I won't be rude*, I think. I don't want to upset Mum. But I'm not going to make it easy for him either. I watch Mum moving around the kitchen like somebody who knows it far too well. *There's something* off *about this place*, I think. A sense of neglect and lurking menace. A vigilance, like a spider crouching in an unkempt web.

"Your mother is a wonderful person," Father Michael says.

Another nod from me.

"We pray for you together often."

"Um … OK," I say.

"God forgives you for your affliction."

"Um … my *what*?"

Father Michael turns towards the kitchen again and calls through the doorway. "There are biscuits in the cupboard, Mary."

"I got them," Mum calls back lightly.

"Do you pray, Kyle?" he says, turning back to me.

"No," I say. "I'm an atheist."

"Don't you believe in anything?"

"Being an atheist isn't an absence of belief," I say.

This is something I learned on YouTube. A phrase I particularly like.

"Then what *do* you believe in?" Father Michael says.

"I believe in my own uncertainty," I say. "Looking at the world and trying to understand it the best I can. Not making up stories and claiming they're the only truth."

"The fact of the matter is, Kyle," Father Michael says, hunching his shoulders as he leans towards me, "it doesn't matter much what you think. You were made by God and *for* God and until you understand that the world is not going to make much sense to you."

I resist the temptation to snort. Father Michael looks like he's about to say something more but there's a loud bang upstairs and a clatter as a young woman with dyed yellow hair appears.

"Hi, Lacy!" Mum calls through delightedly.

"Hi, Mary," Lacy replies, less enthusiastically.

Lacy is thin in a sickly-looking way. She wears leggings and a stained, old-looking puffer jacket. She darts forward and kisses Father Michael on the cheek. I watch their exchange, unsure what to make of it. Too old to be his daughter? Too young to be his wife? Father Michael seems to enjoy my confusion. After Lacy slams out of the front door he flashes me a knowing wink and says, "My lodger."

Mum bustles in and hands around tea and custard creams. She sits at the dining table next to Father Michael. I catch her eye and give her a desperate look.

"Quiet lad, isn't he?" Father Michael muses as he bites into his custard cream.

"The epilepsy," Mum says. "It affects him…" She trails off, her hands crawling over each other like one is looking for a place to hide within the other.

Father Michael nods. "I'm sorry about the epilepsy, Kyle. God has to put some of us on our backs before we can be looking up at Him."

This time I can't help myself. "Bullshit," I murmur. I watch the look of horror spread across Mum's face as she turns from me to Father Michael. I don't care, I'm tired of Mum's churches treating epilepsy like it's either a punishment or a sign from God. "It's not that," I say. "It's neurology and genetics and science and messed-up brain scaffolding."

I'm about to stand and storm out when Father Michael reaches forward with surprising speed and grabs my wrist. "Don't be fooled by our present circumstance, Kyle. I have big plans. I'm on a mission from God and your mother is going to help me."

"Help you? How?"

Father Michael taps the side of his nose. "For now you see through a glass, darkly. But then face to face... Now you know in part, then you shall know, even as you are known."

Corinthians thirteen twelve, I think. *A well-known one.*

I look at Mum, but she sits rigid. My skin crawls under Father Michael's hand.

"Um ... sure. Whatever," I say.

I pull my hand away, my heart pounding. I'm shaken but I don't want him to know that. Father Michael smiles the mean, happy smile of somebody who thinks they've won. "There are many rooms in my castle, Kyle," he says. "For the worthy."

I glance at the peeling damp-stained wallpaper.

"Castle?" I say. "Funny kind of castle."

ELEVEN

I wake gasping and stare in panic at the cream-coloured walls of the library for a long time before I remember what they mean and where I am.

"Hey, sleepyhead." Farah smiles. "It's OK. You didn't drool."

Chiu is watching me. "Good, huh? Like IMAX Superscreen Deluxe?"

I take a shaky breath. I can still feel the pressure of Father Michael's hand holding on to my wrist.

He's the reason I was out on the street on my own.

The certainty of the thought unnerves me.

Why can I still not remember?

"Is it always like that?" I ask.

"It gets easier," Chiu responds. He jumps up, wobbling unsteadily on his mattress. "Come on!"

"Come where?" I say, confused.

"Chiu wants to show us something," Farah says. "He says it'll help."

"What?" I say.

"It's a surprise!" Chiu responds.

Farah and I exchange a look. Chiu seems both older and younger than the Year Eights I remember from school. He probably started out smarter than an average thirteen-year-old but all that time alone, reading, has made him *scarily* smart. And yet he's still a little kid inside. He bounces slightly on his mattress, boiling with fragile excitement.

"OK, OK," I concede.

We follow him down another long corridor and up a flight of stairs. The walls are decorated differently on this ward. A brightly painted caterpillar stretches the whole length of one wall; a glade of painted toadstools adorns the nurses' station.

"Have you been here before?" Chiu asks.

"No," Farah says.

"This is my favourite place." He frowns, then adds: "But it's scary. You can't stay long."

There's a Captain America mural in the waiting area and I can't help wondering what can possibly be so scary about a children's ward.

We stop outside a pair of double doors.

"You ready?" Chiu says.

"Kind of," Farah replies.

Inside is a much larger room: about twice the size of

the wards, with tables, chairs and bookcases on one wall and a small hatch where I guess they serve coffee and biscuits in the ordinary world. I don't think I've been in this particular day room before, but I've spent enough time in enough other day rooms to recognize the vibe. They've made a real effort with this one: paintings, brightly coloured rugs, soft furnishings. My first thought is that I can't understand why Chiu didn't make this his camp instead of the library.

"Come on, let's choose some games to take back with us," Chiu says. He kneels in a little cordoned-off games area where there's beanbags and a stack of games neatly arranged on IKEA shelves, and starts sifting through the boxes.

"Just don't look at the windows," he adds.

Farah and I can't help ourselves. We look and we see immediately what he means. The day room has been carefully built into the corner of the building so two walls are entirely glass. In the ordinary world it would make it bright and cheery but here the view stretches over the surrounding area and it looks … *wrong*.

Insubstantial. Hazy. A lazy artist's impression of a town that trembles like a reflection on the surface of a soap bubble, threatening to shatter at any moment.

It reminds me of the way a seizure feels: the fraught, edgy energy of postictal shock. Farah trembles next to me.

"What's wrong with this place," she breathes.

"Try not to think about it," Chiu replies.

"It's like it's not finished," I say.

Chiu sighs. "The outside is scary. Didn't you figure that out yet? Why do you think I'm sleeping in a windowless library?" He gives us a withering look. "Now come and tell me what games you want."

Farah's hand finds mine and we help each other over to Chiu. The games section, at least, is somewhat shielded from the windows by a pillar and if I concentrate hard on the games it's possible to not think about the outside for a moment.

"I want to get out of here," Farah says, shakily.

"You need to choose a game first," Chiu insists.

There's a petulant, unwilling to be disappointed, edge to his voice. Farah reaches forward without really looking and snatches up Battleship. I spot a box of Uno and feel a small rush of genuine excitement. Before he died, Grandad and I used to play Uno all the time. I find the rhythmic back and forth of the cards peaceful, the pickups and the put-downs. There aren't many choices in Uno; you just follow the rules and the cards go back and forth. I guess that's why I like it.

We grab our stash and get out of there as quickly as we can.

"Should we take these back to the day room after we're done?" I ask. "I don't like the idea of the kids in the ordinary world not having a pack of Uno."

73

Chiu shakes his head. "It doesn't work that way," he says. "I've tried it. If you go back in an hour or two there will be another Uno in the day room."

"What?"

"It makes sense," Farah says. "What we have here is the *idea* of Uno. A template. But it doesn't matter where the *idea* of it is — the substance of it is in the ordinary world. It's like Plato said: World of Form, World of Substance, all that."

"Completely," Chiu agrees.

"Of course," I say, dubiously.

We play games all afternoon. Chiu is clearly delighted to have company again and he corners us with challenge after challenge. It's fun at first. Chiu brims with energy and he makes it easy to forget (at least for a while) the tightly enclosed walls around us and the vast, awful nothingness beyond them.

I enjoy letting go, having an excuse to be childish. I make loud explosion noises and simulate the sound of distant screams when my battleship goes down. When I catch myself and glance self-consciously at Farah, I find that she's smiling more fondly at me than I'd imagined she ever could. After that, we try to outdo each other with ever more blood-curdling sound effects. "I'm burning! I'm burning!" Farah squeals when her aircraft carrier is lost.

After four or maybe five Battleship tournaments I've had enough and Farah becomes quiet and slides away to browse the stacks of books.

"Chess?" Chiu suggests, tirelessly.

I concede to a game of chess. I used to think I was pretty good at chess, I played board two in the chess club at school for a while. But Chiu is something else. He's fast and he doesn't follow the usual patterns and moves they normally teach you. He plays like he's taught himself, like he's seen every game you could possibly play and he already knows the ending.

"How are you so good?" I say, admiringly.

"I was alone for a long time," Chiu reminds me. "I played with myself a lot."

Farah glances over to us. "We guessed. But how are you so good at chess?"

It starts to feel like evening. We can't be sure without hunger or thirst or daylight, but after a brief discussion we agree that it's at least late afternoon. Who knows what time it is in the ordinary world? I imagine myself lying in the street still, caught in a blinding neurological flashbulb white-out, while living this – all this – in that same instant.

Uno, we all conclude, is our favourite. We slip into a kind of waking dream, watching the cards move backwards and forward. Each with its colour and its number, trying to match another colour or number. And the wildcards – plus-four, reverse, swap – they're like bumps in the road, unexpected twists that can upend a game without warning. Farah and Chiu are fiercely competitive. When Farah switches the colour to red, I know it's because she's been watching Chiu's moves and knows that it's the only colour he doesn't have. When Chiu plays a reverse, I'm sure he's done it only to ensure that he can hit me with a plus-four before I can get rid of my final card.

But I still win every hand.

"You're good at this," Chiu says.

I shrug. "It's a game of chance, you can't be *good* at it."

Chiu looks unconvinced. "No, I mean, weirdly good."

"I'm not cheating if that's what you mean."

Chiu shakes his head. "I read something interesting recently." He puts down his cards and rummages briefly among his pile of journals. "Here it is!" He thumbs the pages until he finds what he's looking for. "Have you ever heard of blindsight?" Farah and I shake our heads. "If your striate cortex gets damaged, you can become *cortically* blind even though you are *optically* sighted."

"Your straight what?" Farah says.

"Your *striate* cortex. It's the part of your brain that processes visual information. Your sight."

"What does this have to do with Uno?" I say.

"Sufferers who are *cortically* blind experience the world as if they're *physically* blind. They have no conscious sensation

76

of sight. But if you ask them to guess what colour something is, they *know*. They just don't know *how* they know."

"And this relates to Uno, how exactly…?" Farah says.

Chiu briefly glances at his hand and drops a yellow four. I have a yellow plus-two: just enough to hold Farah off for another round.

"The point is, your brain is capable of processing information that you are not *consciously* aware of. Like a sixth sense." Chiu looks at us solemnly. "I think Kyle might have a sixth sense for Uno."

Farah and I exchange a look before we burst into laughter.

"Worst. Superpower. Ever," Farah snorts.

Chiu looks upset. "You can look it up," he insists. "There was a really famous case study of a monkey, who—"

"Wait," Farah says, swallowing her laughter. "Are you comparing Kyle to a monkey?"

"*Chiu?*" I say, in mock offence.

Chiu sighs and flicks a card at Farah.

"Uno!" I say, placing my penultimate card. And I know, because I've been counting the cards and not because I have a sixth sense, that neither of them can stop me winning.

Later, after Chiu is asleep, Farah and I lie on either side of the dividing blanket and she tells me about her parents and her grandparents, who moved here from Bangladesh in the sixties. Her dad works as an IT consultant, she says.

They're Muslim but she doesn't know what she believes.

She tells me that she was diagnosed with a low-grade astrocytoma when she was twelve. "The good kind of brain cancer," she says, glibly.

"But you're cured now?" I say.

"I thought I was," she says. "But … something put me here, didn't it?"

"It could be anything," I say, trying to sound reassuring. "Maybe you fainted. Maybe you developed epilepsy like me."

Farah is silent for a moment. "You're never really cured with the big C. They just give you statistics, follow-ups, five-year-survival rates."

"What was it like?" I ask. "Being sick."

"It's normal," Farah replies. "That's the worst thing. Before I got sick I used to wonder what being sick was like. I'm not morbid or anything but you do sometimes, don't you? Like … you see a show on television and you think: *Oh, god, what if that was me?* But then it happens and it's … normal. A conversation in a hospital office, with posters of warts and sepsis on the walls. You're still you. None of the other crap goes away. It's awful, but it's also … *ordinary*. Just another thing. I don't know how to explain."

I think about the moment when the consultant recommended surgery for me. Farah has it right: *ordinary*. No dramatic mood music, no darkening of the sky or crash zooms on my anguished expression. The consultant was a kind, patient, matter-of-fact man with gold-framed glasses that were too big for his face. Mum and I sat there while he told us it was a "relatively straightforward procedure" and "the majority of patients responded well". I remember wishing desperately that my arms would stop trembling and my teeth would stop chattering.

"Were you scared?" I ask.

"I used up all my scared," Farah says. "It sounds weird but I think I *chose* not to be scared."

"You can't *choose* not to be scared."

"You can. If you have long enough. Maybe that's why I was such a pain when I came back to school. I had no scared left."

TWELVE

I dream that I'm being watched.

THIRTEEN

After my GCSEs, when I stopped going outside, my world got small very quickly.

I established a routine: wake, shower, toast and Marmite, back to my room for a couple of hours of online study, mid-morning break with YouTube and maybe a game, toast with beans (and sometimes Marmite) for lunch, a bit more revision, a movie to wind down and get me through the tricky afternoon-evening transition, then dinner (composed of frozen potato and meat products) sitting opposite Mum at our impossibly small kitchen table if she came home after work, or on my own if she went to a prayer meeting. I had everything I needed, even the illusion of a goal in the form of GCSE revision and watching YouTubes about physics and London. It was easy to take my sense of failure, the fear that I might never leave this place, and pretend it wasn't real. *This is just temporary,*

I'd tell myself. *As soon as I get my GCSEs I'll be off and life will begin.*

In the hospital, I feel the same sort of routine setting in. Except it's different because I have Chiu and Farah here. We play board games, lots of board games: chess and battleships ... but mostly Uno. Chiu and Farah don't seem to mind that I win every hand, even when I try my best to lose.

We joke around a lot. Everything makes us laugh, even the silliest thing.

Our situation is awful, but part of me is happier than I've ever been. Somewhere, in another reality, our bodies are dead or dying or trapped in ictal paralysis. But here, life is good.

Between games, Chiu reads medical journals with an intensity that doesn't suit his age, like he's searching for something. Whenever she gets a chance, Farah slips away and checks in on the baby on the neonatal ward.

One day, I decide it's time to experiment with this place.

I've always liked rules. Rules mean predictability, order, safety. I can't shake the idea that this place must have rules just like the ordinary world, just different ones. Science took us out of superstition and fear back there, I think, so maybe it can do the same here.

We've always been able to sense people in the ordinary world. For a while, I could still see them in Casualty.

Now, it's more of a feeling, a sense that somebody has just walked out of the room, or the impression that the space behind a closed door is not empty. I wonder if there's a way to tease apart those feelings and *see* the people in the ordinary world again.

Communicate with them even.

I think of the videos I've watched on YouTube, about the way time flexes and bends when you're not watching it. I wonder if that's the secret to our fragile connection with home. I set myself up in the library like a hunter waiting for his prey. After a long time, my mind begins to relax. Time becomes liquid. I start to feel the people around me coming more clearly into focus. It's not as simple as the idea that time moves more quickly here. Time here and time in the ordinary world are decoupled: free to move independently of each other except in the moments when they don't. I don't know how I know this. The knowledge comes to me as a kind of revelation. A certainty without origin.

If I wait long enough, I think, maybe I'll slip into sync with the people in the library. Maybe we'll connect, even though, in the same instant, I am lying unconscious in the street.

"What are you doing?" Chiu asks, looking up from his journal.

"Trying to see them," I say.

Chiu shivers. "Are you sure you want to?"

After a while, I become aware of a man sitting at the end of the table. The first time I try to look at him, I twist my head too sharply and he's gone. It takes a few more tries before I can hold my nerve long enough for the figure to fully take form: reading quietly, barely visible from the corner of my eye.

I force myself to stay calm as I turn to him. I can see him: studying, lost in intricate thoughts, his mind spread out and seeping like water into our world. I can feel the activity inside his head like spiders crawling around in the darkness. His eyes defocus and for a moment they lock on to mine. My heart stops. I wonder what it must feel like for him. A sense of unease? A shadow? I watch him fighting the feeling – the awareness of something – that his rational mind won't accept. Then, with an urgent spasm, his rational mind loses and he gets up and leaves.

After he's gone, I realize that he's left his notebook. I know, somehow, that if I take my eyes off it, it will be gone too. He still holds it in his mind so it's still tethered to the ordinary world and the *idea* of it is not fully in ours yet.

But maybe it could be?

I stare hard at the book. I feel the silent tug of war, the *isness* of the book loosening from the man's thoughts as he goes about his day, my own mind closing around it. After a while, ten or twenty minutes of my time, the book begins to look more solid. I reach forward and pick it up.

"It's stillness," I call to Chiu excitedly. "That's how

it works. If something doesn't move and people in the ordinary world stop thinking about it, the thing seeps into this world. Buildings, furniture, stale food, but not people."

"Makes sense," Chiu remarks, glancing up again, only briefly, from his journal.

The discovery makes me giddy with excitement. There *are* rules here. Different ones to the ones we're used to, but rules all the same. Rules make the world more solid, less precarious, less terrifying. I am like one of Farah's prisoners, chained up and scratching my theories of the shadows into the dirt, taking comfort in my own stories.

When Farah gets back, I tell her about it and we swig warm Cokes in celebration and christen our world "the Stillness". Farah and Chiu congratulate me. I know they're only humouring me, because they see how pleased I am with myself, but in this place we'll take any excuse we can for a party. Farah sings pop songs – it turns out she has an incredible voice – and we all half dance, half bounce on our mattresses and spin on the spot until we're dizzy and nauseous and it feels as if the whole planet is cartwheeling beneath us.

The next day, after Chiu and Farah have had their fill of losing at Uno, I find myself back in the casualty department.

It's cold and empty, shadows line every corner even

though there's no direct light to cast them. There are none of the glimpses of the ordinary world I saw when I first arrived. Just a heavy, disused feeling. Unease crawls over me. I remember staggering in here, my brain on fire, my thoughts splintered into jagged fragments. I wonder what would have happened if I hadn't met Farah, if her presence hadn't grounded me, helped me hold on to myself. Would I have lost my mind? Would I have torn myself apart? I don't think I'd have been as stoical as Chiu.

All you'll want to do is close your eyes and wait it out.

I approach the big concertina doors that mark the entrance. After yesterday's successes, I think I might be able to pull the same trick again and figure out why the outside affects us so badly. Another experiment, a gradual exposure and a careful observation of my experiences. I imagine myself carving away my fear by creating a clearer picture of this world, a theoretical framework. My own take on quantum mechanics?

But as soon as I come close I realize that I've made a mistake. My muscles tighten and my heart rises into my throat. I stare at the unchanging emptiness of the outside world, the unguarded canopy of the cloudless sky, and I feel as if I'm teetering on the edge of an impossible chasm.

It's just the ambulance bay. A patch of grey tarmac with faded yellow cross-hatching. But there's something out there. It crowds around the dome of the sky, watching us, judging us. It's the same dread I felt before all this, the same dread that precedes my seizures, the same dread that kept me welded to my house.

But worse, much worse.

I think about the weeks that followed my GCSEs. Recovering, taking it easy at first; Mum glad to know I was home and safe while she was out at work. Then the point where it would be normal to declare myself well. A breath of fresh air. A walk in the park. Buy a cake and go sit by the canal. Simple things. But I stood at the door instead and I felt the sky over my head bearing down, desperate to crush me, and I knew right then that I was going nowhere.

That's when I came up with my new plan. Online retakes. It was OK, I told myself. I was regrouping, getting ready to crush my GCSEs after all, preparing for my future in London. But I knew even then that it was a lie: you can study for GCSEs at home, but you can't take the exams at home.

I step back from the doors and let the safety of the hospital walls fold themselves around me. A new, bitter knowledge follows me inside.

This is ending, I think.

The thought comes from nowhere and fills me with fear. The safety of our routines in the hospital is as much of an illusion as the world I created for myself at home. *Something is coming that will force us from this place*, I think. *And it will be terrible.*

FOURTEEN

I rush back to the library filled with unreasonable fear and when I get back I find Chiu pacing around the room, his small, wiry body thrumming with excitement. "Where were you?" he says.

"I went for a walk."

"I found something. Something important."

I look at Farah, but she's quiet and thoughtful, in a way that makes me anxious. "Go on," I say.

"I've been reading. I read all the new journals. Usually it's nothing – minor discoveries, science stuff – but this month it was different."

He moves jerkily, tightly wound energy making it hard for him to sit still. At last, he plops himself down cross-legged on his mattress and folds back the pages of the journal in his hands. He reads aloud: "Brownstein's team at University College London have demonstrated effective use of a specialized MRI to directly modulate gamma wave activity. They've identified three key activation points thought to provide strong neurological correlates of consciousness, suggesting that consciousness may continue to exist in patients previously considered unconscious, albeit in a form that is not able to interact with the outside world. They describe this state as Disconnected Consciousness.

"In one case, the team successfully manipulated the cytoelectric activity of a patient in a persistent vegetative state, fine-tuning their network stability at a subcellular level to restore them to wakefulness. The team hopes that this will one day become a significant new treatment for certain classes of coma patient."

"So?" I say.

"Don't you see?"

"See what?"

"*Disconnected consciousness*. That's *us*! Which means there's a cure; they can bring us back."

I take the journal and read it again. "It's a research paper," I say. "It'll take years to get approved as a treatment, you know that."

Chiu shakes his head. "Not if we go there and find this machine."

I glance at Farah but I can't read her expression.

"Go there?"

"To London," Chiu says. "University College London."

"How are we supposed to do that? We're passed out

somewhere in the ordinary world. *You're* in the hospital. I'm probably still on the street."

"We go there in *this* world," Chiu explains.

A weak, unconvincing laugh escapes my lips. Is it possible I saw this coming? The sense of dread that followed me back here, is this what it was about?

"We can't go to London," I say. "There's no trains or buses, we don't have a car."

"We'll walk."

"You're not serious," I say. "You want to walk to London?"

"It's not too far," Chiu insists.

Panic flutters in my chest. He's serious. I wish Farah would say something, tell him how ridiculous he's being. I think about how awful it felt in the day room, the windows exposed to that unthinking sky, and try to imagine what it would be like to try to walk all the way to London.

"There's something *wrong* with the outside, you know that," I say. I gesture at the walls around us. "You're sleeping in the only windowless room in the building and now you think we're going to *walk* to London?"

Chiu stares defiantly at me. "We'll be OK."

"And what do you think you're going to do when you get there? There's no electricity in this world. You can't use an MRI without electricity."

A flicker of doubt crosses Chiu's face. "I don't know. We'll figure it out."

I shake my head. "It's not happening, Chiu." I don't like being mean to him but I want to squash this idea before it goes too far.

I imagine Farah's already had this argument with him but she wanted him to hear it from me. I watch Chiu's face tighten with disappointment and I start to feel sorry for him. It's easy to forget how young he is. He wraps it up in reading science journals and being ridiculously clever, but inside he's just a scared little boy who misses his parents.

"You're going to be OK," I say, more softly. "We all are. The doctors are taking care of us. They said you're going to recover, remember? You could wake up at any moment."

Chiu is silent for a moment, then he says: "What if they're wrong?"

FIFTEEN

I offer Chiu a game of chess to make up for being mean
and afterwards we all play Uno, but none of us are in the
mood. Talk of going outside has shaken me. I've become
attached to our safe little hideaway in the library.

Stuck here just like I was stuck at home.

Later, Chiu announces that he's going to the day room
to look for more games. After he's gone, I expect Farah to
bawl me out for being so hard on him, but she says nothing.
Instead, she carries on reading her book, which she found
that morning in the tiny fiction section of the library. I lie
on my mattress, staring at the ceiling, trying to remember
what happened on the morning of my seizure. I picture our
little house with the dining table in the kitchen. But there's
nothing to anchor the memory to that particular morning,
all my mornings are alike and washing into each other.

"Listen … about Chiu's idea—" Farah says.

I sit up on my elbow and turn to her. "I should have been gentler with him, I'm sorry."

"I think we should go."

I stare at her for a second. "You're not serious."

"I am."

"How? It's, like, a hundred miles to London."

"Ninety-two," Farah says, matter-of-factly. "Walking will take a week. Ten days tops. Chiu found a map in the patient library. I checked: we can follow the A5 all the way down and cross over the M25—"

"Wait, wait, *stop*."

Suddenly I realize that I was wrong. It wasn't that they'd been fighting. They'd been planning it without me, they just didn't know how to tell me.

"Look, I know you don't want to—" Farah starts.

"*Want?*" I say, incredulously. "This isn't about *want*." Anger whiplashes inside me, surprising me as much as it does Farah. "I never stayed at home because I *wanted* to."

"OK, I know, I'm sorry. I didn't mean…"

"There's something outside, I can feel it," I say, desperately. "I know you can too."

"You made it right the way across town to get here, didn't you? Nothing bad happened."

"It was horrible," I say. "And it was about half an hour. You want to go and spend a *week* out there."

"It'll be better this time. Together."

I shake my head. "Whatever we feel out there doesn't

want us outside. I don't think we should antagonize it."

"Or maybe it makes us scared to keep us in one place."

Keep moving.

"Don't do that," I say. "You're twisting it."

"I get it, OK," Farah says. "You had plenty of good reasons to be scared of going outside in the ordinary world and in this world we all feel exactly the same way."

"Then why are we even considering this?"

"Chiu didn't get a chance to tell you the rest of his theory," Farah says. "He's been reading about neuroscience for a *long* time—"

"Of course he has," I say, bitterly.

"He has a theory. He thinks our consciousness is like a guitar string, a vibration that finds different resonances. He thinks that being *here* might mean we're *locked* in this brain state, this *resonance*. And that being here might stop us from being able to recover in the ordinary world."

"You're listening to a thirteen-year-old's theories about neuroscience now?"

"He's not a regular thirteen-year-old, you know that."

"It doesn't mean he knows more than the doctors."

"He might."

"How?"

"He knows about *this* place. They don't."

I let my head fall back against the wall and heave a heavy, disbelieving sigh. "Whatever is going on here, there's still a Chiu in the ordinary world and the doctors say he's going to be fine. There's no reason to think they're wrong."

"There is. Think about it," Farah says. "Have you ever heard about this place? Read about it? Seen TV programmes about it?"

I shift uneasily. "I guess not."

"But we know we're not the only people who have ended up here. So, it stands to reason. Nobody who ends up here makes it back to the ordinary world to tell their story."

Farah and Chiu are gone when I wake up the next morning.

Panic squeezes inside me.

They left?

I stare at the cream walls and tan carpet of the sad little library and imagine myself here alone. I imagine them discussing it while I was asleep, concluding that I'd never go with them so they should make it easier on all of us and just leave. My heart thuds and the walls feel as if they're closing around me. I can't go back to being that person, living my life locked up and all alone.

I think about what Farah said. We know we're not the only people to come here. So maybe Chiu's right: if anyone ever got back to the ordinary world we'd *know* about this place. There's an awful, undeniable logic to it that Chiu understood right from the start.

When we met him, he thought he was a ghost. He believed us when we told him that he wasn't, but he never believed that he was going to get better naturally. He'd been reading for years with the aim of *understanding* the world he found himself in, since he met us he'd been reading for another purpose: to *escape*.

The note on Farah's mattress is half lost among the detritus of sheets and books: "Hey sleepyhead. Enjoy your lie-in. Gone to see the baby."

I shudder with relief, fighting the urge to break down and cry. I'm such a fool. I panicked, that's all.

I put down the note and go in search of Farah. In the corridor, I can feel the doctors and nurses and patients in the ordinary world nearby, brushing against me, always just out of sight, their breath teasing the back of my neck. It's a claustrophobic feeling, as if nothing exists beyond my immediate field of vision, as if the world is a gaping, black absence and the walls and details are being drawn in only in the instant before I look at them.

I hurry down the corridors, following the signs to Neonatal. I would be scared of getting lost but I know it's on the same level as the library and hospitals are, at least, well signposted.

I hear Farah as I round the last corner, singing softly, the baby burbling along with her as if it's trying to sing too. She stops when she hears me and turns to stare at me.

"Hey," she says.

"Hey."

I offer my finger to the baby by means of a greeting. It squirms, then swings its hand round and takes hold with surprising deftness.

"Oh, wow," I breathe.

Farah laughs. "He likes you."

I know that in the ordinary world this baby is lying in its cot, unconscious perhaps. What we are holding is the *idea* of a child: a new person, a brain just beginning to spark into consciousness and that consciousness already caught in a state that's detached from the ordinary world. I wish I knew how many babies who come through this ward survive. If Chiu's right, then this idea of a life is already doomed.

"Did you take care of your brothers like this?" I ask.

"My brothers died really young," Farah answers. "Twins. They were born with a heart condition."

"Oh, I'm sorry."

Farah sighs. "I used to resent them so badly. When I was growing up, our living room was filled with photographs of them. I mean, they hadn't *done* anything. They were just born and then they died. So all the photographs were the same: Mum with babies wearing blue hats; Dad with babies wearing knitted cardigans; Farah looking grumpy with babies. Over and over, like my parents were trying to scratch together a fake family album from table scraps. I used to think if I were very clever, or very kind, they'd

start to love me more and put up photos of me as well…
Nothing worked. But then I got sick and suddenly photos
of me started appearing. New ones, old ones, they dredged
them out of the shoeboxes hidden under their bed and put
them up everywhere. Until it was *all* photos of me and my
brothers disappeared completely. And now I miss them."

"Farah, I've been thinking—"

She flashes me a tired look. "That sounds dangerous."

"I'll come with you. You and Chiu, I mean … to
London."

Farah's lips press into a smile. "I knew you would."

"But we need to call into my house on the way. I need
to check something."

"Sure."

"And I think we should only walk for a few hours a day
before we find somewhere inside. It'll take longer, but it'll
limit our exposure."

"That sounds sensible."

A feeling bubbles inside me. I don't know if it's
excitement or cold terror. We're going outside. I'm being
brave. Braver than I thought was possible and it's because
of Farah and Chiu.

The baby stirs in Farah's arms and I reach out for it
again.

"He looks better to me," I say, caught in a moment
of unaccountable optimism. "I think this one's going to
be OK."

The baby squirms more forcefully and I realize that Farah's expression has become troubled. She places the baby back in its cot.

"I don't think so," she says.

"It could. Even if Chiu is right—"

"Look away," Farah says, shortly.

The baby's crying becomes more urgent, its arms strain and relax, strain and relax.

"What's happening?"

"It's dying," Farah responds. "I've seen it before."

"Dying?"

"Don't look," Farah says again.

She turns, positioning herself directly in front of me, face to face with her hands on my shoulders so she blocks my view of the cot entirely. I know better than to try to see around her. All I'm aware of is a flurry of movement, a pained sound, an urgency. Flickers of the ordinary world intensify around us. I catch a glimpse of a nurse, two other people. *Parents*, I think. Their sadness. A quickening, brief, fruitless struggle.

Then it's over.

Farah presses her head into my shoulder and I put my arms around her. Her fingers press into my arms and I can feel her crying. Over her shoulder I can see the cot now. Not a body, as I'd expected. A kind of calcified rubble instead. It makes me think of dried bird crap mixed with broken china and the sight of it turns my stomach in a way

I don't fully understand. It's like when you watch a horror movie, when blood and guts and broken bones are exposed and you get the feeling that you shouldn't be seeing it, like it's a secret that's meant to remain obscure.

"What is it?" I say.

Farah sniffs and swipes tears away with the back of her hand. "It's just death. It happens all the time. It's different here. Like it's hidden in the ordinary world, but underneath, it's like this."

I stare at the empty space where the idea of a new human is no longer there. The space seems larger, emptier, somehow. Mum always talks about God and God's plan. She finds it easier to believe that there's a plan.

But I think she's wrong.

SIXTEEN

"You ready?" Farah says.

I nod, weakly.

We stand by the concertina doors and Farah's hand closes around mine. Chiu holds her other hand. "Deep breath, everybody," she says. "Everything's fine... Everything's fine."

I don't know who she's trying to convince most.

As one, we step outside.

The sky is raw and cold like pewter, the air is dead still. I stare back at the grey concertina doors with the giant "ACCIDENT AND EMERGENCY" letters above them and my stomach twists. It's only been four days but this place feels as much like home as anywhere. Being here, with Chiu and Farah, is as happy as I can remember being. And now we're leaving it, heading off into a hostile world.

"We'd better start walking," Chiu says. "We've got a long way to go."

I don't want to think about how far we have to go. Back on the main road, the strangeness of this world asserts itself more clearly than ever. The buildings feel flimsy and unconvincing: detailed in places, blurry and indistinct in others. The colours are vague and leach into the murky distance. A barely perceptible tremor blurs the outlines of the houses like an elastic band stretched to breaking point.

This is the half-done underside of the world, I think. The steel and girders behind the facade, the tangled threads behind the embroidery.

We cross the roundabout that leads into the industrial estate, following the route that brought me to the hospital. I can still feel the stuttering presence of the traffic in the ordinary world even though I know now it isn't really *here*. I imagine the cars pushing against the fabric of this world, ready to toss unsuspecting pedestrians and animals into this place in sudden flashes of bone and steel.

Chiu turns to us, his mouth open in a wide rictus. At first, I think he's as terrified as I am but then I realize that he's grinning.

"This is so *cool*!" he exclaims.

I glance at Farah. She looks pale. She tries, unconvincingly, to smile back.

"Oh, *come on*," Chiu says. "You've got to admit this is pretty cool."

Cool? I think. *The same way falling out of an aeroplane is cool.*

He jogs out into the middle of the road and struts along with his arms flung wide. "Zombie apocalypse, baby!" he whoops.

He looks back at us, his face shining with excitement. Farah gives a strained laugh. After a moment though, she goes out to join him. "Watch the treeline," she growls, quoting a line from a TV show I've forgotten the name of. "They'll be in there, even if you can't see them."

"It's OK, Grimes," Chiu replies, picking up the line. "I'm ready."

They crouch-walk, imaginary rifles poised, watching for lurking zombies. But then they stop and stand looking uneasily around them. I feel it too. Something has shifted and their pretend fear has turned real.

"Do you really think there's something out there?" Farah whispers.

"Not the way you mean it," Chiu says. "Not zombies."

"A feeling though," Farah says.

"Something you know, but you can't think," Chiu replies.

The cold, gritty air clings to me like a shroud. I shouldn't be able to hear Chiu and Farah talking from this far away, but I can. Reality feels thin and brittle. The *wrongness* was obscured in the hospital. The walls shielded us. Or maybe it was the proximity of other people in the ordinary world.

103

Out here there is no such protection. Rawness blazes down on us like standing directly in the sun's glare.

We can't be out here for long, I think. *It'll drive us mad.*

"Come on," Farah says. "Let's get some miles in before nightfall."

We walk on. Over the bypass, down the hill. London feels like a lifetime away. Nine days. A million miles. A trillion miles. At some point it stops mattering exactly how far it is. We keep walking, stranding ourselves further and further from anywhere that might once have felt safe.

A little further and I catch sight of the tiled rooftops of my housing estate.

"My house is down there," I call.

Farah nods. We cut off the main road and down into the warren of streets. Home is one of those little three-bedroom starter houses with the integrated garage and about fifty other homes that look exactly like it. It sits malignantly at the furthest side of a small crescent. It's funny, but my feelings towards home were much more complicated in the ordinary world. Home was safety, predictability, order. I hated it at one level but needed it at another. Here, the strangeness of this world overwhelms any sense of familiarity and I see it for what it is: a self-made prison for me and Mum both.

The front door gives way after a shove, the obscured glass shuddering in protest. Inside, it smells of kitchen bins and carpet.

I know, instinctively, that it is still the morning of my seizure here. The shifting, elusive time of the Stillness has left this place just as it was, regardless of the four days that passed for me, Chiu and Farah in the hospital.

Everything is shadowed. Abandoned.

It's small. Meticulously tidy except for the little kitchen table that heaves under piles of Mum's notebooks, bills and junk mail.

I feel anxious. I never had friends over to my house in the ordinary world and I don't know what Chiu and Farah will make of this place. I don't like the idea of them imagining me here with Mum. A *shut-in*. I don't like the idea of them seeing this version of me.

I head upstairs to my room, trying to make sense of the swirling mixed-up feelings in my head. My room feels alien to me: unmade bed, bunched-up clothes that never made it to the laundry basket, computer, a few piles of books. I thought seeing my room would help me remember the morning of my seizure but all the memories of all the identical mornings of a whole year of living like this are smeared into one. Did I shower first and then go down to breakfast on the morning of my seizure? Or was that the day before? It could be any one of a hundred identical days.

There's a photograph of Grandad holding me as a baby on the hallway wall. He looks grim, I look vacant. I can imagine Mum twittering around, wanting to capture the moment, wanting to *create* the moment, and Grandad having nothing to do with it.

The photograph in the hallway stands as a kind of monument to him now, a reminder that this was *his* house and he gifted it to Mum and moved himself into sheltered accommodation right after my first seizure.

He wasn't an affectionate man; he sometimes gave the impression that Mum and I were nothing but a matching pair of inconvenient liabilities to him. The house was an anomaly: the closest he ever came to letting slip that he loved us.

He liked to remind us about it often enough though.

"Surprisingly easy," he used to say. "Three forms and not even long ones and you can *give* somebody a house." As if his generosity – his love – embarrassed him and he preferred to pretend it was an administrative error instead.

I miss Grandad. It was easier when he was around: partly because he was old-school and he could never bring himself to believe that epilepsy was real. He thought me and Mum were making a big fuss over nothing which was annoying, of course, but helped me pretend along with him that epilepsy didn't have to stop me doing anything.

I head back downstairs and find Chiu sifting through the piles of papers on the kitchen table. It's a ridiculously small table, tucked into the nook between the work surface and the door. Mum likes to keep the house tidy – I think it's the only way she has to exert some measure of control over the universe – but the universe pushes back in the form of junk mail and bills until it bursts out on to this table like a guilty secret.

Nevertheless, Mum insists on us eating there when she's home in time for dinner. So dinner usually involves eating with piled-up bills and junk mail on our laps. I wonder what Chiu thinks of us. Does he realize that we weren't coping? Does he see how terribly precarious it had all become?

"What's this?" he says, holding something up.

I glance at it. "It's a pamphlet. From Mum's church."

"God's Scholars?" Chiu squints at the ten or so pages of inkjet print that have been scrappily stapled together. Shame knots inside me. Father Michael's pamphlets are all the same. They depict the tortures and humiliations that are going to befall the sinners in hell after the End Times, all done with just a little too much … *relish*. Inexpertly hand drawn and coloured in by Father Michael himself. It's too easy to imagine him working on them late into the night, his mind filled with sadistic glee.

"Weird," Chiu murmurs.

He starts to pocket the pamphlet, but I snatch it away and return it to the pile. As I slide it back into the stack of bills and junk mail, I stop.

I know what this is.

Mum's note.

How could I have forgotten Mum's note?

Scribbled on the back of a receipt in her blockish schoolgirl handwriting: "Early prayer meeting – see you for dinner. Exciting news!"

A cold wedge slides into my stomach.

This is it. This is what I came here for.

"What is it?" Chiu says.

"Just a note from Mum," I say.

But my heart is hammering. Panic trembles beneath my skin and I know it's the same awful panic I felt when I read the note for the first time on the morning of my seizure.

Why would this note scare me so much?

Mum goes out to prayer meetings three times a week. There's nothing new there. I read it again: "Exciting news!"

That was new. Nothing exciting ever happened to Mum.

There's something else as well. Something missing.

I sift through the envelopes and fliers. I remember searching through this pile in the ordinary world, sick with panic, but I don't know what I was looking for.

When I found it… No, wait, that's not right. When I *didn't* find it, that was when I knew I had to go outside.

The memory is achingly close, I can almost touch it.

A shout from outside the backdoor interrupts my thoughts. "*Kyle!*"

I look at Chiu and we rush in the direction of Farah's

voice. We find her in the garage, sitting in Grandad's old Nissan.

"Hey!" she says, seeming pleased with herself. "Can you drive?"

"No," I say, flatly. "People with epilepsy don't get to drive."

"Can you?" Chiu asks Farah.

Farah grins. "I don't know, I never tried." She turns back to the wheel and bobs a little, playfully, like a kid pretending. "Do you have the keys?" she says.

"You're not serious," I say.

"Why not? It's not like we're going to hit anything."

"It won't work," I say. "It's been sitting in the garage ever since Grandad died. For one thing, the battery is probably flat and for another, there's no electricity here."

"There's no *mains* electricity," Chiu corrects me. "We never tried batteries."

Reluctantly, I go back to the kitchen to get the keys. I don't much like the idea of getting into a car while Farah learns to drive for the first time. But I *do* like the idea of being able to drive to London. If we drive we can be there by nightfall. We can go to the hospital and find Chiu's machine and then... Well, who knows. But at least we won't have to walk to London.

I find the keys on the hook next to the door. Their presence seems flimsy, almost not there, as if they might vanish if I take my eyes off them. I wonder what that means.

That they're not fully in this world perhaps? That Mum still thinks about them – about the car, about Grandad? Or that she sometimes picks them up by accident?

I have to concentrate and hold them in my mind like I'm pulling them from Mum's thoughts. I reach forward … and have them.

Then I go back to the garage and hand them to Farah and she fumbles them into the ignition and turns the key. There's a low, grinding dead-car sort of noise. We stare at each other.

"That sounded better than I expected it to," Farah says.

"*Something* is happening," Chiu agrees.

I can't quite allow myself to believe this might actually work.

"Try again," I say.

Farah turns the key and the engine makes another slower, lower whining noise.

"The starter's turning, but the engine isn't catching," I say.

Chiu looks surprised. "Do you know about cars?"

I shake my head. "Grandad did. I used to hang out in the garage with him when I was little, but he never really taught me anything."

There's a hollow *clunk* as Farah pulls the catch under the steering wheel and pops the bonnet. She flashes me a winning smile. "That makes you our resident expert," she says. "You better take a look, hadn't you?"

I go round and lift up the bonnet with an air of resignation. I have vague notions of spark plugs and fuel pumps but my memories are hazy and date back to when Grandad was alive. I only know about starter motors because he once had to replace one and he let me play with the old one, connecting the battery and watching the pinion pop out and connect the electric motor.

I open the bonnet and my stomach instantly lurches in revulsion.

What's inside is not an engine.

Its shape resembles that of an engine but it's twisted, tortured and diabolical. I can see the engine block and a mass of thick pipes and wires curling around it. But the wires are in constant motion – reaching like vines, crushing and squeezing – while the engine block itself yields and folds and sinks like it's being swallowed, reshaping itself painfully and becoming liquid at the same time. The wires multiply, reach and grasp like fingers. I can hear their dry, rubbery squeaking. Usurious, avaricious.

A moment later and my eyes saccade and the engine is restored, back to where it started. I watch this process two or three times, transfixed in horror as the engine is sickeningly devoured again and again before snapping back into place. Only the starter motor remains stable. The *idea* of a starter motor is the only fixed point.

I slam the bonnet shut and stride back past the car, suddenly desperate to be out of there. "Let's go," I croak.

"We're walking."

"What?" Chiu and Farah exclaim.

"Car's broken; we should walk."

About forty minutes later, we reach the flyover that leads down to the A5. After I explained what I saw under the bonnet of the car, Chiu and Farah fell into a thoughtful silence.

"In a world of ideas," Chiu says, after a little while, "complex things – mechanical things – lose their way. It's too hard for someone to keep the idea of them in their head."

"Hence no mobile phones, no electric lights," Farah says.

I nod. "It was the starter engine; that was the only part I understood, nothing else. What I saw … it was never going to run. Maybe if we had a book. Studied mechanics, or something…"

We follow the arc of the filter lane as it drops down on to the A5. It's hard to walk because of the slope – something you don't notice in a car. We step on to the hard shoulder and immediately my senses are flooded by an overwhelming sense of speed and movement. All at once I see the traffic again, loud and lethal, thundering past inches away from me.

"Kyle? What's wrong?" I hear Farah's voice as if it's coming from a long way away.

"The traffic," I say. "Can't you see it?"

"Kind of," Fara says. "Try to unsee it."

I swallow. *Unsee* it? Have you ever tried to *unsee* an optical illusion once you've seen one? It's not easy. It takes a moment. I *choose* not to see the traffic … and it goes. It doesn't fade. It's becomes … never there.

We walk along the hard shoulder, none of us fancying the road itself in case our *unseeing* falters. *We're making sense of this world*, I think. Coming up with names for what's happening. The Stillness. Unseeing. Blindsight.

We're making it more real.

Chiu and Farah walk slightly ahead of me, playing a game that involves one of them punching the other on a fairly regular basis. Farah is tall: nearly as tall as me and twice as tall as Chiu. There's a kind of unhurried smoothness to the way she moves, a confidence I know I'll never have. She glances over her shoulder and grins at me and I feel my pulse instantly begin to throb in my ears.

Evening and then late evening come on suddenly. It felt like mid-morning all day, but then, without any of us noticing the change, the air is cooler and the sky has turned from concrete to slate grey.

"We need to find somewhere," I say. "We can't be out here at night."

"I know," Farah says.

Farah folds and refolds the map until she has it centred on our location. We crane over her shoulder to see. I haven't the first clue where to start but Farah traces her finger along the road.

"We passed the M69 a while back," she says. "So we're roughly here…"

"There are some warehouses," Chiu offers. "They might be OK. Or maybe there's another hospital nearby?"

Farah scans the map. Then her face cracks into a smile. "I have a better idea."

SEVENTEEN

The hotel is actually famous. Not that any of us have ever been here before, but it's one of those hotels where celebrities and rich people fly in on private helicopters and publish their experiences on Instagram.

It's an imposing stone-walled country mansion set in vast, perfectly manicured gardens. It takes a while to hike up the long gravel driveway with Chiu complaining all the way. At one point he stands stock-still and threatens to bed down where he stands.

"It's too far," he says petulantly. "There's a perfectly good petrol station at the bottom of the hill."

"Ignore him," Farah says, not breaking step.

I glance back at Chiu and he throws his arms up in frustration before hurrying after us. At last, the building comes into view. Vast and timeless. Ivy-clad stone walls that look like they've come straight out of a period drama. East and west wings that jut forward dramatically like arms held up to shoo us away.

"Are you sure about this?" I say, nervously.

"It looks awesome," Farah replies.

"You're used to this kind of place, I suppose."

"Oh, yes, Mummy is a platinum member, *obviously*."

Even though I know there will be nobody in this version of the hotel, it's hard to break the taboo of walking into somewhere so fancy. I know Farah doesn't really frequent this kind of place, but I bet she's stayed in a hotel before. I don't think I have. Mum and I usually take our holidays in a caravan in Rhyl and we haven't done that for years because being away from home makes us both too anxious.

As we approach, the building seems to get taller and even less welcoming. Our feet crunch on gravel and our steps turn hollow as we realize with a surprise that we're on a small drawbridge that crosses a moat.

We huddle together instinctively as we go through the grand reception doors. I can't shake the feeling that we're going to get kicked out of here any second now.

Slate floors. Dark wood. Stone vaulting. The lights are out as we've come to expect, but there's a warm, comfortable glow that leaks through from the ordinary world. It's different from the hospital and even my house. Warmer. Softer. Perhaps people are happier here in the ordinary world; they feel safer and so the light that reaches us is better.

"This place is *insane*," Farah enthuses. "Did you see the moat?"

Chiu pauses to inspect a suit of armour in the corner, shining with the light from spotlights reflected from the ordinary world. Farah examines the signs on the walls like she's exploring priceless works of art in a gallery.

"Oh, *yes!*" she breathes.

Suddenly she darts off, vanishing down a spiral staircase. Chiu and I exchange a perplexed look.

"Farah, wait!" I call, giving chase.

Chiu and I hammer down the stone steps as fast as we can. Farah is ahead of us, yelling for us to hurry up. My heart thuds, confused, unsure whether we're in danger or if something else is going on. We enter a long corridor with white walls, part of a modern extension. It has a slick, upscale feel.

Then we burst into another space and I stop, aghast to find that we've blundered across the most incredible swimming pool I've ever seen. An expanse of crystal water, stone pillars, multi-coloured tiles, recliners and crisp white towels. There's a main pool and smaller plunge pools and Jacuzzis connected to it. It looks the way I imagine the grand imperial *thermae* might have looked in ancient Rome.

Farah has already shed her jeans and I catch a glimpse

of her long, brown legs as she hurls herself into the pool with a "*Whoop*".

The splash resonates around the stone ceiling and Chiu immediately starts working on his own jeans. I go to the edge of the pool and watch as Farah surfaces, smiling, sweeping her black hair away from her face. I see her bare legs flash beneath the water. Her face appears more angular with her hair wet and slicked back: pretty, but strong and defiant. Her neck is one long curve that I can't take my eyes off. My breath catches in my throat.

She grins at me. Knowing, challenging.

"Stop staring and get in," she shouts.

"I wasn't—" I protest.

Farah laughs. "Come on! It's *gorgeous*!"

She shines in light that doesn't come from this world and I can see the darkness of her skin through the T-shirt that clings to the solid line of her collarbone.

"I don't swim," I say. "Epilepsy."

"It's not deep. I'll keep an eye on you."

"You don't swim either, remember?" I say, smiling.

"Different rules here, remember?" she answers.

I start to object, but I hardly get past my first apologetic syllable before I feel something heavy hit me from behind and I'm pitched forward, my arms pinwheeling wildly as I plunge into the water. I surface, choking and gasping, just as the tight ball of Chiu's body flashes overhead and splashes down directly in front of me, swamping me.

I swallow another mouthful of water and sink briefly below the surface before I realize that I'm actually well inside my depth.

"Are you OK?" Farah says.

I nod vigorously, too winded to actually say anything. I gulp and cough one more time before I'm confident enough to shout, "Chiu! You little *shit*!"

I lurch after him and sweep up as much water as I can and swamp him in payback. He laughs and swings round to swim away from me. I give chase, half walking, half paddling.

We fall into a wild game that has no rules or structure, in which it is as much fun to get splashed as it is to splash. Chiu gets out and hurls himself back into the water again and again, using his body like a depth charge to douse us as thoroughly as he can. At one point, I grab hold of Farah's ankle. She twists in the water, grinning, kicking with her free leg in an effort to swim away. I haul her closer, until the warm curve of her calf grazes my side and I let go sharpish.

When we're tired, we step over a low separating wall and plunge into a small spa pool. I wonder at the heat of the water, how it's possible for us to feel it. But then I realize that it makes sense: the water in the ordinary world is *always* hot and so the idea of heat has seeped across like everything else.

Farah leans her head back against the edge of the pool and closes her eyes. Chiu copies. I gaze around at the dancing patterns on the ceiling from the water and at the recliners that border the pool.

One of them is occupied. A small woman bundled up in a dressing gown. For a moment, I feel ice forming in my chest. I imagine her dying here, the hotel discreetly dealing with her body so as not to alarm the other guests. But then I see that she's not dying. Just relaxing, her thoughts spaced out and leaking into our world like the man in the hospital library.

Farah notices me staring and turns. "You see one of them?"

"Don't you?"

Farah squints. "Kind of. Now you mention it."

"I think she's just dozing," I say. "Maybe dreaming a little bit."

"Do you think she sees us?" Chiu asks.

"If she did, she'd be freaking out by now, wouldn't she?" I say. "Maybe she *feels* us."

"Blindsight," Chiu says, sagely.

"Maybe she can't understand why she's feeling so irritated," Farah says.

We laugh at this, without really knowing why. It feels like a delicious sort of mischief to haunt a posh old woman when she's trying to relax at her fancy pool.

"Interdimensional trespassers," I say, dramatically.

At which Chiu and Farah lose themselves for a while in silent, heaving laughs. After we've calmed down, Farah says, "You've got to admit, this is better than the hospital library, right?" I smile and refuse to answer and she leans forward, her face suddenly determined. "Oh come *on!*" she taunts me. "Admit it … *Farah was right.* Go on … I want to hear you say it."

"Fine, if it makes you happy," I say. "This is cool. But it's all just some messed-up coma dream anyway, so it doesn't matter."

Farah's manner shifts and she moves towards me. Provocative, magnetic. Like she has a secret and she's deciding whether or not to share it. She pushes off from the side of the pool and comes closer and places her hands on my chest.

A rush of warmth floods my face. I can feel the heat of her hands even over the heat of the spa. Close, the lower part of her forearms grazing my skin. She allows the bubble and fizz of the water to nudge her closer, much closer, so that our wet faces are nearly touching and I can see the tiny lines and vessels in the domed whiteness of her eyes. I can feel my heart thudding under the pressure of her palms and I'm desperately embarrassed by the knowledge that she can feel it too. She waits a moment, that slight, knowing smile lingering on her face. She looks like she's going to kiss me and I'm desperately scared I'm going to make a mess of it.

Then she smirks and slides backwards, reaching out with one lazy arm to drench me.

"You need to get a better imagination, my friend," she says.

We dry off and relocate to the bar, where we claim a vast leather armchair each and bathe in the warm glow of a log fire that doesn't exist in our world. Instinctively, we sit as far from the window as we can. There are no curtains and the blackness outside presses against the glass like a weight. It has a presence to it. A heft. Darkness, in this world, is not just the absence of light. It has an irksome quality: a brooding intent, a vast, breath-freezing emptiness.

"It's worse at night," Farah remarks.

"People have always been scared of the dark," I say.

"But we're closer to it now," Chiu agrees.

We fall into uncomfortable silence, trying and failing to avoid looking at the blackness beyond the windows.

A jittery, paranoid feeling spreads inside me. I'm scared that leaving the hospital was a mistake, that we've left the one place that felt safe and now there's no going back. But then Chiu rummages in his pocket and pulls out his deck of Uno cards with a flourish.

"Game?" he says.

"Hell yes," Farah says, sighing with relief.

We fall gratefully into a game. I imagine that we're lost in deep space and somehow that feels better. If we're lost in space, then it's because we built this ship and so we have some control over it.

"You know, we could be here for eternity," I say, perhaps a little wishfully. "This could actually be the afterlife."

"Oh. My. God," Farah says, dramatically. "My dad was right all along... There *is* an afterlife! I'm in Muslim hell. Playing Uno for eternity with an atheist and a ... a ... what even are you, Chiu?"

Chiu looks confused. "I'm a ... boy?"

Which, for some reason, we find unbearably funny.

Later, Chiu has fallen asleep. Farah and I are lying on neighbouring sofas. I listen to her breathing as it becomes slower and I wonder what falling asleep feels like for her. Does her mind roam, as mine does, down side alleys and back streets of thought that seem to make complete sense ... until, suddenly, they don't?

"It was weird being in the pool with you today," I say.

Farah gives a quiet snort. "Don't tell my dad, please."

"Are you not supposed to?"

"I'm not really a rule follower, Kyle, you know that." Her voice is slow, on the edge of sleep. "Besides ... you're different ... special..."

My heart starts to beat more heavily in anticipation. "Oh?"

"You and Chiu," Farah drawls sleepily. "You're like my brothers."

EIGHTEEN

Brothers?

It was inevitable, I suppose, that I would develop a crush on Farah again. I mean, why not? It's not as if our lives aren't messed up enough already.

It's petty and it's childish, but ... *brothers?* Seriously?

I don't sleep. My thoughts turn over and over. I always liked Farah, in spite of the sneering and bad attitude. And now I know a different Farah as well. We're on the underside of the universe, the stitching behind the embroidery, and we're starting to see the stitching behind each other as well. There's the Farah everyone knows and there's the Farah *I* know. A glowing core of kindness that she tries to hide. A clarity, a strength, a *certainty* that takes my breath away.

Stop it, I think.

By the time I look up and realize that I haven't slept,

the sky has turned to the colour of wet rock – a colour that makes me think of sheer cliff edges and sudden, cold, jagged death.

I've had enough of lying here.

I creep away from Farah's and Chiu's sleeping forms and prowl the silent hallways. I pass the business centre and a large event hall. I can imagine people getting married here: all the white flowers and dancing and bridesmaids like you see on television.

I find the staircase and head up a level, where I find a restaurant and another bar. Even in the ordinary world it would all be abandoned at this time, but, for once, I'm enjoying the quiet. It gives me space to think.

And of course, I think about the pool. Farah. Standing close, her hands on my chest, her breath on mine. She was breathing as tightly as I was. Surely it wasn't all an act.

Grow up, Kyle. You have bigger things to worry about.

Like dying. And walking to London. And a sky that wants to eat me.

I should tell Farah I like her. And then what? It's not like we're going to go out on a date. A cinema that has no films? A restaurant with no power? In a world where we don't eat and an unspoken malevolent force lurks outside?

But at least she'd *know*.

I go up another level, a surprisingly stark column of stairs that dog-leg round and round and were presumably added on when the building became a hotel.

But what if it goes wrong? What if things get weird between us? It's not like there are lots of other people in this world to hang out with.

Slowly, I'm beginning to realize that my prowling isn't aimless. I'm looking for something. I'm in one of the corridors: deep pile carpet, gold leaf wallpaper. This place really is *fancy*. I have an idea that I want to give Farah a present. Something small that she can carry with her. A keepsake. I'd never dream of doing it in the ordinary world, but it feels OK here. A gift to a friend: something to make us brave.

"Here."

"What's this?"

"Just … something I found. I thought you'd like it."

I have a picture in my head and I don't know why I think it's here, but it's—

There.

A gold necklace hangs from the arm of an ornate bronze lamp on a half-moon writing desk set against the wall.

It can't be an accident, I think. It's like I *knew* it was here, even if I didn't know that I *knew*.

Blindsight, Chiu would say.

I wonder at the chain of events that led to this necklace being left here: a guest dropped it, I imagine, and then a cleaner picked it up and hung it here so it could be more easily spotted. Then … it was forgotten. The guest never found it, the cleaner never came back this way and other cleaners couldn't risk taking it for themselves in case they were accused of stealing.

It's beautiful. I reach out, slowly, scared that it's going to vanish before my hand touches it. A gold chain with a single golden dolphin curled round a tear-drop pendant. I don't know if it's just that I've never handled something so expensive before or if gold is somehow different in this world. It does more than reflect the light of this and the ordinary world: it captures it, transforms it, returns it as something more iridescent, more *complete*. I never really understood gold until now, but I feel like I'm seeing something here that people in the ordinary world only half see: that gold cuts across the worlds, thousands, millions of them, it gathers light from them all.

I stop suddenly. A noise nearby. I listen, hoping that I've imagined it. Did somebody whistle? A soft, fluting warble? Surely not. I want to call out, I want to believe that Farah has woken up and come looking for me.

He'll sniff you out.

I pocket the necklace, my head swivelling up and down the corridor. Alert, expecting any moment to see … something. My pulse races. A primordial fear inside me reaches back to the ordinary world and stretches forward, beyond this one.

Blindsight. The ability to see round corners.

A floorboard creaks. I've felt this in the ordinary world too: that shivery, unnerving sense when you're all alone at night and some instinct tells you that you're not really alone. In the ordinary world it's only ever an illusion, perhaps a whisper of this world. Your heart rises into your throat and you throw open the living-room door and there's nothing there.

Another creak.

A man appears from round the corner and stands, solid and completely here. He turns his head a little to the side, as if double-checking that I'm fully here as well.

"It's OK," he says. "Don't be scared."

I take a step backwards. He's tall and slender, but powerfully built, lean and sinewy. He wears combat trousers and a lank camel-coloured shirt, open at the collar. I watch his heavy motorcycle boots compress the luxurious carpet.

"I can help you," he says. "What's your name, lad?"

He's walking towards me. Every instinct in my body wants me to run, but my legs won't let me. He's built of menace, overpoweringly dark.

"Young lad, eh?" he says, thoughtfully. "Sad. Cut off before you ever got a chance, right?" He's reaching behind his back, the tight knots of the muscles in his arm twisting and rolling over each other. "I don't suppose you've got any hobbies, have you? Do you like technical things?"

I shake my head, slightly. His face is grim, haunted looking.

It's the clear, cold eyes that finally do it for me.

I bolt. I don't look back; my legs lurch out like they're grasping at the carpet and pull me after them. My mind is frozen, a rigid spear of terror thrust through my heart.

"Hey, wait up," the man calls. "I need to talk to you—"

I grab at the wall as I turn the corner and swing into the next corridor. I'm a mouse caught in a trap, filled with uncomprehending terror and nothing else. I fling myself at a door, hoping desperately that it's open...

Locked.

Obviously, it's locked.

I'm not thinking straight.

I hurl myself off the short flight of stairs that connects the old part of the hotel with the new wing. I land heavily, almost fall, stagger, struggle to maintain balance, keep running. I can feel him coming, I can hear his feet pounding down the stairs after me. I can't outrun him.

I swing round another corner and throw myself at another door.

Why would a hotel door be unlocked? I'm a fly batting itself against a windowpane.

The chances are a million to one, but...

Somehow, I know the next door will open.

And it does.

My fingers shake as I drag the security chain into place and twist the deadbolt. I back away from the door, listening to my own panicky, gasping breath, swallowing and swallowing like I'm drowning.

He'll sniff you out.

I can't stay here. Whoever he is – *whatever* he is – he's either going to find me or he's going to head downstairs and find Farah and Chiu.

I go to the window and press my forehead against the glass. *Third, fourth floor?* I don't remember exactly. The sheer face of the stone wall drops beneath me, offering nothing. There's ivy reaching up to the next window along but it's too far. I'd have to climb out somehow, balance on the window ledge and jump for it. I look down: gravel path, a few bushes. I wonder what happens if you die in this world.

The window is not an option.

I rush over to the door and peer through the peephole. No sign, just the empty hallway, twisted by the lens into something that looks more like a fairground ride.

The room is like nothing I've seen before: wood-panelled walls; a sofa; minibar; vast four-poster bed. I imagine what Farah would make of this place. I imagine her parading around and pretending to be a rich guest planning her day.

I turn from the door to the window and from the window to the door. If he's gone, then I need to get back down and warn Farah and Chiu. If he's not, then all I've done is corner myself.

I look at the door. And I *know* he's there. I catch a glimpse of him turning. I don't see, not exactly, but I know he smiles, takes a step back.

A moment later the door shudders and bucks against its deadbolt.

He's kicking the door down.

Any last shred of hope that I might be imagining the danger is swept away. Regular people don't kick down doors.

Another loud crash and the door shifts a little in its frame. It won't hold.

The window is starting to seem more appealing.

I rush over and pull up the sash. It bangs uselessly against a safety bolt, refusing to open more than a few inches. There's a catch and an intricate, childproof mechanism to unhook it. My fingers tremble and fumble, but I eventually figure it out.

SLAM!

It's too late.

"Don't worry, mate," a voice says. "I got you."

I spin round and the man is moving towards me. The sweat on his face shines with reflected light from the ordinary world. He moves quickly, unnaturally so. A series of jump cuts instead of steps.

Just do it. Jump!

But I'm too scared. I hesitate.

The man slams into me and keeps going, smashing me against the wall next to the window. My head snaps backwards and crunches painfully against the plaster. A bolt of lightning cracks through my skull. The wind whooshes out of my lungs and I feel as if my chest has crumpled into itself.

The man stares at me. *He'll sniff you out.* His eyes are light blue. He smells of woodsmoke and sweat. He reaches behind his back and produces a knife.

No, not just a knife. A hunting knife.

Its thick blade is as long as my forearm, sharp and curved on one side, serrated on the other. Its vicious, elongated point presses against my chest.

"Just a boy," the man whispers regretfully. His face is close to mine, inhaling me, studying me. "No use to anyone."

He has me pinned. One arm is pressed across my chest, holding me, the other angled back so he can hold the knife at a perfect right angle against my chest, ready for a single shove to drive it right through me. I try to push him off, but he doesn't move. He's so strong he hardly seems to notice.

I have about five seconds to live unless I do something, but my mind is frozen.

I don't even have enough thoughts to be scared of dying anymore. Just a faint, distant regret that I wish I'd had a chance to tell Farah how I felt about her.

"Shh, shh, shh." The man hushes me, his voice almost kind as he leans forward, his face very close to mine. His breath smells damp, like an old cellar. "Time to meet your Maker, son. You ready?" he whispers.

Then...

He stops. His nose curls and he sniffs, once, quickly.

His expression changes and I feel the pressure against my chest loosen. He smiles and suddenly everything is different. The knife vanishes and he takes a step backwards, almost apologetic. I stumble now that I am no longer pinned and he reaches forward to steady me. He smiles again, gives me a concerned look.

"You're OK, son," he says. His voice is warm. His eyes study mine. "You're safe now. You're lucky I found you."

NINETEEN

I'm still trembling as we head downstairs. The man sticks nearby, holding my upper arm, keeping me close.

"You're new here, I guess?" he says.

I nod, weakly, swallow, try to say something and find that I can't. I should be running; I should be doing everything I can to tear myself away from this person. But I'm paralysed.

"I'm Jonah," he says.

"K … Kyle," I respond.

He smiles. "You OK, Kyle? You're not going to do anything silly now, are you?"

I shake my head unsteadily. I don't understand what's going on. Being a prisoner would be one thing, but this is much scarier. His smile is troubled, almost anxious. He shows no sign of having just tried to murder me.

He squeezes my upper arm more tightly, carefully

meted-out strength. "It's a bit disorientating when you first get here," he says, amiably.

I start to wonder if I imagined the whole thing. But then he reaches forward to open the fire door and I see again the knife in a tan leather holster, strapped to his back. The world rocks around me, my mouth fills with cotton wool. Jonah catches me as I stagger backwards. His hand rests against my back.

"Don't worry, lad," he whispers. "Bit of a scare, that's all."

He leads me back to the bar and when we get there my heart stops. There's three more of them, sitting on the leather furniture, waiting with Farah and Chiu. One of them, a small, plump, muscular man with feral eyes, is playing Uno with Chiu. I lock eyes with Farah and I can see the tension in her body, her calculating look. Chiu glances up, but then looks back to his cards. I can tell he's scared, but he's concentrating hard on the cards in order to keep himself under control.

Jonah claps his hands together. "Well, well! It's a party!"

"This is Farah and Chiu," one of the other men says – a tall, athletic man with long legs, bare arms and a narrow, mournful face. "We found them in the bar."

"I can see that," Jonah says, glancing at me like we're sharing a joke. "Funny how you lot always search the bar first, isn't it?"

The man playing cards rearranges the glasses in front

of him self-consciously. "We didn't know what to do with them, so we waited—"

"Right, right," Jonah snaps. "Of course you did." He turns to me. "Kyle, I want you to meet my friends. A more feckless bunch of layabouts you'll never set eyes on." He pauses again, like he's waiting for us to laugh. "This black javelin of a man is Ose," he continues after a moment. "And the chunky little Sherman tank here is Levi."

Ose nods, holding my gaze, sizing me up.

"Wotcha," Levi says, with only a cursory glance.

Jonah turns to the last man, sitting silently in the armchair with a glass of something golden in his hand. "The sickly-looking fellow here is Tongue."

"Tongue, tongue," Tongue says, nodding and jabbing his thumb to his chest.

"You'll have to excuse Tongue," Jonah adds. "He came to us as damaged goods and he says not a word except 'tongue'."

"Tongue," Tongue agrees.

Chiu looks up from his cards, intrigued. "Broca's region?" he says. "It's part of the brain, I read about it. This happens if Broca's region gets damaged."

"Tongue! Tongue!" Tongue nods, with sudden enthusiasm.

Jonah laughs. "Well! That *has* made him happy. And you've taught us something that we managed not to learn in all the time we've been here." He heads behind the bar and inspects the bottle that the others must have left out. He whistles softly. "Twenty-five-year Macallan? Lads, this is the good stuff."

He takes down a glass and pours the liquid to the very top.

"Tongue," Tongue agrees with satisfaction.

Jonah drops heavily on to the sofa next to Farah, sandwiching her between himself and Ose. There isn't enough space but he doesn't seem to care. Ose does his best to make room, although he, in turn, is limited by the arm of the sofa.

Jonah takes a large swig of the whisky, swills it in his mouth and then spits it back into his glass. "*Gah!*" he gasps. "No eating or drinking in this world, I guess you figured that out by now? I still *miss* it though. I drink the *idea* of whisky. I drink to *remember.*" A cold smile breaks across his face. "Get it? Drink to *remember*?" He looks at me impatiently. "Sit, sit down," he says.

I slump into the remaining armchair, opposite Tongue.

"You OK, Kyle?" Farah says, guardedly.

"We're fine," Jonah answers for me. "Bit of a misunderstanding, that's all."

I catch the question in Farah's look and turn away. I keep thinking about the way Jonah looked at me when he pressed the knife against my chest. No compassion, no regret.

Why did he change his mind?

"So ... tell us about yourselves," Jonah says with false joviality. "What brings you to this god-forsaken place?"

We exchange a look, me, Farah and Chiu. What can we do except play along?

"I fell off a roof," Chiu says.

Jonah grins appreciatively. "Ha! Wonderful. What a way to go!"

Even Ose cracks a slight, reluctant smile.

"What about you?" Jonah asks Farah, like we're playing a party game.

"A headache," Farah says. "I guess I passed out in Casualty."

Jonah looks intrigued. "So you might be with us a little while?" He gives Farah a Cheshire-cat grin. "A lot of people here are just passing through, some of them don't even know they're here. But you three are different, aren't you?" He turns to me. A piercing, shrewd look. "And you, Kyle, what's your story?"

"I don't remember," I say shortly.

"Come on, Kyle," Jonah cajoles me, an edge in his voice. "We're sharing here, right?"

"I have epilepsy," I say. "I pass out a lot."

I expect him to be irritated by my non-answer but he seems oddly satisfied. "That you do," he muses. "That you do."

"Tongue?" Tongue says, questioningly.

"Leave it," Jonah warns. He smiles, falsely. "Let's have another drink, shall we?"

It seems to go on for an age, Jonah filling the room with his one-sided banter, a kind of strained, scripted act. *What does he want?* I wonder. *Where is this leading?* He fetches the bottle and refills his glass.

"Want some?" he asks, holding up the glass for me. "Or Coke, or whatever. There's no rules in this world, that's the wonderful thing about it."

Jonah tells us that he came off his motorbike. He doesn't know what's left of his body in the ordinary world, what fragment of wrecked brain matter is keeping him tethered to this world, but he's been here for decades. Ose was hit by a car and Levi was a maintenance worker for the railways. Their brains in the ordinary world are still dying or wrecked beyond repair and clinging on to life. They have no way of knowing for sure but, somehow, they've reached the same conclusion as Chiu. In the ordinary world their brains are igniting in gamma activity, catapulting them here, keeping them here. Hours, days, years… It's irrelevant, the time in one world is unaffected by the time in the other.

They tell us this in passing, as if the nature of this place was never in question.

"I woke up on the tracks in this world," Levi says. "Not that I knew it was this world. I couldn't figure out why the lads had left me. I was still walking the length of the tracks, going nowhere in particular, when Jonah found me and explained it all."

"How long have you been here?" Farah says.

Levi shrugs. "More years than I can count."

"There's a machine that can help us," Chiu says suddenly. "We read about a machine that can—" He stops when he catches a look from Farah.

Jonah's eyes are vigilant and cunning. "A machine?"

"It's nothing," Farah says. "Just kid stuff."

Chiu looks furious but he doesn't say anything.

"Is that where you're going then?" Jonah asks. "To find a machine?"

"We're going to find my family," Farah says. "In Islington."

Jonah nods slowly. He doesn't believe her.

He throws his head back and drains his glass, then slaps his hands on to his knees and stands with sudden decisiveness. "Well, no rest for the wicked," he says. He catches my eye, as if we're sharing a secret. A warning, I think, not to tell them about what nearly happened upstairs. "Levi, Tongue, you're with me. Ose, stick around and keep our new friends company, will you?"

He gives Tongue and Levi a nod and they follow him out, leaving us alone with Ose. Ose watches them, his face inscrutable.

"Where are they going?" Farah asks.

"They're searching," Ose says.

"Searching for what?"

Ose shrugs lazily. "Anything we can make use of. Anyone passing through."

Farah stands slowly. She flashes me a *play-along* look. "Well," she says. "We'd better be leaving as well, I guess. I was visiting my friends when I passed out. We have a long way to go to get to my family's house."

"Why are you going to your family's house?" Ose says. "They are not in this world."

"No, I…" Farah falters. "I want to see the place, that's all. It's home."

Farah glances at me and Chiu and we stand. Ose holds his ground, blocking the way between us and the door. There's a deep, deep sadness in him, a ponderous despondency.

"It's better that you stay here," he says.

"I don't think so," Farah replies, her voice hardening.

"Better to stay," Ose insists.

Farah looks at me. For a moment I'm scared she's going to rush him. She doesn't know what happened with Jonah, she doesn't know how dangerous these people are. I give a slight shake of my head and we share a moment of silent debate. She glances at Ose, sizing him up. He looks like a marathon runner who chops down trees for a hobby. Her mouth pinches in frustration and she sits.

We wait in tense silence. Ose doesn't want to chat in

the way Jonah did and that, at least, is a relief. But the air is thick and melancholy, the grey sky and manicured lawns beyond the window wait pensively. When Ose wanders over to the bookcase on the far side of the room and starts perusing the small collection of antique-looking books there, Farah shifts over quickly and sits next to me. Chiu leans forward to join in.

"We need to get out of here," Farah hisses.

"We should wait," I whisper.

"There's only one of them now. We'll never get a better chance," Farah says.

"She's right," Chiu agrees.

I'm sure Ose is listening to us. The way he pulls a book from the shelf is *too* casual. But I don't suppose there's any use pointing that out to Farah. I think about her truculent departures from French lessons and hope she doesn't try that here. I lean closer, speaking as quietly as possible in the hope that Ose can't hear.

"You don't understand," I whisper. "Tonight. That's our best chance."

The sky has turned to the hopeless grey of an electricity pylon when Jonah and the others return in high spirits. Jonah's movements are sharp, filled with unexpended energy. "A good day," he announces. "A very good day indeed."

"What makes it a good day?" Farah asks.

"Those that end up here sometimes need our help," Jonah says. "I perform a public service. I find them, I help them."

"Help them how?" Farah says.

Jonah gives an off-hand shrug. "It depends."

"Did you find anyone?" I ask.

"Tongue," Tongue says, his voice edged with an inscrutable bitterness.

Jonah lifts his hands as if to show us they're empty. "Does it look like we found anyone?" He goes behind the bar again and takes down a fresh bottle of Scotch and fills his glass. He takes a swig, gags and spits on to the floor behind the bar.

"We need to be getting on," Farah says. "There's somewhere we got to be."

"Oh?" Jonah feigns innocent interest. "The machine?"

"My family."

"Of course." Jonah nods, as if the memory is coming back to him. "Well you don't want to be out walking at night," he says. "This world might feel quiet, but ... it's worse at night." He glances at the others. "You should come back with us. We know a safe place."

"We're fine," Farah says. "We're safe here."

I brace myself for a confrontation. Violence watches us. I'm scared Farah is going to do something rash. *We're playing a game*, I think. But we all know the pretence could slip at any moment.

Jonah smiles wolfishly. "Come on. I want to show you something cool."

Farah starts to shake her head, but I interrupt.

"Sure," I say.

"Smart lad," Jonah replies.

We follow him and the others back out through reception to the front of the hotel. Four motorbikes are parked on the gravel, gleaming and slick looking. They look out of place, like their colours and lines are sharper and more *real* than everything else around them. The evening sky has leached the colour from the building and the gardens but the sleek red and blue bikes still shine like its midday.

"Do they work?" I ask, baffled by the unexpected sight.

"Work?" Jonah laughs. "They go like the bloody clappers!"

"How?" I say.

"Tongue!" Tongue says. He jabs his chest enthusiastically. "Tongue!"

Ose puts a hand on his shoulder. "What he's trying to tell you is ideas and things are closer to each other in this world. Technical things only work if you have the knowledge to make them work."

Tongue nods vigorously. "Tongue!"

"And Tongue is the best mechanic I ever met." Jonah grins.

Jonah's voice is admiring but there's a mocking edge

to it as well. Tongue drops to one knee and places his head close to the engine of the first bike. He might be checking spark plugs or oil, but he looks more as if he's coaxing a nervous horse into a race. He mutters under his breath, "Tongue ... tongue." A sound that seems full of longing, like a child whispering secrets to a soft toy. I catch a glimpse of the engine beneath his fingers: components shifting and easing into place. The unruly mess I saw under the bonnet was a reflection of my own ignorance and, here, Tongue's knowledge bends and warms the ideas into place. No wonder the electricity doesn't work. No wonder our phones don't.

Tongue silently moves on to the next bike, while Jonah swings himself on to the first and the engine gives a guttural purr and rumbles into life.

"Kyle, you're with me," Jonah says. "Farah better go with Ose. Chiu with Levi."

One last look from Farah. I can imagine her sprinting across the gravel. She'd be fast, but I can see Jonah striding after her; one or two lurching strides and he takes her down—

I move quickly, before she has a chance to react, and climb on to the back of Jonah's bike. Farah's body tenses like she isn't sure what to do, but when Ose climbs on to his own bike she climbs on behind him.

TWENTY

Dark and rushing, like falling. The thrill of riding with Jonah is oddly familiar. Reminiscent of my seizures.

We move so fast, so close to utter annihilation, I can't help the swell of excitement that rises up in my chest. I watch the road dash beneath us and I wonder what it would be like to touch it. It seems blurred, almost insubstantial, like I might reach out and carve a wake around my fingers like it was water. But then Jonah leans the bike steeply into a corner and his knee comes within an inch of the ground and the unyielding concrete reasserts itself. I imagine the tyres losing their grip, plunging down and being torn apart by the speed.

There's something beguiling about it. Fear, for me, has always been a diffuse thing, leaching into everything. Here, fear has the surgical precision of a scalpel: focused on a single flickering patch of rapidly moving concrete.

It's terrible, but comforting as well, because this kind of fear is small enough to hold in your hand, small enough to crush if you squeeze hard enough.

Jonah's "safe place" turns out to be the South Mimms Welcome Break: a service station just off the M25. It feels like a warehouse or an airport. There's a central food court, with cheap-looking Formica chairs and tables and big plastic self-service bins. Around the outside of it there's a series of roofed-off areas, each one with a frontage displaying its logo: Starbucks, McDonald's, Burger King, Wetherspoons.

"You're right," Farah says, deadpan. "This is definitely better than the hotel."

Jonah laughs sharply. "Don't mock what you don't understand, girl. Give it a minute, you'll feel it." He strides across the food court, his arms raised like a preacher giving a sermon. "This place only half exists in the real world. People shelter here, nothing more. It *belongs* to no one, which means it *belongs* to *us*."

He's right, I think. The crawling, uneasy feeling in my chest is easier here. Like the library was easier than the canteen, the hotel was easier than my house.

"Levi!" Jonah shouts. "You know what to do!"

Levi walks off. They've rearranged the leather sofas from the Wetherspoons, added roll mats, beanbags and an eclectic assortment of table lamps, and made a ramshackle sort of living room for themselves. A giant flat-screen television forms the centrepiece, black and insectoid in the half-light of the food court.

"Ose, if you would do the honours," Jonah says.

Ose moves slowly from lamp to lamp, switching each one of them on in turn. A gasp escapes my mouth. *Light?* I look at Farah and Chiu and Farah looks amazed. The finishing touch is the television and for an incredible moment I'm caught by the wild and almost incomprehensibly wonderful idea that we might get to sit and watch for a while. But when the screen powers up it has nothing but a kind of digital static. Broken, frozen, disjointed filmic images.

"Ose is as moody and uncommunicative as they come," Jonah remarks, mocking as before. "But there are advantages to having an electrician on the crew."

"You're an electrician?" I say.

Ose's face twitches with a look that might be one of irritation. "I know enough of the basics to get the lights working."

"How do you do it?" Chiu asks.

"How do you wake up?" Ose replies.

Levi appears again, holding a large bellowed instrument that I recognize as an accordion. He starts to play, a wheezing whine like a dozen harmonicas played slightly out of tune with a higher, sharper melody playing over it. Each sound would be grating and unpleasant on its own, but together they create a weaving, wonderful, discordant chaos.

Jonah disappears behind the bar and returns with a crate of bottled beer that he slams on to the table. "Plenty of old stock in a service station as well," he remarks. He cracks open a bottle, takes a long swig and then spits it upwards, over and behind him like a geyser, before wiping his mouth with the back of his hand. "No decent Scotch though."

Tongue cracks open bottles for himself, Levi and Ose. Then he cracks open another and hands it to me. He offers one to Farah but she shakes her head slightly. A moment later, Ose appears with a crate of Coke and gives one each to Farah and Chiu.

"Come! Come dance!" Jonah calls.

He takes up a spot in the main food court, just outside the bar, and begins a slow, side-stepping kind of dance: heel–toe, heel–toe, his arms floating above his head. Ose lets himself sink into an armchair and closes his eyes. Tongue does the same. Levi plays and plays, utterly absorbed by his music.

Farah and I sit on the spare sofa opposite Ose, and Chiu takes the armchair nearby. I take a sip of the warm, flat beer. I've never been a big fan of beer, but I'm beginning to understand Jonah's point about drinking to remember. I'm not sure if it's the body or the brain, but some part of me remembers the *idea* of drinking a beer, some part of me hankers after that feeling. I sip and watch Jonah dance. Heel–toe, heel–toe. Incongruous but oddly fitting. Chiu has been distracted by the television, the steely-grey light reflecting off his rapt expression.

"Our lives are brief flickers," Jonah says. "We matter to no one. But we have a choice. We can huddle in the darkness like timid little mice ... or we can throw our arms out into the night and yell: 'Come on, you sadistic wanker! Show yourself!'"

A debilitating, drug-like tiredness falls over me. There's something about the music, the lights and the television. I know at some level that I'm with a man who nearly murdered me. I know that just underneath the surface we are prisoners. But those troubles seem distant.

"This is not a death dream." Jonah's drawl intrudes into my thoughts. "'For now we see through a glass, darkly; now I know in part, but then I shall know even as I am known.' Do you know what that means?"

The familiar words pull me back into wakefulness.

For now we see through a glass, darkly.

Father Michael. I remember him saying those words. Anxiety twists inside me. Fragments of memory push themselves into my mind. Mum's note. *Exciting news!* Searching through the papers in the kitchen.

Why was I outside on my own? What was it I was trying to do that was so important?

All I know is that it was urgent. The longer I stay here, the more likely it is that it's going to be too late in the ordinary world to do whatever it was I was trying to do.

Levi's accordion music goes on and on. The melody stretches over the notes like a sheet: smooths them out, turns them into liquid glass inside my head.

"*We* are on the *other side of the glass*, Farah, do you see?" Jonah continues emphatically. "That which you call *reality* is the universe of reduced awareness, it is a measly trickle. *This* is living."

Farah looks uncomfortable. Jonah notices and his face tightens with annoyance. "Relax, Farah. Your boyfriend doesn't mind us talking, does he?"

"He's not my boyfriend—" Farah begins.

"I'm not her boyfriend—" I say at the same time.

Jonah laughs loudly. "Oh, *jeez!* Kids! You two are broadcasting hormones halfway to the moon." His voice becomes hard. "You still don't get it, do you? It doesn't *matter*. None of it *matters*. We can do *anything* we like here."

He reaches for Farah, grabs her wrist. She lets out a yelp and twists away from him. Ose's eyes are suddenly open, his face alert. He flashes me a warning look.

"Leave her alone," I say, standing.

Levi stops playing and the air becomes abruptly empty. A grin splits Jonah's face as he squares up to me, like a panther stalking his prey.

"Well, well, the mouse squeaks," he growls. "There, you see, Farah? You see what I mean? Anybody can do anything? Even this little one. That's the wonder of this place." He turns back to me, his eyes narrowing. "But I expect some respect around here, boy. You stay, you make nice, OK?"

"We're not staying," Farah says. "Actually, we're leaving. Right now."

Jonah points a finger in her direction without taking his eyes off me. "You'll leave when I bloody well say you can leave."

There it is, I think. At last, no more games. It's almost a relief.

He's right in my face now. "I can't decide about you, Kyle," he says. "I don't know if you're going to be worth the effort or not."

His face twists and he raises his arm ready for a backhand swipe. I've been hit plenty of times before, but never by a grown-up.

Don't flinch, I think. *I will not flinch.*

His muscles clench and his eyes tighten. I'm used to people picking fights with me but this is different. This man has killed plenty of times, he's not afraid of it.

You can do anything in this world.

A sharp, pained cry from behind stops him.

Jonah turns, irritated by the distraction. Tongue has stood up and is clutching his stomach, staggering unevenly away from the sofa. "Ahhmmmhhhh," he groans.

"Get hold of him," Jonah says.

Levi and Ose spring into action, closing on Tongue from both sides with a swiftness and confidence that can only come from practice. Tongue tries to shake Ose away but Ose pulls him towards the nearest armchair. Tongue squirms, sweat shines on his forehead and top lip. Ose grunts with effort as he adjusts his position to make sure Tongue can't slip away. Levi pins his other arm.

I exchange frightened looks with Farah and Chiu. *What's happening?*

"Come on, old pal," Jonah says. "You know the drill. Let's not make a fuss now, eh?"

Tongue's face crunches up, he closes his eyes and shakes his head, moaning in fear and pain and sheer loathing for whatever is coming next. I take a step closer, fascinated, horrified. Jonah takes out his knife and slices Tongue's shirt open, letting it fall away from his chest like a waistcoat.

Immediately he leans back, repulsed. The smell hits us a moment later: pungent, rancid, foul, like rotting meat.

"Sweet Jesus, Tongue," Jonah scolds. "We talked about this. You're not supposed to keep this stuff a secret, are you?"

I think, at first, that Tongue's chest is covered in boils. There are three or four clusters of them, protruding, red and angry from yellowish skin. One batch swells from the curve of his muscle near his armpit. Another, composed of three or four small mounds half melded together, peeks out from beneath his ribs. A third pushes from behind the waistband of his trousers. Farah lets out a cry of disgust and a moment later I see it myself. They aren't boils. They're eyes.

Living, blinking, swivelling, watching eyes.

I can't move. The set of eyes in Tongue's armpit twist in my direction and fix on me. They stare, bulging with fear, pleading. Wiry eyelashes protrude from swollen flesh; the oily surfaces of the whites swell and swell.

Jonah reaches behind his back and pulls out his hunting knife. He leans forward and, without a pause, uses the tip of his knife to lever out the first eye.

Tongue swings his knees left and right trying to curl up into a protective ball but Jonah and the others have too firm a grip on him. I watch the tip of the knife slide into the flesh just below the next eyeball and a great welling up of dark blood.

"Ahhhhhh! Aaa!" Tongue cries.

There's a gelatinous *slurp* and a brief squirt of more blood as the eye pops out and drops to the floor. Jonah barely pauses as he moves on to the next.

"Stop it!" Farah shouts. "You're killing him."

"We're not," Ose answers, without looking up. "We're saving him."

Jonah begins to work more quickly, more roughly. He levers out two more eyes.

"Aaaeae! Aaa!"

Chiu slaps his hands over his ears to block out the sound

and turns away, Farah presses her face into my shoulder. But I can't stop watching.

Evil, my mind whispers, *has only ever been an abstract thing before*. The biblical evil they used to rave about at church. The evil of wars in other countries and child soldiers and history books. This is different. This is evil. *Right here*.

For evil to flourish, it requires only that good men do nothing.

Jonah palms another eyeball and tosses it to one side. Tongue's torso strains and relaxes, strains and relaxes. His foot slides over one of his own eyeballs and smears it into the ground, leaving a torn remnant on the floor like a crushed grape.

I should do something. But what? Run at him? Tear him away?

I've felt Jonah's grip; he's strong like nobody I've ever met before. And the truth is, I'm weak.

Fear squirms inside me like a poison, rooting me to the spot.

And then, it's over.

Jonah rocks back on his heels and sits on the floor, his legs splayed out in front of him, laughing silently. He looks elated. His hair is matted, his chest heaves from exertion. He wipes a slimy hand on his chest and then turns laboriously on to all fours before he can bring himself to standing.

He catches my eye, flashes me a wink.

Ose and Levi slide back, similarly spent. Tongue's chest is slick with blood, rising and falling with his shallow, trembling breaths.

Jonah reclaims the bottle of beer he was drinking and takes a long swig. For a moment I think he's going to come back and pick up where we left off, break my jaw after all, but he staggers away instead. I watch him fade into a darker corner of the bar where they have their roll mats laid out. "Get some sleep, everyone," he calls. "Me and Kyle are taking the bikes out tomorrow."

TWENTY-ONE

Levi rolls Tongue on to his side and covers him with a blanket, tucking it around his shoulders with a surprising tenderness. Then he follows Jonah over to the roll mats, mutters a half-hearted and weirdly ordinary "g'night" and collapses.

Ose picks himself up, uses his long fingers to extract two beers and two Cokes from the crates nearby and comes and sits with us. He hands me a beer, hands the Cokes to Farah and Chiu, then sits on the sofa next to me and cracks open his own drink.

"I'm sorry you had to see that," he says softly.

"I don't understand what happened?" Farah murmurs. "What were those … things?"

"We call them Puzzles," Ose explains. "Tongue's dying. That's what it looks like here when we're dying."

"We grow *eyes*?" Chiu says.

"It's different for everyone," Ose says. "We treat the

symptoms, like in the ordinary world. A cancer grows in your brain, you cut it out. A cancer grows in your lungs, you cut it out."

"Not with a hunting knife," I say, incredulous.

"Not eyes," Chiu adds.

"Cutting them out will keep him going for a while," Ose says. "If we tried something like this in the other world he'd fill with bacteria and he'd go septic. But bacteria aren't a problem here."

We sit in numb silence for a while. My drink tastes like I'm drinking a bottle of my own saliva but I'm intensely grateful for it.

I drink to remember.

This is my blood, drink this in remembrance of me.

Tongue moans softly in his sleep. Beyond that, the heavy, sleeping breaths of Levi. Jonah lies nearby, silent. I guess even Jonah likes to be near other people when the sky turns black outside.

My eyes search the metal framed roof, the panelled windows showing a blackness so complete it terrifies me if I look at it for more than a moment.

"Is that going to happen to us?" Chiu asks.

"Maybe," Ose concedes. "But Tongue has been here for a long time. He was here before I came. Time's different here, but it's not for ever."

"How long do people last with Puzzles before they … you know?" Farah asks.

"Everybody is different," Ose says. "Some last a few moments. Some last for days. Tongue … with our help … several months now." He shrugs. "We don't know, really."

I'm sure Farah is thinking about the baby, wondering if she could have saved it.

"It's awful," I say.

Ose takes a long, bitter drink. "Nobody knows when they're going to die, Kyle. That's no different here than it was there."

TWENTY-TWO

You're not supposed to know when you're dreaming. It's a secret your brain likes to keep from you. But I've seen Grandad in my dreams so often it's become a dead giveaway.

"What about these?" I say.

I hold up a jam jar filled with assorted bolts. They look like silvery maggots, gummed to the glass with grease.

"Box," Grandad replies.

I'm fifteen and Grandad has come over to clear out the garage. I drop the jam jar into the cardboard box where it clunks against a pile of screwdrivers.

"Careful," he scolds. "You'll break it."

He adds his own jar to the box, delicately, almost lovingly, even though we both know we're taking the whole thing straight to the tip after this.

"You don't have to clear out the garage," I say. "We don't use it."

"Better I do it than leave it to you and your mother after I'm dead," he replies.

I bite back a twinge of annoyance. He insisted I spend my Saturday helping him while Mum was at work but now we're here he's acting like I'm getting in the way. He always does this, treats us like we're both equally useless. It's his burden, I guess, to care about us no matter how disappointed he is in us.

I pick up the starter motor from the workbench. "I remember you showing me how this worked when I was little. I spent ages trying to fix it."

Grandad glances indifferently at it. "That thing was never going to work."

He takes it from me, drops it in his box and opens another drawer.

My earliest, warmest memories are of being in the garage with Grandad, tinkering with various car parts while he tells me about his job as a fitter at the Jaguar plant. I think it maybe only happened once or twice but the memory has grown so much it feels like more.

"Ah! That's what I'm looking for." He pulls out a sheaf of papers. "This is important."

"What is it?" I ask.

He lays out the papers on the workbench: *ID1: Verify Identity – Citizen. TR1: Transfer of Whole of registered title(s). OFFICIAL COPY: Register of Title.*

"Very easy to give somebody a house, you know," he

161

remarks. "Just a couple of forms, nothing else. You could almost do it by accident if you weren't careful." The joke is so old he doesn't even bother to wait for a reaction. He turns on the spot, scanning the bare brick of the garage. "Now ... where should we put it?" He stops, his eyes alighting on a dark corner of the garage. "That'll do." He stacks the forms together and slides them into the space between the electricity cupboard and the wall. "I'm putting them up here, OK? Keep them safe."

"Safe from what?"

He gives me a small, dogged sigh. "I won't be around for ever, Kyle. And your Mum ... well, you know what she's like." I nod. I know, but he's going to tell me anyway. "She's suggestible," he says. "People take advantage of her."

He's talking about Dad again, I think. I never met Dad, but the story has come out in fragments over the years. A churchman – evidence that Mum was fond of the churches even before I came along – a youthful affair and that's all ... never to be seen again.

"I do what I can," Grandad goes on, gesturing to the garage and, by implication, the house. "But I need you to step up, Kyle. Do you get it? I need you to look out for her."

So that's why he wanted me here today. I'd be pleased that he's putting so much trust in me, except I can see in his face he doesn't trust me in the slightest.

"She could shift the house without the papers," he

says. "But there's no reason to make things easy for her, is there? Look out for her when I'm gone. She's dangerous when she gets an idea in her head, you know that." He gazes steadily at me, a pessimistic look. "Just do your best, son, OK?"

TWENTY-THREE

"Kyle." Farah's voice, low and urgent. "Kyle, wake up."

My eyes open, my body drags itself out of sleep. "Farah?"

"It's time," Farah whispers.

Chiu is quietly pulling on his clothes nearby. I look up and the blackness of the skylights catches my eyes. "Are you sure about this?"

"You'd prefer to wait around until Jonah starts prising body parts off you?" Farah says.

I slip on my shoes. Jonah and the others are still sleeping, a little distance away on their roll mats. I watch Jonah for a few moments. I can't shake the feeling that he's not really asleep.

The *slip-scrape* of our footsteps as we creep away is terrifyingly loud in the silence.

Any minute, I think, *Jonah will be on us.*

But then we're outside and the cool air and the darkness swallow us like we just dived into the ocean. No streetlights, but always just enough light to see by. The black, undecorated sky looks like eternity; the darkness rushes around us in a continuous swoop-and-return, devouring us, again and again. Farah holds the map in her hand but it's clear she's already made her plan.

"Across the bridge and down on to the motorway," she whispers. "We've got one junction on the M25 and then we can get off the main roads. Even if he bothers to come after us, he'll never be able to find us among all the side roads."

She makes it sound too easy; I don't trust her confidence. We're about to start walking when there's a movement behind us, a scrape of gravel. I spin round and find Ose standing in the doorway. Perfectly still, he looks like a tree that's been struck by lightning.

"You can't leave," he says quietly.

"Please," Farah hisses back. "Don't try to stop us."

Even in the dim light I can see the conflict in Ose's face. *He's scared of Jonah*, I think. But that doesn't mean he's going to help us.

"He won't let you leave," Ose says, stepping closer. "It's better you don't try."

Farah flashes me a look. We're both thinking the same thing: we could make a run for it. But we both know it would be hopeless. It plays out quickly in my mind: a clumsy, panicky bolt; Ose's long, strong legs propelling him forward, scooping up Chiu under one arm, pushing Farah to the ground.

"He's asleep," I say, guardedly. "We'll take the back streets; he'll never find us."

Ose shakes his head slightly. "He has the bikes. He'll track you down."

He'll sniff you out.

"Why?" Chiu says. "What does he want with us?"

Ose hesitates. I'm sure his eyes flash briefly to me and then look away, but if there's meaning in the look it's lost on me. "He'll find you," Ose says again, refusing to be drawn. "And he'll punish you."

"And you would help, I suppose," Farah says, bitterly.

Ose flinches but he doesn't deny it. "I've hurt and killed many people to save my own skin. But you're children … I don't want that."

"Then *help* us," I say.

"I *am* helping," Ose responds. "This is the best I can do."

Jonah wakes in a furious good mood. He strides around the service station, kicking Levi awake and shaking Tongue into consciousness. "Right, right, come on, everyone – come on, busy day!" He calls over to us. "Sleep well, love birds? No disturbances, I hope?" He smirks, then leans closer to Tongue, his hand on his shoulder. "How are y', Tongue? Feeling better?"

Tongue nods groggily.

"Can you ride?"

Tongue nods again, hauls himself to his feet. *There are no bacteria in the Stillness.* Seeing as Tongue is still alive, I guess there's no traumatic shock, cardiac arrest, blood clot or sepsis, either. *But there's still pain*, I think.

Jonah slaps me on the shoulder – rough, friendly, like he hasn't twice come within a breath of murdering me. "Kyle, you're with me." He turns to Levi. "Levi, keep an eye on these two."

Levi nods.

"Where are we going?" I ask.

Jonah taps the side of his nose. "You'll see, boy. You'll see."

I enjoy riding with Jonah more than I like to admit. My muscles sing with the strain of holding myself inches from the murderous road. The motorbike seems faster and more lethal in the morning light. I imagine what would happen if I fell: shoulder first, then my head slapping on to the tarmac and bouncing back, my momentum rolling me forward, smashing my collarbones one at a time as each shoulder hit the road in turn, twisting my spine until it tore and my legs flailed out at hideous angles and my knees hinged backwards. The image plays over and over in my brain, so vivid it draws me towards the ground.

"You did good last night," Jonah shouts over the wind.

The words whip around me like scraps of cloth, only enough to get the meaning. "Standing up for your girl like that."

"She's not my—"

"It's the right attitude," Jonah continues. "That attitude will keep you alive in this place … if it doesn't get you killed first."

Threat or compliment? I'm not sure. I shouldn't care what Jonah thinks but it's hard not to. It's instinct, I suppose, survival of the fittest. Millions of years of evolution have taught me that craving Jonah's approval is what will keep me alive here. But there's something else … a connection I don't understand. I know he feels it just the same as I do. I think it might be why I'm here.

The piercing wail of Tongue's bike follows close behind, shadowing us. He needs to be close – it's him, or his understanding of engines, that keeps us running. I don't know how close he needs to be; the lights faded last night as soon as Ose went to bed. They seem to be taking no chances though. I catch glimpses of Tongue from the corner of my eye as he drifts closer and closer. I hope to hell he has a good working knowledge of angular friction and tyre pressure tolerances.

"We are the Founding Fathers, Kyle," Jonah shouts. "This place belongs to *us*. You and me. We can do *anything* we like. We *define* this world."

We accelerate into the turn and keep accelerating. I wonder if motorbikes are always this fast or if Jonah or

Tongue somehow *will* them to move more quickly. A feeling swells inside my throat. A kind of rapture. Like a stone skimming across the surface of a lake.

"Faster," I whisper, the words coming from somewhere else. *"Faster."*

And does the bike accelerate? Do I feel the kick of extra speed, sense Tongue falling back and fighting to keep up?

Jonah lets out an ecstatic howl. "Yes! Yes!" he hollers, laughing. "Yes!"

It's over too quickly. I lurch forward as the bike slows, pinned briefly against Jonah's back. We veer to the left and the woods give way to a housing estate. Boxy brick house-hutches flash past as we weave down first one side street and then another.

They remind me of home. Our tiny little house filled with tiny little people. Mum at the tiny kitchen table making margin notes in her bible. Me, upstairs, working through GCSE notes, wondering what the point of it all is if I'm never going to leave this place anyway.

We stop outside a bungalow with a scruffy, overgrown garden. Jonah flips down the kickstand and I step shakily on to solid ground.

"You like that, eh?" Jonah grins, stepping off. "I can tell."

I allow myself a weak, trembling smile and Jonah slaps me on the shoulder. "Don't look so nervous, Kyle. You're with me now. You're safe."

"What are we doing here?" I say.

Jonah sniffs sharply. "Don't you smell that?"

I sniff. Nothing. In the other world you might smell bins, or cars, or stale grass, or dog mess. Here: nothing. I shake my head.

"You do smell it," Jonah says. "You just don't understand it yet."

He takes a crowbar from the pannier on his bike and cracks open the front door as swiftly and simply as if he'd used a key. Tongue stays with the bikes. He's leaning a little to one side like he's still in pain, but his colour is better than it was yesterday.

I follow Jonah inside.

This house isn't empty.

Jonah heads up the narrow staircase, I follow him. I feel like a thief, but I know we're not here to steal anything. Jonah pauses halfway up the stairs and whistles. That soft, fluting warble. The same sound I heard in the hotel.

"Not everybody has the courage to adapt to this world," Jonah murmurs, his nostrils flaring. "Some people hide away. They need our help."

I know which door he's heading for before he takes another step. He presses his finger against his lips, his eyes wide and alert. He turns the handle. Now I smell it. Except it's not really a smell, it's more like a feeling, a sense of nausea, a memory...

My mind is running at a thousand miles per hour, I take

in the details of the room in a second. The television bolted to the wall; the window looking out on to a small, square patch of lawn that tessellates against the other lawns around it; the chest of drawers; the pile of dirty laundry heaped up against it like a snow drift; the bed with the crumpled grey sheets; the mirrored doors of a fitted wardrobe in which I see the terrifying silhouettes of Jonah and myself.

"Help... Ple ... ase ... he ... lp..." a dry, breathy voice calls out.

Jonah moves to the bed. The man who's lying there looks to be in his sixties or seventies – thin and attenuated. He's not under the sheets, his pyjamas tent around his thin frame. Jonah leans close, combs his hand through the man's thin grey hair.

"You're OK, mate," he says softly. "I got you."

"I'm ... I'm sick."

Jonah nods. "You're very sick, mate."

"I need a doctor."

"Oh, you're way past that," Jonah says coolly.

"Please ... help."

"I know, I know," Jonah whispers, still stroking the man's hair. Jonah glances around, takes in the meagre room. "Pretty nice place you got here, my friend. Are you some kind of businessman?"

The man coughs a wry laugh. "You're kidding, aren't you?"

I watch Jonah rethinking. *He's after something. But what?*

"Ah, right, right." Jonah muses. "What do you do, my friend? You like to build things? Fix things?"

The man shakes his head, getting agitated. "I need a doctor, not twenty bloody questions."

"Help is coming," Jonah reassures him.

The man relaxes, lets his head rest against Jonah's hand as Jonah delicately smooths his hair. *Help isn't coming*, I think.

"I bet you're a technical person, am I right?" Jonah says.

The man shakes his head. "I'm a cleaner, OK? I work for the bloody council."

"Cleaner?" Jonah casts me a regretful look I don't understand. He turns back to the man. "You got any hobbies, cleaner? What about guns? Do you like guns by any chance?"

The man groans and begins to shake his head. "Please… I'm scared."

"Of course you are," Jonah says, soothingly. "You got a good reason to be scared."

The tendons on his forearm shift as his grip tightens. The hand that was stroking the man's hair becomes firmer and suddenly Jonah is holding him down instead. He reaches behind his back with his free hand and draws out his hunting knife.

"It'll be over soon, don't worry, mate," Jonah mutters.

I take a step forward, then freeze.

I know what's coming next.

For evil to flourish, it requires only that good men do nothing.

I imagine myself leaping forward and pushing Jonah away. But I don't move. The man seems to sense what's coming as well. He draws on some last reserve of strength and struggles, contorting under Jonah's grip.

"Shh, shh, shh," Jonah whispers, leaning closer. "It's OK, you can let go now."

"N … nn … n…" the man grunts, trying to resist.

Jonah presses the hungry point of his knife against his chest. The man tries to squirm away. It reminds me of Tongue's desperate attempts to escape, but this man is much weaker and Jonah seems oblivious to his struggles.

For evil to flourish…

I look away just as Jonah pushes in the knife.

I hear the man's chest give way with a dry crunch like a crust of stale bread. A cloud of dust from his disintegrating body billows out and engulfs us. I feel it catch in my throat. I see it settle in Jonah's hair. Then life and movement go out of him.

Jonah steps back. He's sweating. His breath comes in short animal grunts, his shoulders rock with each exhalation. He wipes the blade of his knife against the bedding and returns it to its sheath. He wipes a hand down his face, smearing the white ash and mud into white-grey streaks that look like war paint.

He glances at me and smiles.

TWENTY-FOUR

Jonah strides across the food court, pumped with febrile energy. He strips off his shirt and drops it on the ground, sweat shines on his twisted muscles in the non-light. He goes to the sink behind the bar and runs the tap. When the sink's full, he cups his hands and drenches himself, rubbing without soap at the engrained white-grey ash from earlier.

He gasps when the cold water hits him, a triumphant yell, half laugh, half battle cry. He gestures for me to join him. "You need to wash as well, boy."

I stand frozen. I feel hollowed out, the world feels slow and dream-like. I keep seeing the old man falling into dust in front of me, his chest crumbling. I can feel the oiliness of the ash from his body ingrained into my skin. It's in my hair and on my clothes, it tastes sour in my mouth.

Is this what happened to the babies? Is this what Farah didn't want me to see?

I'm aware of Farah and Chiu watching from the sofas, Ose and Levi too for that matter. I can't bring myself to look at any of them. I pull my T-shirt over my head, repulsed by the feeling of the ash and oil as it presses against my face. The sink is too small, round, stainless steel. I scoop water on to my face and scrape with my fingernails to try to remove as much of the oily residue as I can. It's useless, my efforts smear the ash around without getting rid of it.

Jonah has cracked open a beer and is dancing. Levi isn't playing, but Jonah doesn't care. He sways as if the music is already inside him.

As I lean forward to scoop more water on to my face, I notice that a small fruit knife has slipped down behind the sink and been forgotten. I glance up and check that nobody is looking my way, then I reach forward and slip the knife into my pocket. I don't know what I'm going to do with it. The thought of trying to attack Jonah with it feels laughable.

I go to the sofa and sit down. Ose hands me a beer and I drink, feeling the flat, insipid liquid fill my throat.

Chiu flashes me a brief greeting. He's holding something – a laptop. The incongruity is shocking. "How did you—?" I start.

"Ose made it work," he says.

"How?"

"This was my job," Ose says. "Chip designer. It doesn't always work."

"Do you have the internet?" I ask.

Ose shakes his head, smiling sadly. "No. Just the corporate site, a few games."

"They have Snake!" Chiu says, gleefully.

Farah appears. She hands me a new T-shirt that she's fetched from the Marks and Spencer on the opposite side of the food court. She doesn't say anything. She waits while I put it on and then she sits next to me.

"He killed him," I say.

"Who?" Farah asks.

"Just ... somebody. I couldn't stop him."

I can feel myself crying. I don't want to cry in front of Farah, I don't want to cry in front of anyone, but the tears keep coming. I feel Farah's arm reach around my shoulder and I lean my head against hers and she leans her head against mine.

"You'll be OK," I hear Jonah say. "A bit of a shock the first time, that's all."

"Why?" I say. "Why did you—"

"People get stuck here sometimes. I help them on their way," Jonah says.

"It's murder," Farah breathes.

"It's God's work," Jonah replies.

"That's bullshit," I spit.

"Now, now, let's be nice," Jonah warns. "God has a plan for me, Kyle. Big plans. And you can be a part of them if you pull yourself together."

I shake my head slightly. "Never."

"Oh, come on." Jonah looks disappointed. "You did good today. You felt it, didn't you? You felt it watching us? Tell me you did." I don't answer. "This place isn't further from reality, you know," Jonah continues. "It's *closer*. You know that, don't you? The things we do here matter more. When we kill, it doesn't go unnoticed. This place can make you strong, Kyle. That's what you want, isn't it? To feel strong? I can help you with that."

He turns away.

Did you feel it?

Yes, I felt it.

I felt something close by. I felt its gaze. I couldn't see its face, but I could feel it watching us, curious, like it was trying to make sense of us. Noticing us.

But I'm not going to tell Jonah that.

Jonah cracks another beer and flaps his hand to tell Levi to hurry up and start playing. Farah's eyes burn into me. *She hates me*, I think. Of course she does. I let Jonah murder someone, right in front of me. Farah wouldn't have done that. She'd have stopped him. She'd have tried, at least. But I didn't have the guts.

That's what you want, isn't it? To feel strong? I can help you with that.

177

Jonah is dancing more energetically now, bare-chested, lost in whatever this ritual is to him. Levi is lost too, heaving rhythmically on the bellows, his fingers dancing on the keys, his eyes blank and unsettling. Tongue, I notice, has taken himself to his roll mat.

What is the hold Jonah has over them? I wonder.

"Why does he do it?" Farah says. "Why is he searching for people?"

"He's a collector," Ose replies.

"A what?"

"He collects people like us, people with skills who can be useful to him. If they're not useful to him, he … helps them."

I remember all the questions Jonah was asking the man. Are you a builder? Are you a technical person?

"He was asking about guns," I say.

The word *gun* somehow cuts through the music and Levi glances in our direction. Ose tenses. He waits until Levi is once again distracted by his music before he says in a low voice: "You think Jonah is happy with motorbikes, table lamps and an accordion player?"

"What will he do if he finds somebody who can work a gun?" Farah says.

Ose shrugs. "Take over. We're not the only ones here, you know. Not everyone is hiding in their beds and we come across other groups like ours sometimes. Jonah has big plans for this place. He wants us to get organized.

Imagine what a man like Jonah could do if he had weapons."

A shiver runs through me. Imagine Jonah building his gang, raising an army, ready and waiting for every poor sod who wakes up in this place.

"Why are you with him?" Farah says.

"We were dead men," Ose says. "Jonah taught us how to live here."

"This isn't *living*."

The weight of the fruit knife presses against my leg. I got us into this mess because I was too scared to run before, so now it's up to me to get us out.

"I'll kill him," I say.

"You wouldn't stand a chance," Ose replies.

"I'll wait until he's asleep."

Ose shakes his head. "When he said this place makes you strong, he meant it."

"Strong how?"

Ose glances at Levi. He's saying too much, but a part of him needs to get it out. "Like I say, sometimes we run into other people. Sometimes we fight. But with Jonah, it's not really a fight. He's ready for them, always. He smells them coming. They hit him and it's like they're nowhere near him. Like he *chooses* not to be hit. Then he hits them and they fall apart. What he does here, the killing, it makes him powerful. It attracts attention."

"Attention? From who?" I say.

Ose shakes his head slightly. I'm half relieved he won't answer.

"What are we supposed to do then?" Farah says.

"Don't cross him," Ose says. "You're important to him, Kyle. That's the only thing keeping the three of you alive."

TWENTY-FIVE

Wake. Up.

TWENTY-SIX

My eyes snap open into undarkness. My pulse throbs in my ears; cold sweat prickles my face. I expect to find Farah shaking me awake, but, when I turn, I see that she's sound asleep.

Her lips are slightly parted as she inhales and exhales, she looks calm, younger than she looks when she's awake. Her eyelids flicker like she's having a dream and I feel a rush of unexpected tenderness.

I imagine waking her. *We would be alone*, I think. I imagine her sharp intake of breath, her watchful look. I imagine that she might start to sit up, but if I put my arm around her and slide on to the sofa next to her, would she understand? I imagine her resting her head on my shoulder so that I can hold her. Half-formed feelings churn inside me, feelings that are exquisitely peaceful and feelings that are not so peaceful as well.

I wish for a moment that we were back in the ordinary world, that we could hang out like normal people. Perhaps I could tell her how I feel then. But it's a futile dream, because we were never friends in the ordinary world and we never would be, let alone anything else.

I stand up, every creak of the leather sofa sounding like a tiny detonation that must surely wake the whole world. My heart races, my shoulders tremble.

He'll find you and he'll punish you.

I don't know to what extent Ose, Tongue and Levi are prisoners like us. But they are culpable, they allow Jonah to keep on murdering people in order to save their own skin.

I don't want to turn into them.

I don't want to stand by and let Jonah murder anyone else in front of me.

You wouldn't stand a chance.

We'll see about that, I think.

What he does here, the killing, it makes him powerful. It attracts attention…

Whose attention? God's? I think of the ancient Greeks riding into battle with their gods in tow. I think of the crusaders, with their cruciform swords and their symbols. Maybe God is drawn to bloodshed and horror in both worlds.

Fine, I think. *Maybe if I bring the bloodshed he'll side with me.*

I smile in the darkness, amused by my own rushing thoughts.

The voice in my dream still rings in my ears. *Wake. Up.* Was it a sign? I snort bitterly under my breath. A lifetime of being an atheist and suddenly I think God is talking to me.

I approach the roll mats where Jonah, Ose, Tongue and Levi sleep. A neat row huddled together, side by side, like a Scout camp.

Jonah's asleep. His lips are pressed tightly shut. His face is marked by age and anger, pockmarked and fleshy, a Martian landscape. The sense that his eyes might flick open at any moment.

Levi lies next to him, then Ose, then Tongue. Tongue's T-shirt is still covered in uneven stains from the surgery Jonah administered two nights ago.

Enough thinking.

I hold the knife tightly against my chest, clutching it like some kind of amulet.

He's ready, always.

I practise my attack with the tiny fruit knife, thinking through the angle I need, the way I'm going to spread my weight.

I need to not mess this up.

I imagine Jonah's hand flashing up with impossible speed, twisting, snapping my arm...

I take a step.

Others must have tried and failed, I think. *Why should I be any different?*

I don't know. But I have to try. Because if I don't, then sooner or later Farah or Chiu will try and then their death will be on my hands too.

You're important to him, Kyle. That's the only thing keeping the three of you alive.

I step forward. It has to be fast.

What he does here, the killing, it makes him powerful.

I know Ose is right. I know it won't work.

Just walk away.

But now a new idea comes. A flash of inspiration. It's so quick and so clear, it feels as if it comes from somewhere outside. This time I don't have to think. I act.

I dart forward, raise the knife…

And it's done.

I stare at the dark handle of the knife in my hand and my hand pressed against the naked flesh of Tongue's neck and the blade is gone because it's deep, deep inside.

Tongue's eyes flick wide open. His arm flashes up and grabs my wrist. I'm terrified he's going to shout. But he just gives a slight, wheezy intake of breath.

I try to pull my hand back but Tongue holds me where I am, my hand pressed against his throat. "Tongue," he says quietly, emphatically.

He looks at me with an extraordinary, profound, oddly familiar expression, his eyes shining in the undarkness with an amazing lustre. Then I feel the pressure of his hand, not pushing me away, but drawing me forward, ensuring that I finish.

I don't dare look at Jonah. I walk, fast and silent, across the food court, back towards Farah and Chiu.

My body is rigid with fear. I shake Farah awake. She starts, sitting up quickly.

"We need to go," I say. "Right now."

I shake Chiu and press my finger to my lips to silence him. He and Farah clock the look on my face and don't ask any questions.

Just go, I think. *Don't stop. Don't think. Just walk.*

Out into the night and whatever waits for us out there.

TWENTY-SEVEN

We walk fast, desperate to break into a run but scared to, in case the noise of our footsteps gives us away. We're lucky Farah has this part worked out already. She leads us through the car park and across the motorway bridge. There's an airy, grasping sort of non-space in the air. The night sky feels like falling. *It's worse at night*, Jonah said. He was right. I glance over the side and catch a glimpse of the traffic in the ordinary world, cutting in and out of my vision like faulty wiring.

"You killed Jonah?" Chiu asks, breathless, trotting to keep up.

"No," I say.

Chiu looks panicked. "But the bikes? He'll come?"

"The bikes aren't a problem now," I say.

Chiu casts Farah a questioning look and I see the realization dawn on him. The thought of it swims sickly in my mind. *I killed a man. I killed Tongue.*

"Down here," Farah says.

We follow the ramp down on to the M25. I keep my eyes fixed on the hard shoulder, knowing that if I let myself see the traffic, I might not be able to unsee it this time and I don't have the luxury of freaking out right now.

The road gleams in the night, the weight of the traffic in the ordinary world presses against us. I keep seeing Tongue's eyes, wide and fearful.

"This one," Farah says. "Barnet, A1081."

"Are you sure?" Chiu says.

"It'll take us south, towards London."

"What if he comes after us on foot?"

"We'll get off the main road as soon as we can," Farah says. "We'll be into the housing estates before morning. He can't search that many roads without transport."

We drop down, leaving the M25 behind us. The four-lane junction peels away and we're left with a single-lane road, grass verges and a thick line of gorse bushes on either side. The thought of the housing estates and hundreds of side roads to get lost in draws us on, but right now there's only this road. This road and fields either side and an impenetrable line of spiny gorse corralling us to this one and only route. I'd hoped we'd be able to get into a field or something and be hidden by bushes until we're into the suburbs. But there's no way.

Keep moving.

We pound down the tarmac without speaking. We

know we're too exposed, visible for the entire stretch of road until it curves ahead of us half a mile away; visible from the motorway that stretches over our heads. If Jonah's awake already, he has a fifty-fifty chance of picking the right direction on the M25. But our odds are worse than that because it wouldn't take much for him to guess that we'd take the most direct route towards London. We told him we were going there after all.

He'll sniff you out.

"We should have doubled back," Chiu says. "Thrown him off the scent."

"We're going this way," Farah answers. Resolute.

We scan the verge, looking for a break in the gorse bushes and a way off the road. We pass a caravan park. I almost suggest finding a caravan and hiding out for the night, but I know it's better to put some distance between us and Jonah. Even I don't fancy the idea of cowering in an abandoned caravan while he prowls around outside.

He'll sniff you out.

"Maybe he won't bother," Chiu says. "Without the bikes, maybe we're not worth it."

"Only if we get far enough away," I say.

"I shouldn't have told him about the machine," Chiu says. "I'm sorry."

"It's fine," Farah says. "We didn't tell him anything. Not really." She glances at me. "Besides, I don't think it's the machine he wants."

Tiredness starts to override our adrenaline and our steps start to come more slowly. It feels as if we're not getting anywhere, like dreams where the distance grows as quickly as you cover it. We're spent. Chiu has started limping. We need to stop, but we know we can't. Not on the road. We push ourselves onwards. I take Chiu's arm and he leans his weight into me. He won't make it much further.

All the while, the night enfolds us. It presses against us. *We can't be out here for long. It'll drive us mad.* I can feel the fear needling at me, picking me apart.

A slight thinning in the gorse off on the right catches my eye.

"Wait here," I say.

I clamber awkwardly up the verge, slipping, nearly face-planting in the long, slick grass. I pick my way into the line of bushes. Thick spikes catch on my T-shirt and I stumble and feel something snag and tear at my calf. I spot a thinner patch I can push through and get further up the slope. For the first time I can see over the brow to where the land drops away.

"What is it?" Farah calls, noticing that I've fallen still.

"It's a golf course!" I call down, a laugh bubbling up inside me. "Come on, we can get through."

The undulating outline of the fairway falls away from us and the oval greens cluster further off. On the far side, I can just see the shifting reflections of a small lake. Farah and Chiu scramble excitedly up the verge, Farah grabbing

Chiu's hand and hauling him after her. I duck down and force my way into the hedge, twisting and manoeuvring myself to escape the clinging branches. When I finally break through, I turn and find Farah right behind me. She's snarled up and I have to carefully unpick a barbed creeper from her hair. I pull her through the last few branches and we stand and gaze in wonder at the expanse of open green stretching away towards a dense treeline.

We're smiling. We're kidding ourselves, because we're still easy pickings for Jonah, but it feels like a win to be off the road, and the neatly sculpted slopes of the golf course look so *silly* in this place.

We head off at a diagonal. We hike, half run, down the steep slope, crossing between thick, rough and perfectly tended green, skirting a large sand trap. The prospect of disappearing into the treeline spurs us on, but it's still heavy going. Our breath rasps in our throats and breaks our words into ragged gasps.

"My dad plays golf," Chiu says. "I'll have to … tell him about this place…"

"I'll give you a game … when we're back," I gasp.

"Do you play?" Chiu asks.

"I don't know … I never tried."

Chiu and Farah laugh. It's not that funny, but then … somehow it is. We can't stop ourselves. The euphoria of being off the road takes over.

By the time we reach the line of trees, my head is

throbbing and my leg aches from top to bottom. Bacteria might not exist in this world but blisters do. Lactic acid, cardiovascular distress, pain. My calf is a wall of blinding agony. We drop heavily to the ground and I pull up my trouser leg and inspect the cut. It's deep. If we were in the ordinary world I'd be thinking about infection, tetanus, sepsis... In this world, I check the jagged lip of torn skin for the tell-tale black seeds that might be the first eyes; I check that the skin isn't growing hard, cracking, or turning white.

"Are you OK?" Farah asks.

"I think so."

I pull my trouser leg down. The air is cooler here, the grass has given way to dried leaves and a bed of soft mulch. In the ordinary world, it would be pitch-black. Here, we can still see, but the light is flat and textureless, coming from everywhere and nowhere at once. *It's not light*, I think. It's the absence of darkness.

We're silent for a long time. We shouldn't stay here. It feels like resting in the jaws of a bear trap. But we don't have any choice.

I lean back and lie, staring up at the treetops that stoop over us. This is how the world looks when I come back from a seizure. The weight of the ground beneath me, the crowded faces looking down at me, wondering if I'm dead. *This will happen to us someday*, they think. They know it; they just don't like to think about it. For most people, death is a faraway, abstract idea. But for me it's always been different.

I'm closer to this world than the ordinary world.

Do you want to know what death feels like? I think.

I'll tell you: it feels like *nothing*.

I think of Jonah. *What he does here, it makes him powerful. It attracts attention.*

Yes, I think. I've always felt the attention of something. Ever since I was a child and It visited me in my auras. But that attention is different now. Stronger. Closer. I think in the ordinary world we'd call it "guilt" or "shame", but here I see that those feelings are just a reflection of something much worse.

The cold breath of God on the back of my neck.

God... Mum... The thoughts connect and I remember the rhyme she used to say to me every night. *Now I lay me down to sleep, I pray the Lord my soul to keep.*

"You really killed him?" Chiu says.

I sit up; a hollow feeling fills my chest. I can't look at Farah and Chiu because I'm scared of what I'll see on their faces. Disgust? Fear?

He wanted me to... I was helping *him...*

But that's exactly what Jonah would say. I keep quiet. After a moment, Chiu lies down and rolls on to his side, his back to me, and curls into a ball with his arms folded across his chest.

"Thanks," he says.

Farah shuffles backwards, sitting with her back against my chest. I put my arms round her and hold her like that.

"I'm cold," she says, leaning her weight against me.

We don't feel the cold in this place, but I don't bother to point this out to her. She presses her cheek against my forearm and I'm filled with silent gratitude for her. I think that sleep will be impossible like this, but it comes quickly, a dark purple like anaesthesia.

And if tonight I should not wake, I pray the Lord my soul to take.

I dream.

TWENTY-EIGHT

I'm young, seven or eight, and I've been spending a lot of time in the hospital lately for reasons I don't fully understand. Now Mum's started going to the hospital as well, which is why Grandad is picking me up from school instead.

"Does she have the same thing as me?" I ask. "Epilepsy?"

It's a new word. An ugly word that reminds me of the figure I see watching me sometimes and I hope desperately I won't have to see again.

"No, mate," Grandad says. "What your mum's got is different."

"Can I go and see her?"

"Not right now."

He upends a tin of beans into the pan and stirs them vigorously. He stoops down to check the toast. I don't press any more. When I ask too many questions, Grandad gets moody, and I never get anything useful out of him anyway. The most I've ever got out of him is that she "needs a bit of a rest", whatever that means.

"Uno?" Grandad says.

He sits at the tiny kitchen table and stacks and re-stacks a pile of Mum's papers to make space. I take a wad from the main pile and place them on my lap so Grandad can start dealing. I don't mind that Grandad is looking after me for a little while. The world always feels edgy around Mum, filled with a manic energy that I've always been instinctively uncomfortable around. "Stop the world, I want to get off!" she used to cry.

"Those forms still safe?" Grandad asks. His voice is casual, but I'm not fooled. "Those ones in the garage."

I narrow my eyes. Dream Grandad always gets things wrong. "You're getting muddled. You hid the forms later. This is before."

Grandad is unfazed. "Oh, right. Sorry."

He picks up a yellow seven and drops it immediately on to the pile.

"You need to get inside," he says. "You've been out here too long already."

I look up and find him watching me. His voice is calm, unhurried. In my dreams he usually plays along, acts like he doesn't know he's dead, to keep things nice and cosy. But there's a serious note in his voice now.

The warmth of the moment leaches away. "You should

have fallen through by now," he says. "The walls of the world are too thin here. You can't last."

"Why not?" I say. "What's out there?"

"Everything."

TWENTY-NINE

"We should get going," Farah says, stirring.

The morning air is damp and clammy and we can't completely see the edges of the golf course. We stick to the treeline, walking slowly, our bodies heavy. The ground is uneven and littered with dried branches and hidden ditches. I lose track of how long we walk. There's no movement of the sun or pressing need to eat or urinate. Only heaviness and the sky's whiteness turning brighter whenever we're not looking at it.

I guess about an hour later we hit the fence at the end of the golf course and track left until the grass gives way to the car park and the clubhouse.

There's a high street on the far side with rows of newsagents and fruit shops, a phone shop, a kosher takeaway and a music shop with guitars hanging in the window. The shops are ordinary shops but they're also thrillingly different. Souvlaki – *what is that? Greek?* This is my first glimpse of London. The shops are not purpose-built blocks of concrete like at home; they're set into the frontages of what look like old Victorian terraced houses.

People must live up there, I think, a flight of stairs from a Spanish bakery and a Portuguese cake shop. The buildings have a weirdly satisfying, intricate look. The ageing brickwork creates delicate patterns and the big sash windows look grand, even though they are caked in grime.

"What's wrong with you?" Farah says, bemused by my expression.

"It's nothing," I say. "It's just that I've never been to London before."

Farah laughs. "This isn't London, mate. This is Barnet."

We cut away from the high street as soon as we can and weave into the suburban side roads. We turn frequently, zigzagging left and then right. Farah keeps looking at her map, navigating us south as the winding streets curl around each other.

Chiu hops from paving stone to paving stone, avoiding the cracks. Farah joins him. If we keep going this way, weaving through the side roads, only occasionally crossing main roads when we have to, we'll reach UCL before nightfall.

They think they're safe, I think.

They're imagining Jonah staring fruitlessly at the high street, trying to guess which of the side roads we've taken.

But what if he's not guessing?

I try not to think about the way he led us to the old man's house. *You smell that?* It's not like he had to search door to door, is it?

But I don't mention it to Chiu and Farah. There's no point, so why worry them? We'll keep going, we'll get to UCL and then … I don't know.

When Chiu first told us about the machine I thought he was kidding himself. But now, somehow, I'm pinning all my hopes on it too.

The knife I used to kill Tongue is still in my back pocket. It presses uncomfortably against my backside as I walk but I keep it there anyway. I like feeling it close.

We come to a T-junction and Farah consults the map, then starts to the left.

I stop. "Wait."

Farah gives me a worried look. "What is it?"

I shake my head. My body thrums suddenly with a sense of dread I don't understand.

"Jonah?"

"No."

"Then what?"

"I don't know."

Farah and Chiu exchange a look.

"We need to keep moving," Farah says.

I shake my head again. I look down the street to the left. It has a high wall on one side where it borders the train line and a huge block of red-brick flats on the other. The trees that line the road are stark rods of grey wood, cut back and bare.

"We can go right instead, can't we?" I say, my voice trembling.

Farah glances at her map, shakes her head. "We need to get past the train line. It's like … an extra three miles that way and then three miles back. It makes no sense."

I can't explain. But I know. That way is death, death and more death. Nothing more. I don't know *how* I know, but I do.

Farah stares at me, scared and irritable at the same time.

"What is it?" Chiu says.

"I don't know."

Farah's irritation comes out now. "You need to do better than that."

She glances at Chiu like she's expecting him to back her up, but he remains silent. I look at the road curving away from us again. It's like the aura I get before a fit, the certainty that something terrible is coming.

"Jonah could still be behind us," says Farah. "I'm not walking six miles out of our way because you're scared of the bloody trees."

The trees *are* terrifying now that she mentions it. They look like people who have been strung up to die and hung there so long there's nothing left but bleached white bones. But it's the big, blank windows in the red-brick apartments that really scare me. There's someone waiting for us in that darkness. I don't know if he's seen us yet but if we go that way he will and we won't stand a chance.

Farah glances at Chiu and then back at me.

"I think we should go Kyle's way," Chiu says at last.

"*What?*"

Chiu looks unapologetic. "Kyle's getting good at this sort of thing."

We walk more quickly now, our earlier good spirits lessened. Farah strides ahead, her strong, long legs pounding across the pavement. She's angry at me. Chiu falls into step at my side.

"I'm sorry," I say, uselessly.

Chiu shrugs. "Blindsight?"

"Maybe. I don't know."

"Any other … feelings?"

That we're walking into something terrible. That we may have avoided immediate death but we won't avoid it for long.

I shake my head.

It's all residential houses here, big leafy trees and grand brick properties. One house we pass has actual battlements and I want to point them out to Farah but I figure she's not in the mood. Right next to it, there's a modern, six-storey apartment block and across from that, the heavy grey complex of a council estate. I remember reading somewhere that the reason you get so many different styles of houses in London is because of the Second World War. The bombs plucked entire rows of terraces – and entire families – out of the universe and London's planners have been desperately trying to fill in the gaps ever since.

I like the effect it's created. I like the way each street has the capacity to hold a secret. A strikingly modern building with a small lawn on the roof sits next to a dignified-looking semi, next to a vacant plot, next to a pub, next to a shop that sells fishing tackle.

I'm in London, I think. I can't help the whisper of excitement inside me. The vast, throbbing, layered energy of it all. London has weight, just as the traffic on the A5 had weight. It's more real, more *there* than the town I grew up in. London fizzes and crackles across worlds. The constant rush of life and death, the tightly packed minds and hope and love and hate. It bends the walls of the world.

I wonder if that's why I was always drawn here. Because I understood, intuitively, that London straddled both worlds just as I did.

The streets are still empty though. I catch occasional glimpses of people in the ordinary world: an old man shuffling along on the opposite side of the road and then disappearing behind a tree and never re-emerging; a woman watching me from a living-room window before vanishing in the shifting reflections of the glass. There should be more people, more *life*. But this world is not *life*, I think, it's the absence of life, the before and the after, the realization that all of us have already been dead and will be dead again and the thing we call life is just the briefest spark between eternities of blackness.

And all the time, the dull, featureless dome of the sky watches us.

You've been out here too long.

I feel it come on all at once. The disequilibrium of the Stillness.

"I need to stop," Chiu says, a moment later as we cross another main intersection.

He sits heavily on the ground, his legs crossed, his hands in his lap. He stares numbly at his fingers as if he hardly recognizes them.

"No," I say, panic rising quickly. "We need to keep moving."

Chiu shakes his head belligerently. "I'm tired."

Farah walks back to us. "What's he doing?"

Chiu rolls on to his side and curls into a foetal ball.

"We've been outside for hours," I say. "We need to get out of this light."

Farah nods. At the same time, I watch the energy slip out of her and she leans against the low wall of the front garden next to us and puffs out a heavy breath.

"We shouldn't have come this way," she breathes.

I think about the old man Jonah killed, too weak to

step outside his bedroom. I think about the man I met on the street when I first woke up: *all you'll want to do is close your eyes and wait it out…*

That's what happens to people here, I think. Their minds unravel; they curl up and they slip through the cracks in the world. It was happening to me until I met Farah and it was happening to Farah too. I think we saved each other. I have no idea how Chiu lasted for so long on his own, but maybe it was because he's younger, or maybe his books saved him.

Chiu's back is turning brown. Dry and crisp like an autumn leaf.

"We can't stay here," I say.

Farah offers me a weak smile. "You were right. We shouldn't have left the hospital."

"It was the right thing to do," I say.

The ground tilts under my feet. The walls of the world recede and suck the air from my lungs. I can feel It watching me. It watched me when I was young, It watched me kill Tongue and It's watching me now. That presence. It feels like the aura before a seizure, the metallic taste at the back of my throat.

Long and muscled, Its head tilted to one side like It's puzzled.

"If we stay here, we'll die," I say.

"I can't…" Farah shakes her head. "I can't think."

People think you can fight off a seizure the same

way you can fight off falling asleep, but it's not true. Something comes and sucks the ichor from you. I see it now in Farah: unblinking strength bound together by steel and snark, and yet ... she's beaten.

"I'm done, mate," she says, looking regretfully at me.

"No," I insist.

"Let's just stay here a little while."

I look at Chiu. His back is entirely brown now, one corner of his elbow cracked and threatening to flake off. Something shifts inside me, a new understanding. The reason why the outside is so awful here is not because there's something here that doesn't exist in the ordinary world, it's just better hidden.

You cannot see my face, for man shall not see me and live.

Exodus 33:20. One of Mum's favourites. It's the layers of detail that protect us from It in the ordinary world. Food to counter stillness. Love to counter emptiness.

"Dying is OK," Farah says. "We shouldn't make such a big deal of it."

"*No.*"

"Why not?" she responds, irritably.

Because I love you.

The thought cracks through my mind like a whip. "Because it's just getting good," I say, instead. "Don't you want to see what happens next?"

A weary half smile curls the corners of Farah's mouth. It's such a small thing: other people. I used to think I was a nobody, I was nothing, because I'd never *done* anything. I used to think no one would pay any attention to me because of it. But something happens when you get to know somebody: a connection forms. It's the most human thing and it's what binds us together even when everything else is gone.

Farah sees it in my eyes and I see it reflected in hers. I offer her my hand and she takes it. "Help me with Chiu," I say.

She pulls herself to her feet. Her shoulders are stooped forward and her footsteps scrape on the pavement but she's moving. I roll Chiu on to his back and slide my arm under him. Farah helps me, taking the other side of him.

He's rigid, crisp and fragile. As light as a sheet of paper.

Oh god, we're too late.

"Be careful," I warn.

We lift him, delicately, terrified that he might break and fall into dust.

This is it; this is how he dies.

It's shocking how quickly death comes. You're fine and then you're not.

The road is wider here, with a stretch of low, modern buildings on one side. I scan the signs, casting around for somewhere we can go. Somewhere out of Its glare.

An Indian restaurant…

A garage…

And then I find exactly what we need.

THIRTY

SLEEPY HOLLOW CO.
SOFAS, BEDS AND CARPETS

I don't remember how we got into the shop. I don't know if I carried Chiu or if he walked or if Farah carried us both. All I know is that if we hadn't got inside when we did, we wouldn't have made it.

I wake in the cavernous interior. Silver heating ducts and electrical conduits snake around the ceiling above me; rows of beds extend in every direction, giving way to a lake of sofas in the middle distance and, a little further off, a coastline of fake offices and what might be fake kitchens. There's an alarm clock on the bedside table next to my head, its fake time stuck for ever at 7:59. The shelves next to Chiu are stacked with perfectly folded towels and empty picture frames.

The memory of being outside feels like a fever dream. If I'd lain down, if I'd told myself I was just going to close my eyes for a second… Just a second…

That's how it would have ended. Nobody remembers themselves falling asleep.

Farah stirs on the bed next to me and then Chiu. They sit up like space travellers waking from a century in deep freeze. For a long time, none of us know what to say. We sit in incredulous silence.

At last, Chiu asks, "What happened?"

"You sat down and refused to move," Farah says, offering Chiu a crooked smile.

Chiu shakes his head. "I was so tired."

"It's OK," Farah says. "I was too."

"Why weren't *you* affected?" Chiu says, looking at me.

"I was," I say. "It's something I've felt before though."

Chiu gets up, moves tentatively towards the door. I can see him deliberating with himself. The open sky broods outside. "It's getting late," he remarks. "It's at least, um … quarter-past dark grey. We must have slept most of the day."

"Then we'll stay here," I say. "Leave first thing."

The others agree readily. None of us is in a rush to go outside again. Chiu smiles and he fishes for something in his jeans pocket. He pulls out a small, battered box. "Hey! Who's up for a game of Uno?"

*

We play Uno and gradually our fear recedes. Uno is our sacrament, the secret we keep from God. The brightly coloured cards go back and forth and we sit cross-legged on a giant king-size bed that Farah has taken as her own. We might be kids on a sleepover.

I win and keep winning, but nobody wants to stop playing so we go again and again as the whispers of the ordinary world flicker around us. Chiu is the first to call it a night. He drops his cards mid-hand and declares that he's exhausted. He rolls off Farah's bed and crawls heavily to the next one along and falls instantly asleep, face first.

"I'm done as well," Farah says.

We clear the cards and I move to the next bed along. Farah flops extravagantly on to her back and pulls the large, white-and-purple duvet around her. "My bed is my best friend," she sighs. "It gives me warm blanket hugs."

"G'night," I murmur.

I lie on my back and stare once again at the twisting silver pipes above my head. Sleep reaches out for me hungrily. I roll on to my side and my thoughts start to fall apart.

There's a sound and a movement and suddenly I'm aware of Farah lying next to me. The warmth and weight of her presses against my back and I can feel the slight pressure of her knees against the back of my thighs. She puts her arm around me and presses her forehead against my neck.

"Is this OK?" she says.

"Um … yeah … of course."

My chest feels as if somebody is kicking over oil drums inside it and my stomach twists and turns. I'm scared that she can feel how tense I am. I don't want her to think I don't want her here.

"Thank you," Farah says quietly.

"For what?"

"For saving us."

I half laugh. "It's the Carpets that saved us."

"You saved us," she replies. "And I'm sorry about what you had to do to Tongue."

I don't answer right away. The image of him is still too vivid, the movement beneath me as he died feels like a stain on my memory that I'll never be rid of.

"Are you OK?" Farah says.

"Honestly?" I say. "I'm a little scared."

Farah squeezes me tighter and my body wants to dissolve into hers. "No you're not," she whispers. "You're courageous."

If I was really courageous I'd turn round now and kiss her, but I don't move.

Farah shifts, leans forward and kisses the back of my neck. I can feel the shape of her lips, her breath scalding my skin.

Brothers? Is she serious?

"Sleep well," she murmurs.

Not a chance, I think.

But I do sleep. I must have, because the next thing I know, I hear Farah screaming.

I sit up, staring desperately around at the rows of beds. No sign of her.

An icy quench drops through me. I leap out of bed and I'm scrabbling on the floor but the knife is gone.

Jonah?

Chiu is up too. "This way!" he says. "This way!"

"Farah!" I shout.

We run, dodging between the beds and then between sofas and coffee tables. It's hard to pinpoint the sound in the warehouse-like space. We stop next to a fake kitchen with a fake sink and dishwasher and listen, disorientated and panicking. The noise is nearby: a reedy, horrified noise, half sob, half moan. It's an appalling sound – the noise of a rabbit caught in a snare, the noise of something badly hurt, dying.

"Over here," Chiu says.

We bolt. It's a trap, obviously. I don't know why Jonah didn't just kill us in our sleep but I guess he wants something else. He wants to make us suffer; he wants to punish us.

Think, Kyle. Be smart.

But my body is fizzing and crackling with fear and I can't stop. I bolt through a fake kitchen that has a bowl of fake fruit on the dining table. There's a fake television, a set of cookery books that have no pages, a stack of brightly coloured ceramic bowls that will be forever empty.

I wish I had my knife. Not that it would do me any good against Jonah, but I still wish I had it. I spot Farah at a desk, part of a squared-off area designed to look like a teenager's bedroom with a single bed and a rack of storage units. She's scrunched forward, clutching something close to her chest, rocking slowly, forwards and backwards, sobbing.

"Where is he?" I gasp, scanning the room. "Where's Jonah?"

Chiu is at my side a moment later, his body tense, ready to fight. *He's a good kid*, I think. *As brave as they come.*

I move closer, cautious now.

Where is he? What did he do to her?

I see the blood first.

Then my knife on the desk and the blade and handle slick with yet more blood.

Then Farah: her T-shirt drenched in it, her jeans black with it. "What did you do?"

Farah looks up and stares at me like she's seeing me for the first time. There's more blood flecking her cheek. She pushes her hand forward, flat on the desk. Among the treacle-streaks of gungy blood I can see that she has seven … no … eight fingers.

"What's happening?" Chiu whispers.

"It's Puzzles," I answer.

"Help me," Farah gasps.

She grabs her wrist with her free hand. There are more fingers now, nine … no ten … they swell and split, bulging from under the skin and then bursting out, contorted and malformed. I draw an empty breath.

"Cut them," Farah pleads. "Please cut them."

"I can't."

"It *hurts*…"

I can hardly bear to look at the hand, the thought of cutting into those twisted, alien fingers makes me sick. But I know what will happen if I don't. Already her wrist and the lower part of her forearm are beginning to bulge and shift, before long her hand will be gone altogether and then her arm and then … her.

Treat the symptoms.

I have to do what Jonah did for Tongue.

I step forward and pick up the knife. It's slick with blood from Farah's own failed attempts at stopping the disease. I clamp my hand over the back of Farah's, my knife at the ready.

"Are you sure?" I say.

Farah nods.

"Do it, quickly!" Chiu urges.

I press the knife down on to the back of one of the fingers. It writhes and flexes like an animal trying to escape. It reminds me of the time I held the school hamster when I was little. No one could understand why I was so freaked out by it. But I remember thinking about all those fragile organs and liquid beneath the springy skin of its engorged stomach and I remember thinking, just for a moment, that I might *squeeze*...

It's the same pliable softness under my knife now. I imagine myself squeezing the hamster of my childhood until its smooth, round stomach split. I turn away.

Farah screams.

When I look again it's like our hands are islands in a lake of black blood. The severed finger squirms a moment, then stops, then is gone. When I go for the next finger, Farah pulls back instinctively. I hook my elbow over her arm and pin her in place.

The next finger is easier. It feels like slicing through chorizo.

I slice again and again, and the excised fingers curl away and then melt into the black muck that no longer looks like blood, and that drips in slick rivers on to the floor. Farah's breaths come in torn mouthfuls like she's struggling to get enough air. I'm terrified she's going to die. I'm terrified that I'm killing her. But I cut and cut and cut.

Gradually, finally, the new fingers stop appearing. The ones that are already there fall limp like they're resigned to their fate. I slice them off one by one. Farah's breathing slows, her head flung back.

I loosen my grip and step back. Farah curls into a protective ball around her hand. I help her to stand, guide

215

her to the sofa. I take a T-shirt that's draped over the sofa in a parody of a messy teenager's laundry and wrap it tenderly around her damaged hand.

She doesn't resist. She sits, stupefied and inert, and when I'm finished she rolls on to her side and falls asleep.

THIRTY-ONE

Puzzles.

We all know what it means. It means Farah is dying. She's dying here and she's dying in the ordinary world; after all, each world is just a reflection of the other.

I think of Chiu's theory. That being here might prevent us from being able to recover in the ordinary world. If he's right, then nothing the doctors do there will be of any use. It'll just be one of those things they don't fully understand. The limits of science. *We're doing everything we can,* they'll tell her parents. *She's not responding to treatment.*

Idiopathic organ failure.

They're just words we use to describe the things we don't understand.

We need to get her back.

It's morning, or at least something that approximates the damp grey of a February morning. But Farah isn't going anywhere. She's sitting on the same sofa as she was sitting on hours ago, staring numbly at her bandaged hand. Chiu and I sit on the edges of our seats. Waiting. Watching. She looks scared. But worse than that, she looks resigned. Farah, the *fighter*, looks beaten.

"Farah," I say, softly. "We need to go and find the machine. It's our best chance of getting home, getting better."

She barely responds.

"Farah, *please*. We can be there in a couple of hours."

She starts unwrapping the T-shirt we used as a bandage.

"Don't," Chiu says. "Leave it."

But she carries on, unwinding the dark, stained material with trembling fingers. Her hand, beneath the bandage, is misshapen and discoloured. Gnarled bulges rise from the skin like new knuckle bones where I removed the extra fingers. They look like the scarred bulges that appear on trees when a branch has been cut. They look dead.

"It might not mean anything," Chiu says hopefully. "Tongue was sick for months. Ose said we don't know."

"He's right," I say. I try not to think about what it would be like to have to hack off Farah's fingers on a regular basis. "We can handle it. We know what to do now."

"You don't understand," Farah says. She stares at us both with savage, distrustful eyes. "I'm not like you two. We know what happened to Chiu. His body is fine and if we can get him out of this place, he'll be able to recover just like the doctors say he will. Kyle, you have epilepsy; you do this kind of thing all the time. But me … I got sick because the tumour is back. I'm dying in the ordinary world because my brain is being squashed by a mass of abnormal tissues. Being stuck here is the least of my problems."

I shake my head. "We don't know that."

"I'm not going back just to be sick," Farah says.

I look at Chiu and his eyes are wide and worried.

"I'm not doing it," Farah insists. The scary thing is I believe her. "I'm not going back to have surgeries and treatments and then die anyway. I'm not doing that again."

"Farah," I say, trying and failing to keep my voice calm. "Listen to me—"

"You can't change my mind."

"Just listen. You don't know this but I used to watch you in class all the time. I'm sorry if that sounds creepy but it's true. But you were *so* cool. I used to want to be like you. Then I got to sit with you in swimming lessons and I *can't believe* I made such a mess of it. But I was *so scared* I could hardly breathe around you, let alone talk to you normally. And now … it's wild but I got another chance. And it's different because I know you now. I've come to bloody London for you! And I'm not scared anymore, do you see?" Farah stares defiantly at me. I'm not getting through. I see flashes of her storming out of the classroom, the bewildered teacher left in her wake. Farah, who won't let anybody tell her what to do. But I carry on anyway. "But now I know you and I want *more*. I want to see you in the ordinary world as well. I want to go to the park and have a picnic with you. I want to go to the cinema and watch a crappy movie with you. I need you back in the ordinary world, Farah, where there's actually *stuff* to do beyond playing bloody Uno."

Farah watches me silently, her lips tight. The words are words I thought I'd never have the courage to say, but they come easily.

"Jonah was right," I say, changing tack. "There's something watching us. I've seen It before, in my seizures. And now we've caught Its attention and It thinks It can control us. It tells us that the outside is bad, so we lie down and sleep—"

"How do you know all this?" Chiu says.

I shake my head. "I don't know how, but I know I'm right. The point is, you're not someone who gives up and lies down because something tells you to, Farah. You're not someone who lets anyone, or *anything*, claim authority over you. And neither am I … not anymore."

"Or me," Chiu says.

"Right," I agree. Farah's mouth twitches in that half smile of hers. She must think I'm ridiculous, but I feel a rush of hopefulness anyway. "I don't even care if It wins in the end," I say. "If It wants to eat us, then fine. I'm still going to spit in Its eye first." On impulse, I pull out the tiny fruit knife from my pocket and brandish it. "And I'm going to stab It in the bloody face and Chiu is going to tear a chunk off Its goddamn ear!"

Chiu nods his enthusiastic agreement.

"That's quite a speech." Farah smiles.

"I'm serious," I reply.

"Will you kick It in the balls for me as well?"

"Absolutely!" I say. Then I add, "If I can reach. I mean, I think It's probably quite big, whatever It is, and if It's trying to eat me I'm going to be up high and so I might not be able to reach all the way down to—"

"I get it," Farah says. "It's OK, I get it." She stands, slowly, shakily. "Let's go find this bloody machine then."

We reach the bridge that cuts beneath the railway line and then we weave back through the side roads, making our way diagonally towards where the map tells us UCL is. I watch Farah anxiously. We've promised to keep an eye on each other and get inside at the first sign of any of us flagging.

But Farah is different since last night. She's distant. There's something broken about her, like cracked china. We pass a larger road and a strip of shopfronts and I make a mental note of them so we can get back there quickly if we need to.

Chiu picks up a stick and lets it rattle along the panels of the garden fences. It's hypnotic, more complex, more absorbing, than the sound would be in the ordinary world. Farah walks ahead of us, checking her map frequently, unwilling to talk or make eye contact for too long.

The houses get steadily grander as we get nearer the centre. They look like giants compared to the little matchbox houses at home. They're so huge it's hard not to imagine the rooms and the furniture inside as equally oversized: an armchair you have to climb on to, a dining table you need to scale like a mountaineer. It makes me wonder how anybody could possibly need that much space. People buy these houses because it makes them feel safer, I think. Like ballast, they tie themselves to them in the hope that nothing, not even death, will be able to sweep them off the face of the earth.

We walk and walk.

And, suddenly, we're lost. I look back to where we've crossed a main road and find that the road isn't there anymore. There's only the wide arc of another road filled with houses, fading into the distance.

Farah pauses, takes a closer look at her map.

"What's going on?" Chiu says. He turns to where I'm looking and stops. "Oh."

"That's not right," Farah says, quietly.

We walk on, more urgently, none of us wanting to say out loud what we're all thinking. Falloden Way. Ballards Lane. Wainwright Road. The roads smear and blend into each other. The fear grows between us.

Farah murmurs as she walks, checking her map. *No, no, no, no...*

"What's happening?" Chiu says.

"There should be ... there should be a road."

Farah stops, her chest heaving. My own head throbs. We can't get stuck out here again. We won't survive this time. Chiu looks quickly between us.

In the ordinary world we'd ask a passer-by, or we'd use the sun to point us in the right direction, but we have none of that here. We're lost, and not because we took a wrong turn, but because things have changed, because they keep changing. The strangeness of this place crawls through my hair.

"It's trying to test us," Chiu says.

"Or trap us," Farah replies.

"This way," I say.

I sound more confident than I am. Farah and Chiu don't question. I walk and they follow and I have no idea where I'm going, but we feel better for walking. More roads. More indifferent houses. It doesn't want us to get out of this estate.

The houses here are all semi-detached and have big bay windows and the road stretches on into the distance with no sign of any junctions.

"What do we do?" Chiu says.

"It's this way," I answer, taking a turn that has come into view without warning.

"Do you feel something?" Chiu says hopefully. "Is it blindsight?"

I don't have the heart to tell him that I don't. I'm just walking, trying to buy us some time by keeping them from despair. My feet are screaming and time seems to be sliding around beneath us. The sky was the same colour as a fifty-pence coin when we set off, now it looks more like ash. Late afternoon, I guess, or what passes for it in this place. We need to rest, but if we stop, we won't get up again. It's ready for us this time.

"Kyle," Chiu calls. "Kyle, I need to stop—"

"Come on," I say. "It's just at the end of this road."

I start to wonder if I *do* feel something. I think at first it's wishful thinking. The urge to see round the next corner is a kind of agony, a blend of hopefulness and despair, a sense of anticipation. I don't know if I really believe Chiu and his blindsight, but there's *something*, isn't there? Something pushing me on.

When we reach a T-junction, I turn left without pausing.

The tree-lined road bends and then opens out, and across the slightly larger road ahead of us there is a wall. A high brick wall, dark like slate, slightly curved.

It's not much, but it's different at least.

"Seriously?" Chiu says, dismayed.

"We're walled in," Farah says.

"No," I say. "Look. The curve is convex. We're *outside* the wall."

"Is that any better?" Chiu says.

"I think so," I say. "If we can find a way inside."

I set off. I know I'm right now. I can *feel* the arc of the wall and I know that the gates are up ahead somewhere. On our right, the bay-windowed houses with apple trees and magnolia trees watch us resentfully. They know we're escaping and they can do nothing to stop us.

I can feel Its surprise. Its head tilted to one side inquisitively.

We walk for a long time. On our left, the wall arcs round and it feels like an anchor, a single fixed point in space and time. *It made the rules, but It has to follow them like we do.* I think about a physics YouTube I watched once about a beetle walking across a football. It doesn't realize that space is curved and so it keeps going, thinking it's travelling in a straight line, until it inevitably loops back round and ends up where it began.

If the beetle wants to get somewhere it needs to fall off first, I think.

"Kyle, please," Chiu groans.

I glance back and Farah has slowed down as well.

"*Kyle*," Chiu says again. Irritable now.

"We're really close," I say. "I'm sure of it."

The treeline is thicker up ahead and for a heart-stopping moment we lose sight of the wall. But then we round the outcropping of bushes and on the far side there is a gate.

Standing open.

Tall: three times my height at least. Made from wrought iron and ornamented so extensively that it reminds me of a storm that's been frozen in time.

"That doesn't exactly look inviting," Chiu says, doubtfully.

"It's fine," I say. "It's where we want to be."

I can't exactly explain the excitement rushing inside me. *Escape*, my mind says. *Deliverance*. It didn't want us to get this far. I turn and grin at the others. They seem less impressed than I'd expected them to be.

On the other side of the gate is a park of some kind. Winding paths cut through dense treeline, cutting back and forth, rising up a steep hill. I take the map off Farah and look. There's lots of green spaces on the map and it's impossible to tell which one we're in, if any of them. But I'm certain that if we get to the top, it'll become clear.

I'm sweating and my breath is tight in my throat. I stumble, scramble my way up the hill. We're close. Chiu and Farah call from behind me, but I don't stop. They're following, that's enough and we're moving faster again.

It's not exactly a mountain, but I'm thinking about all the mountains Mum and Father Michael like to talk about. "Mountains are closer to God," they like to say. Like Mount Sinai where God gave Moses the Ten Commandments and Mount Nebo, where he saw the promised land. This is *my* mountain, I think. But it's not taking me closer to God. It's taking me somewhere better.

I've given up on the paths now and I'm scrambling through the brambles and the ferns. They catch on my jeans and claw at my T-shirt. I stumble into a patch of stingers and feel the angry needles like tiny electric shocks across my palm. The others are calling after me. They sound scared as well as angry now.

Then the brambles give way and we're in a wide-open field. It's been well looked after, more of a park than a field, with a broad, gravelled path and trees carefully planted to obscure the view until you are at the very top.

We climb. And then we're there and beyond the brow, between the trees.

London.

Laid out, like a meal on a plate.

Just like the photos I've seen on the internet, just like all the tourist information and visitor sites I've trawled over the years. There's the Shard, spearing upwards like it's slicing the sky in two. The dome of St Paul's below it. The Gherkin off to the left, swollen and unlikely, like a seed pod ready to burst. To the right, the Walkie Talkie, which could be a regular tower block except that it's somehow warped and half melted in the heat.

The breath leaves my lungs and I feel for a moment as if I'm floating.

The London skyline has always looked unworldly to me, but seeing it now, after everything we've been through in this world, I find it hard to imagine that the architects who built this place haven't spent some time in the Stillness.

"It's Parliament Hill," I say.

"It's *London*," Farah says firmly, as if to say: *This isn't Barnet.*

I sit, feeling my own exhaustion now, but elated as well, because here is the place I've wanted to come for as long as I remember and here I am, towering over it, as if I could reach down and pluck one of the ripe, succulent buildings and eat it like a grape.

"We can't stay here," Chiu says, his voice tinged with panic. "We need to get inside."

I shake my head. "We should rest here. It's OK."

"But we're *outside*," Chiu says.

"Don't you feel it?" I say. "The danger isn't about inside or outside, it's something else. People come here; they feel safe here. So long as a place has weight, we're OK."

I can feel It considering me, appraising me. I know I'm right.

Chiu contemplates this for a moment, then his face flickers with relief. He sits and I experience another one of those moments where I'm surprised by how young he is. Farah sits too, cross-legged with her hands on her knees. She smooths back a strand of hair, wraps her arms around her stomach.

Chiu lets out a shivering breath. "This calls for a game of Uno."

THIRTY-TWO

We're exhausted, but we play anyway and then we sit for a long time, until the sky starts to turn sooty with the onset of night. It doesn't change gradually like it does in the ordinary world. It changes in discrete steps, one minute it's a particular shade of turbid grey, the next, it's another. Somehow, you never *see* it change. You blink, or you look away, and the colour of the sky becomes different.

The darkening, starless dome recedes, becoming more impossibly vast with each step. I'm caught by a sudden insight, a vision of myself: a flicker, a guttering candle, an astonishingly small moment. Darkness before and darkness after.

I blink and the feeling is gone. The brain is like that, I think. It's attuned to notice change and proportion. If you close your eyes and hold a penny in one hand and ten pence in the other, you can tell the difference; but if you hold a brick in one hand and a brick with ten pence on it in the other, you can't. If you spend your life locked in your room, then going to the shops is, proportionately, terrifying; but if you feel, for a moment, the vertigo of falling through all of space and time and the immensity of your insignificance, then nothing in the ordinary world feels like such a big deal anymore.

All of which is to say, I think things are going to be different when we get back to the ordinary world. Small comfort.

As night falls, we drift back into another game of Uno. The cards are our version of music: they bind us together, create a space that is for us alone.

But I feel It always now. My aura. That implacable force brooding over an inscrutable intention. It notices me now. I don't know whether it happened when I killed Tongue, or when I got us here, but I've definitely caught Its attention.

"How did you do it?" Chiu says.

"Do what?" I say.

"Get us here. *Escape*."

Farah nods. "It didn't want us to get out, but you *knew* how to get us here."

"Blindsight," Chiu says. "It's getting stronger, isn't it? Ever since Jonah."

"I don't feel any different," I say.

Chiu pulls a card from his hand and holds it up with its back to me. "What card am I holding up?"

I half laugh. "How should I know?"

"Tell me what card," Chiu insists.

"But I can't see."

"*Guess.*"

"Red, seven," I snap.

Chiu flips the card and we fall silent.

"Lucky guess," I say.

"This one," Chiu says, holding up another card.

"Reverse turn, any colour," I say.

Farah holds up one of her cards.

"Plus-four," I say. I wince because that card was coming for me.

"What's going on?" Farah says.

"Blindsight," Chiu says, with satisfaction. "Like I said, you have a superpower, Kyle."

"Not much of a superpower," I say.

Farah grins. "Not unless we take you to Vegas."

The sky is black and nothing, and we can only see by the grey sheen of unlight. It doesn't frighten us here though. This place is safe, tethered by the weight of people who hold this place in their mind.

"I think we're going to be OK," Chiu muses.

"OK?" Farah sounds dubious. "That sounds like a stretch."

"Kyle is going to get us to the machine and get us home." He nods. "With his superpower."

"No pressure then," I say.

"I'm going to see my parents again," Chiu says, his eyes shining in the unlight.

Farah doesn't respond. I'm worried about her; she picks absently at the makeshift bandage wrapped around her damaged hand. For a moment, I imagine staying here for ever. I can go outside here. I have friends. I have Farah.

But Farah's dying in the ordinary world and if she's stuck here, there's nothing they can do to save her there.

And I have unfinished business in the ordinary world. Things I need to get back to, even if I don't completely remember what they are right now. There's Mum and the question of what I was doing in the street that day. Father Michael. Her note on the kitchen table. "Exciting news!" The memory of searching through papers and my panic. I was looking for something: something important enough to make me leave the house for the first time in a year. I have to find out what it was before it's too late and the longer I spend here the worse my chances get.

"That's it," Chiu says, after I drop my last card on to the pile. "I'm going to bed."

He rolls away from us, curls into a tight ball and falls instantly asleep.

"He's pretty incredible at that," I say.

Farah shuffles closer to me and rests her head on my shoulder, looking out over the London skyline. "Can we watch for a little bit? I'm not sleepy yet."

We sit quietly, the black expanse above the narrow arc of the Earth looks more like the absence of a sky than a sky, but it's not as terrifying as it used to be. London glows beneath it with a heavy grey-orange light – not the city lights I've seen on television, but a liminal sheen, like the pith of the city is bleeding through into this world.

"The one everyone calls Big Ben is really St Stephen's tower," I say. "It's the bell that's called Big Ben."

"I knew that," Farah says.

"Did you know that the real name for the Gherkin is its street name: 30 St Mary Axe?" I add. "And next to it, the Walkie Talkie, that's 20 Fenchurch Street." I glance at Farah and see that she's smiling ruefully. "Rubbish names, right?"

"Please tell me the Shard is really called the Shard, though?" she says.

"Yeah," I say. "It is."

"Phew. That's my favourite."

I point down towards the murky basin of London. "UCL is down there, I think it's a straight run from here."

"What if we get lost again?"

"I don't think that's going to happen. I can feel it from here. We're close."

She narrows her eyes. "You're creeping me out with all this zen mystic stuff, you know that, right?"

I laugh. "*I'm* creeping *you* out? You can talk, octopus-girl."

She doesn't find it as funny as I thought she would.

Her smile fades. "I'm sorry," I say. "I don't know why I said that."

"It's fine," she says.

"How is it?" I ask, gesturing towards her hand.

She unwinds the makeshift T-shirt bandage and inspects her hand, the spot where I cut off several of her fingers. The wounds have begun to seal over but the hand is still swollen, like it's been slammed in a car door.

"Fine, I guess."

"Does it hurt?"

"No … but I can feel it, I know it's going to come back." She hesitates. "Thank you for what you said in the shop. About how I had to get back so we could hang out in the ordinary world. It helped." She wraps her hand slowly, methodically. "You know, it sounded for a minute back there like you were asking me out."

I feel myself turn red. "Oh … I didn't mean…"

She darts forward and kisses me on the cheek. It's gentle, brief, but not exactly *sisterly*. I freeze and she draws back, looking a little embarrassed. I realize a second too late that maybe that was my moment and I blew it.

Then I remember something. I lean awkwardly to get my hand into my jeans pocket and I find the gold dolphin necklace I found in the hotel. I hold it out in the palm of my hand for her. "I got this for you," I say. "It's a present."

Farah stares at it. "It's beautiful." She picks it up so it hangs loose. "It's the most beautiful thing."

She turns, lifting her hair so I can put it on her. My fingers tremble as I drape the necklace over her shoulders and join the clasp. The back of my hand grazes the smooth nape of her neck and her skin is so hot it feels like I might scald myself. She turns to face me, smiling, admiring the small, shining dolphin that curls round a drop of pure sunlight.

"I've been meaning to give it to you for ages," I say. "Since the hotel. Dolphins are a symbol of a free spirit, like you. But they're also a sign of luck and protection. They were the messengers of Poseidon and there are tales of dolphins saving sailors who were lost at sea and taking them back—"

"Please stop talking," she says. She kisses me. I'm ready this time and I don't freeze. She kisses me, delicately, two or three times, like she's picking her spot and when I finally collect myself enough to kiss her back, our lips come together and the world detonates inside me and for a moment I swear that the sky is filled with stars again.

I know that some things are brighter in this world and some things are brighter in the other world, but kisses, I decide, are like music. They are more here. Much more.

THIRTY-THREE

I wake with a crisp brightness that I have never felt before, not in this world or in the ordinary world. At first, I don't remember why, but then I see Farah curled on the grass next to me and it comes back in a rush.

I can't shake the nagging fear that I might have dreamed it, but I know it was real. "Real", of course, is a risky word in this world, but kissing Farah, I'm sure, was real by any definition.

I want to kiss her again, but I figure I should wait until she wakes up first. Chiu is still asleep, curled in a ball with his back to me, a thin slice of his backbone visible where his T-shirt has ridden up. London is a hazy cluster of buildings on the horizon, the colour of apricots. I know I'm biased, but it looks astonishingly beautiful this morning.

I'm caught by a restless energy. I don't want to wake

the others, but I can't just sit around here and *wait*. I walk a way down the hill and then glance back and see them still lying there, achingly defenceless. There's a cluster of trees just off to the left and the strangest urge creeps over me to go and explore them.

I know the sensible thing to do is stay with Farah and Chiu, but I can't ignore the feeling, suddenly magnetic, that draws me on.

Blindsight.

I quicken my pace, walking with purpose now, turning back frequently to check on Chiu and Farah. The brow of the hill takes them out of sight sooner than I would have thought. I reach the trees and find a little clearing with a bench that I hadn't seen before. Oddly, the bench faces the wrong way: not out towards the city, but back down the hill towards the undergrowth and the layered banks of trees that we came through to get here.

The bench is overgrown with creepers and lichen, weather-beaten and half rotted like it's destined to fade into the earth some time very soon. I wonder if the bench in the ordinary world is actually gone altogether, destroyed a long time ago and what remains here is just the slowly degrading idea of it. I turn and look at the banks of trees and the arching dip of the grass as it drops away in the middle distance. It causes something to swell in my throat, a sense of wonder, of awe, as if the sweeping folds of land might swaddle me if I knew how to let them.

"Beautiful, isn't it?" a cracked, dry voice says.

I startle and reach instinctively for my knife. An old woman is sitting on the bench. She's been there all along but she is so weathered herself, so much a part of the bench and half buried under fallen leaves and branches, that she is hardly visible.

"I met an angel here once," she continues. "I think they come for the view. We *think* we come for the view as well but we don't. We come because of how it feels to be near the angels."

"Are you … OK?" I say.

The woman smiles tiredly. Her skin looks like bark, her white hair looks like a spider's web that's breaking under its own weight. "I'm dying, dear," she says, kindly. "But other than that, I suppose I'm doing OK." One arm has grown its own shoots and leaves and begun to merge with the bench so that she can hardly lift it; the other, I realize now, is gone entirely and looks to have blended with the bench a long time ago. "I used to come here with my husband, you know. I like to imagine that he came here as well after he died."

"I can help you," I say, moving towards her, my knife outstretched. "I can remove the Puzzles, cut you free—"

The woman makes a sudden effort to shake her head. "No, no, I'm past all that. I was surprised to find myself here at all if I'm honest." She laughs dryly, returning to her previous thought. "Most people came to Parliament Hill to see the city, but my husband and I always sat here. We preferred the green. Silly really, to live in London all that time. We should have moved out to the countryside as soon as we got married. We used to talk about it often enough, but we always thought there was more time… People always think there's more time than there is, don't they? We live like we're going to be here for ever and then suddenly we're not."

"Please," I say. "Let me help you."

"Yes," she says. "Yes, I think you are here to help me."

She catches my eye with a warm, regretful look and suddenly I understand what she means. "No," I say. "I … I can't."

"Come on, dear, I need you to be brave now." I start to back away and she stretches her head forward, as if trying to reach out to me. "The view is very nice and all," she continues, matter-of-factly. "But I've been here too long. I'm done."

"I can't," I say.

"You're afraid? Look at me … so scared I'm rooted to the spot. But it's such a small thing, really. Fear. I've had a long time to think about it and I'm ready to move on."

"Where will you move on to?" I say.

Her laugh is playful, an echo of a younger woman. "How could I possibly know a thing like that?" she says. "Probably nowhere, but that's not a reason to hang on indefinitely, is it? The only thing wrong with dying is doing it when you don't want to."

I could leave, I think. Go back to the others and head down the hill. She'll fade away soon enough.

"He's still coming for you, you know," the woman says.

I turn quickly and stare at her. Jonah. "How do you know?"

She smiles. "The same way as you know, my love."

"I have to get Farah back," I say. "She's sick, she needs treatment."

The woman's face breaks into a smile. "Young love!" She beams. "You are lucky, my boy, to feel that. Oh, I was wretched with it in the early days." Her eyes mist as the memory comes back to her. "I remember it so well. I remember the feeling, but I can't for the life of me remember *why* it felt that way." She frowns. "You think you're in control of your brain, you think you're a pilot flying an aeroplane. It's not true. You're more like a jockey riding a horse. You can direct it, you can hold it back, nudge it this way or that, but really you're just holding on for the ride for as long as you can." A pause. "If it's not you, then it'll be him. He's not far behind and he's been busy."

"Busy how?" I say.

"Please," the woman insists. "I'd rather it was you."

I can't stand it any longer. The sound of her crackly dry-leaves voice. Begging me. I do it in one quick motion. I take out the knife, step and thrust it into the side of her neck.

"It's only death," I whisper.

The old woman lets out a breathy sigh. "Nothing to be afraid of."

Roots and leaves begin to sprout from her shoulders and arms, pooling and running into the slats of the bench like blood. The woman's mouth moves like she's trying to say something. I lean closer to hear.

"You need to be careful, son," she whispers in a sepulchral voice. "You have caught God's attention. It's not a good thing."

"I don't believe in God," I say.

"It didn't believe in you … either," she murmurs. "It was better for you that way."

THIRTY-FOUR

We drop down off Parliament Hill on to another row of bay-windowed terraces. The fear of getting lost again bats against the inside of my head like a moth.

Fear of dying. Fear of forgetting. Fear of being trapped. Fear of the unknown.

The fear of Jonah.

He's still coming for you.

My footsteps beat a rhythm in my ears and I hold on to it. *Just. Keep. Walking.*

The road opens out into a wider road and a huge 1970s block of flats extends in both directions, alternating red and white garages and strips of balcony behind faded glass. We cut right and then left and the next road has shops, a park and a church.

I recognize the brutish stone hulk of a Church of England church. They never lasted long for Mum: too much equivocation, too much compromise and the songs weren't a patch on the Seventh-Day Adventists.

London gets heavier, more potent, as we walk and the buildings grow more sure of themselves. These are buildings that have been here for more than a hundred years; they've seen entire lifetimes come and go – they've earned their place in this world.

The people seem closer too, sparking and fizzing into existence as we walk. The basketball courts ring with the sound of bouncing balls and the heavy rumble of a bus causes Chiu to leap back in fright.

We reach Camden and the sound of people and shops and traffic snaps into focus. Pedestrians step crisply into view and then vanish, traffic cuts in and out of frame. The painted shopfronts. The tattoo parlours. The souvenir shops packed with London memorabilia. My heart thrums with it.

I catch a look from Farah.

"Pretty cool, huh?" she says.

"I wish we could see it for real," I reply.

"What's real? This is Camden, baby!" Something catches her eye and she grabs my arm playfully. "Hey, look – there's a sign for the zoo. Shall we go?"

I laugh at first, thinking she's not serious. But then I see it in her face.

"We need to get to UCL—" I say, guardedly.

"Oh, come *on*, we've got time for the zoo!" She widens her eyes. "I reckon elephants will be pretty wild here,

I've always thought they're more in this world than the ordinary world… They might *talk* in this world!"

I feel the mood shift as she senses my reluctance and reacts against it. Suddenly she's filled with febrile energy.

"Chiu, you'd like to go to the ghost-zoo, wouldn't you?" she says.

"I want to go to UCL," Chiu says. "I want to go home—"

"Oh, *oh* and then we can go to the palace," Farah continues, ignoring him. "We can take a *dump* in the queen's toilet! We could—"

I stop walking and face her. "Farah, what's going on?"

Her eyes flash angrily, the look she used to give teachers when one of them tried to tell her to quieten down. "Nothing," she says. "We're in *London*, Kyle, isn't that what you always dreamed of? And we *own* this place. Look at it! Don't tell me you're not up for a bit of fun before we go back?"

"That wasn't the plan," I say.

"I'm changing the plan."

Defiant. Dangerous.

"We don't have time," I say. "You're sick."

Wrong thing to say. I spot her resolve tighten. It was one thing to convince her to get up and leave the carpet shop, it's another thing to convince her to walk away from all of London.

"You're just scared," she says.

"Farah, stop—" I say.

"No, *you* stop." Suddenly she's furious at me. "Stop *hiding*. That's all you want to do. You want to hide away and do as you're told." She turns away from me. "If you're going to be my boyfriend, Kyle, you're going to have to up your game."

My heart clenches. Chiu and I have to walk fast to keep up with her. She's leading us down on to the canal towards the zoo.

The world whirls around me. We don't have time for this. Farah is sick. Jonah is coming. He's going to sniff us out. Our only hope is to get to UCL and get back before he catches up with us.

"Farah, wait—"

"Oh, Houses of Parliament," she calls over her shoulder. "Then the zoo."

I reach forward and snatch at her arm, stopping her, turning her towards me. She glares at me. "Let go of me," she says.

I let go. We stare at each other. A silent stand-off with the smell of Camden – cigarettes and sweat and cheap perfume – fading in and out around us.

"Farah, UCL. That's the *brave* move, you know it is."

A hard, uncompromising look.

"Please, Farah," Chiu adds, breaking our stalemate. "I want to go home."

I see Farah's eyes dart to him. He seems so young again. A child who misses his parents. Farah softens. She casts a regretful look towards the canal. "Fine," she says, at last. "UCL first. But if it doesn't work out, I'm taking a dump in the queen's private bathroom."

"UCL and then you can take a pretend dump wherever you like," I concede.

"Promise?" Farah says.

"I promise."

We press on, past Euston where the trains sound like monsters bellowing from below us and down towards Queens Square. There's a special prehospital feeling I get when an appointment is coming up and I feel it now. Whatever was left of our optimism from last night has faded. I glance at Farah.

"You OK?" I ask.

"I don't like hospitals," she replies.

"Same."

The roads are quieter here. The grand Georgian houses look as if they think they're better than us because they outlast us so easily. We follow a gently curving crescent past a coffee shop and a bar that look deserted in this world. Then we're standing in front of the unwelcoming facade of the building we've come all this way for. Five rows of big sash windows, sandy-coloured columns flanking a heavy wooden door and a sign:

UCL INSTITUTE OF COGNITIVE NEUROSCIENCE

"Have you ever been to this one before?" Farah says.

"No."

We climb the couple of steps that lead up to the door and the black-and-orange sign. Farah and Chiu look at me expectantly and I wonder when they started treating me like the leader. I nod towards the door.

"Shall we?" I say.

"You first," Chiu replies.

"This was your idea."

"*You*," Chiu says steadfastly.

I press my hand against the brass panel. I expect – halfway hope for – it to be locked, but the wooden door swings open easily.

A small reception area. Walls panelled in light wood. A couple of armchairs that have seen better days. A table with a small pile of scientific journals.

The desk, computer and shelf filled with box files look out of place beside the grandiose decor. In the other world I suppose somebody sits at the desk and checks people in as they come, but it's empty here. I wonder if they sense us … if they feel the same uncomfortable presence as we do.

"Hello?" I call.

Nothing.

The door straight ahead leads into a corridor. The stateliness of the reception is left behind, the walls are painted with the same thick cream paint as a hospital, the floor is wood, battered and creaking. A window on the left gives us glimpses into a cluttered lab, the desks busy with microscopes and ambiguous-looking equipment, the walls crammed with shelves of pipettes and sample trays and glassware and plastic packets I can't even begin to guess the contents of.

We pass a pair of heavy-looking fire doors that are pinned open on magnetic fittings and stop because the corridor beyond them is sealed by another pair of fire doors, pinned shut.

A moment of uncertainty catches me – *why two sets of fire doors on this short stretch of corridor? Is that normal?* One set looks like they were added recently. The wooden frame is unpainted and the screws that hold it to the wall have been drilled clumsily and at angles, like the DIY projects Mum sometimes starts and never finishes.

I notice a security camera in the corner near the ceiling, its wire tacked to the wall and running through a hole in the frame above the fire doors.

I stop.

Farah turns. "What is it?"

"Out, *out*—!" I shout.

Then everything happens at once.

There's a *click* and the fire doors behind us slam shut.

Then a white-hot flash so intense it feels as if somebody has cracked open my skull.

BANG!

A sound so loud it pounds against my chest cavity.

Then two more people are in the room … no, three.

Weapons raised above their heads.

Shouting, "Get down! Get *DOWN*!"

Something hits me, hard, in the shoulder and my head slams into the wall. I hear Farah scream. I whirl round, trying to catch sight of whoever is attacking us but something heavy hits me again, from above this time, and I go down, my world a lightning strike of pain and dizziness.

My ears ring, I can hardly see past the searing scorch marks in my eyes. I blink and look up to see a figure looming over me.

Jonah! I think. Lying in wait for us.

But it's not Jonah, it's hardly human. It's a lumpen, clumsy creature. *It might be a bear,* I think wildly, *or some kind of human wardrobe.*

"Stay *down!*" it shouts again, its voice muffled. "*Stay* DOWN!"

Then, murky recognition: it's no bear. Just a man in strangely bulky clothes. Gradually, the shape resolves into the padding that goalies wear in ice hockey. He looms closer, his hockey stick raised high above his head.

Coughing, I lift my hand, doing my best to convey the fact that I have absolutely no intention of going anywhere.

Somebody else has Farah around the waist and she's

struggling. The third man holds Chiu. Then the second fire doors swing open and the air currents suck the smoke away just enough to catch a glimpse of yet another man standing in the doorway, wafting the heavy door as hard as he can to clear the smoke.

"For heaven's sake, Marcus," he shouts, severely. "They're *children*!"

The scorch marks in my eyes are beginning to fade, but blue dots, like ink stains, still drift across my vision and my ears won't stop ringing. My head and my shoulder throb from where I was hit. Chiu has a bruise on his lip and stares sullenly into space. Farah looks unharmed but her face is stony.

We're in a lab off the main corridor. Four rows of blue-topped Formica workbenches stretch its length, strewn with papers, racks, sample bottles and white-panelled machines. We're sitting on office chairs, lined up in a row along the workbench, while the one who hit me – Marcus, I think – hovers over us, guarding us with his hockey stick close at hand.

Now that he's taken off his hockey gear, I can see that he's in his late twenties. A broad, bland face and a mop of wavy blond hair. Something about his style and his mannerisms makes me think of the posh kids who used to go to the private school on the opposite side of town. He looks anxious – more anxious than he should be, given that we're kids and *he* has the hockey stick.

The far side of the lab has been partitioned off by a glass wall and behind it there are seven folding beds arranged in two neat rows.

Seven?

There are four people here. So there must be more of them.

Farah catches my eye and flicks her head towards the door. It also has a glass panel and on the far side of it we can see the other three who jumped us. The older man who yelled at Marcus earlier is talking. Late fifties, I guess. He has tight, wiry black hair, an untidy beard and a crumpled suit beneath a white lab coat. He seems agitated, pressing the blade of one hand repeatedly into the palm of the other as he talks. The man listening to him is tall and thin, Indian or Pakistani I guess, slouched against the wall with his arms folded. The third is a woman, young like Marcus. She has a stern, gaunt face, framed by long hair that's been dyed pure white.

They're obviously discussing us, deciding what to do with us. I feel the knife in my back pocket, pressing against my leg. *All that and they didn't even check us for weapons.* I shift my weight experimentally, gauging how quickly I could get to the knife if I had to.

At last, they file in. Scientists, I decide, from the lab coat the older one wears. He has a name tag pinned to his lapel that reads: PROF. BENEDICT BROWNSTEIN. He must be the one in charge. My brain puts the pieces together. They must work in this lab. But what are they all doing *here*? In the Stillness?

"You're trespassing," Professor Brownstein says abruptly.

"We're sorry," Farah says. "We'll go."

She starts to stand, but the other man holds his ground, blocking her path.

"What are you doing here?" the woman asks.

Farah does a good job of looking bewildered. "We wanted somewhere to rest. Please – we didn't think anyone would be here."

The woman and the older man look at each other.

"Benedict?" the woman says.

Professor Brownstein – Benedict – frowns suspiciously at us. "You expect us to believe you just blundered in here by chance?"

Farah nods. "Yes, we—"

"We're looking for the machine," Chiu interrupts.

Farah clenches her teeth in irritation. The others look from one to the other in befuddled silence. "What machine?" Benedict says at last.

Chiu fishes in his back pocket and pulls out the folded sheets of paper he tore from his journal before we left. He hands them to Benedict. The others cluster around him to read. I watch their eyes scanning the words. Then the woman takes a step back, her hand rising to her mouth, her eyes wide with shock.

"Devon made it?" she murmurs, a weak, hopeful smile flickering on her face. "He made it!"

"We shouldn't jump to conclusions, Abi," Benedict warns.

"But it has to be him, right?" Marcus says. "'The team successfully manipulated the cytoelectric activity of a coma patient … restoring them to wakefulness.' That's him. Devon. Abi's right."

"What do you think, Vikram?" the woman named Abi says.

The man named Vikram shrugs, his eyes still scanning the pages. "It's possible…"

"It *has* to be him," Abi insists. "It worked."

A tense silence. They fall back to reading, muttering, pointing out passages to each other. *Chiu was right*, I think. Something important is happening here and these people are a part of it.

"Where did you get this?" Vikram says at last, looking up at Chiu.

"We were in a hospital when we first arrived," Chiu says. "I found it in the library."

"What does it mean?" Abi asks.

"It means they went ahead and published without us," Vikram says bitterly.

"Why would they do that?"

"Look at the date," Marcus says. "And they've used our names. We're all co-authors."

"Oh, the damn fools," Benedict says. "They're trying to keep up the cover story."

"Oh god—" Abi sits heavily, her face pale.

"Excuse me?" Chiu says, interjecting. "Who's Devon?"

The others look at us like they'd forgotten we were there. Abi offers us a weak smile. "Devon Wang is one of our colleagues," she says.

"Don't tell them too much," Vikram interrupts her. "It could be a set-up."

Abi gives an exasperated sigh. "They're kids, Vik."

"Kids who happen to have found and correctly interpreted an academic paper?"

"Chiu isn't like most kids," Farah says firmly.

"Suspicious," Vikram says.

"For god's sake. What do you want to do?" Abi says. "Turf them on to the street?"

"We can't risk that," Vikram responds. "They'd go back to whoever sent them."

Abi turns to the older man. "Benedict, please, talk some sense into him."

"Of course," the older man – Benedict – says. "I apologize for the … poor start. This world has more than its fair share of trouble. Allow me to introduce myself. My name is Professor Benedict Brownstein, I run this lab and allegedly I wrote this paper, which was an impressive trick seeing as I was unconscious at the time. These are my colleagues: Dr Abigail Peradams, Dr Vikram Shah and Dr Marcus Lancaster. We are – er, were – part of a study to explore disconnected consciousness." He gives us an awkward little half bow and then looks around, brightening. "Marcus, maybe this would be a good time to put on a nice pot of tea, don't you think?"

THIRTY-FIVE

They show us through to another room behind the main lab. It looks like some kind of common room, cluttered to the point of being filthy: pizza boxes, takeout containers, half-eaten sandwiches; electronic circuits, soldering irons, dismantled equipment. It's hard to tell how much exists in this world and how much has leaked across, forgotten in the common room of the ordinary world. In the spaces between the equipment, there are piles of loose papers: ring binders and notebooks, all filled, as far as I can see, with densely packed writing and intricate diagrams. The windows, I notice, have been covered with cardboard and masking tape.

We sit on three long, low, moth-eaten sofas, arranged in a U-shape around a coffee table strewn with yet more scientific journals and notebooks. Marcus bustles over to a small kitchenette and flicks on a kettle.

"You have electricity?" Farah gasps.

Marcus grins like a schoolboy. He gestures to the far corner where a large section of the room has been given over to a stack of car batteries, all wired together with high-voltage cable. "Just a hand-crank generator, I'm afraid. I wish I could get the LiPos working but lead acid is about my limit."

"How?" Chiu says.

"We're scientists," Benedict replies, looking affronted. "Neuroscientists, to be fair, but between us we have enough working knowledge to get a few things running."

Marcus fusses over mugs and tea bags and starts pouring tea. "Milk?" he asks. "I'm sorry it's only long-life. The fresh stuff never makes it through before it's gone off."

I grin at the absurdity of our sudden change in circumstances, as Marcus slops milk into each of our cups.

Something catches Chiu's eye and he lets out a yelp of delight, leaping up and rushing over to the large flat-screen monitor on the workbench next to the kitchenette. "You've got a *television*?" He examines the flat-screen, which is showing a grainy image I can't quite make out. "Can you get TV? Movies?"

"DVDs are a bit outside my field of expertise," Benedict admits. "We have a hard wire to the CCTV camera in the airlock, that's all."

I recognize the scene on the monitor now. Not the broken filmic images we saw in the service station, but the white and cream walls of the hallway where they ambushed us. *That's how they did it*, I think. This screen, an arrangement of magnetic locks on the doors and some kind of … explosive?

We make ourselves comfortable on the mismatched sofas while Marcus offers around a plate of biscuits.

"Ah! Tea and stale biscuits," Vikram remarks caustically. "No one eats here, no matter how many times we've tried, but Marcus keeps at it. He thinks it's good for morale. Typical upper-class Englishman."

Marcus scoffs, haughtily. "You went to a better school than I did, Vik. And if I described you as a typical Indian, it wouldn't be acceptable, now, would it?"

Vikram waves him away.

"It makes the place more homely," Marcus insists.

Benedict sits next to Farah and gestures towards her bandaged hand. "May I?"

Farah casts me an anxious look but allows Benedict to take her hand and gently unwrap the bandage. "Hyperdactyly?" he says. "But … what happened to the extra fingers?"

"We cut them off," I say.

Benedict glances at the others. "You cut them off? Why?"

"We were told that you could treat the symptoms. Slow it down."

Abi comes over and sits on the far side of Farah, her

face a mixture of scepticism and hopefulness. "It's possible. *Anything* is possible in this god-forsaken place."

"Surgical removal?" Vikram remarks, impressed. "Why didn't we think of that?"

"We lost Alistair to hyperdactyly," Marcus explains.

Farah withdraws her hand and wraps it again. "What are you all doing here?" she says. "You said you were studying ... disconnected...?"

"Disconnected consciousness," Vikram says.

"This is our lab, in the ... real world," Benedict continues. "We've been studying the nature of consciousness for many years now." He sips his tea and watches us intently. "We discovered that in certain circumstances, patients who appear *unconscious* sometimes display neurological activity that's *indistinguishable* from that of somebody who is fully conscious. We believed – and now we *know* – that it signifies a new state of consciousness."

"Not dreaming, not hallucinating. Just ... not there," Vikram says.

"You mean *here*, in *this* world," Chiu says.

"Exactly," Vikram says.

Chiu nods excitedly. "I read the journal article."

"Our biggest breakthrough was when we discovered that people in this state could communicate with each other," Benedict explains. "We ran a study with twins who had epilepsy. One pair in particular, their seizures always happened at the same time and they were able to pass messages to each other while they were, supposedly, unconscious."

"How do you know?" Chiu asks.

"They would tell us when they woke up." Benedict smiles. "Ask one of them to think of a secret word, over and over. Think it, but don't share it unless and until you realize that you're in a seizure. Then they would come back and the other would know the word."

"It's like a radio," Vikram adds. "Everyone you've ever known is tuned to Radio One. But sometimes, like right now, we're all tuned to Radio Two."

"That still doesn't explain how you're *all* here," Farah says. "It means you're all unconscious in the ordinary world, right? Like … was there an accident or something?"

Benedict's mouth pinches, he seems uneasy.

Vikram answers for him. "It was all theoretical. Naturally, we needed to test our hypotheses under experimental conditions."

"Which means?" Farah says.

"Medically induced coma," Marcus says.

Farah looks shocked. The scientists shuffle awkwardly.

"You did this to *yourselves*?" I say, incredulous.

"Officially this is a sleep study," Benedict explains. "But we're not really sleeping, we're sedated, in the beds you will have seen in the sleep lab next door."

"That can't be legal," Farah says.

Abi exhales: a short, bitter note.

I look around at the trashed room, the car batteries that power the kettle and the CCTV. I think about the seven beds for four people. "Something went wrong, didn't it?"

"It went wrong from the moment we arrived," Abi says.

"How?"

"Our plan was to spend two weeks here," Benedict says. "Enough time to record our observations and establish communication with the ordinary world."

"We lost Alistair to hyperdactyly right away," Abi says. "We presume he reacted badly to the anaesthetic."

"Reacted badly to the anaesthetic in the ordinary world or slipped through the cracks in this one," Vikram muses. "Depending on which way you look at it."

"Either way, he died in a few hours," Abi says.

"We were attacked a few days after that," Marcus says. "We were idiots and left the lights on. It seems that some people arrive here and get together, form gangs. Of course, we didn't know that at the time."

"They killed our colleague Jessica, and took Eduardo," Abi says. "But we killed one of theirs in return and managed to drive them off."

"After that we got serious," Marcus says. "We armed ourselves. Built the airlock. Benedict and I got the security camera working. We've rigged the place so if they try again, we're ready for them."

"How long have you been here?" I ask.

"Two and a half years," Abi replies. "Our best guess, anyway."

I take a breath, understanding at last the unspoken tension in the room. Abi's eyes, I see now, are tight, tired and angry. But there's still something they're not telling us.

"Why haven't you gone back?" I say. "If some of you were dying, why didn't your colleagues revive you in the ordinary world?"

"Natural occurrence of this brain state is very rare," Benedict says. "But we used a cocktail of medication and deep-brain stimulation to trigger it in ourselves. You're right, our colleagues in the ordinary world should have revived us by now. Our best guess is that being *here* is preventing them from reviving us in the ordinary world."

Chiu flashes me a brief, triumphant look. "That's what the machine was for, wasn't it?" he says. "If reviving you in the ordinary world didn't work, it was meant to get you back from this side…?"

He trails off, his voice pinched with the fear of disappointment.

Farah places a hand on his shoulder. "We thought the machine might get us back?"

"That is what it's designed for. But I'm afraid it's not so simple," Benedict says. "Our plan was to establish communication with the ordinary world, modulate our cytoelectric impulses and use our brains as aerials. But our maths was off. We hoped that the machine would provide a route back if our colleagues couldn't revive us. But without being able to talk to them we have no way to know if the machine is safe."

"We *had* no way to know," Abi corrects him. "We have new evidence now." She picks up Chiu's paper and quotes from it: "'The team successfully manipulated the cytoelectric activity of a coma patient, restoring them to wakefulness.' That's Devon, right?"

"It's possible," Benedict says. "It's not certain."

Abi looks incensed. "Not *certain*?"

Benedict turns back to us, ignoring Abi's challenge. "When our communication failed, we agreed not to use the machine until we'd further developed our theories. That's what we've been doing these past two years: trying to understand where we went wrong and establish whether or not the machine is safe."

"We did use it once though," Vikram says. "Our colleague Devon was badly injured when we were attacked. He was dying, so we took a chance and used the machine."

"And—" Chiu says.

Vikram shrugs. "And ... he disappeared. We have no way of knowing whether we helped him back to the ordinary world or helped to finish him off."

"Exactly my point," Benedict says.

"But the journal you showed us changed that," Abi

says. "We know now that he survived. Which means the machine is safe to use and we can go home."

Chiu sits a little straighter, but I can see from Benedict's expression that he doesn't agree.

"We know nothing of the sort," he says.

"How can you say that—?"

"It's conjecture, Abi." Benedict leans forward, his eyes sharp and blazing with intelligence. "We still have no way to know what really happened: whether Devon made it back successfully or what condition he was in. There are still too many variables. Don't you see? We need to go back to the fundamentals."

Abi glares furiously at him. "Don't start with the academic crap, Benedict. I'm not in your study group anymore."

"I'm serious," Benedict says. "Work the problem rationally, Abi. It will help, I promise. Hypothesis: Devon survived and they successfully revived him." He gestures towards Abi. "Now: evidence?"

Abi sighs irritably but relents. "Evidence: our colleagues published a paper describing how they revived a coma patient by modulating their cytoelectric brain patterns."

"Counter hypothesis one," Benedict responds immediately. "It wasn't Devon, it was some other patient and they referenced a loosely related result from our lab in order to maintain our cover story." Abi opens her mouth to object but Benedict talks over her. "Counter hypothesis two: Devon regained consciousness but died shortly afterwards, a detail that would be natural to omit from such a paper." Abi tries to interrupt but Benedict is on a roll now, his voice rising. "Counter hypothesis *three*: Devon has regained consciousness but is severely brain-damaged and unable to communicate."

"*Conjecture!*" Abi practically shouts, rising from the sofa.

There's a pause, before Benedict responds calmly, "Evidence?"

Abi glances at Vikram for support but he gives only a resigned shake of his head.

"*Counter* evidence," Benedict says, unable to hide his triumph. "If Devon had survived intact, he would have told them of his experiences here and it would have changed *everything*." He looks around at us. "Don't you agree?"

THIRTY-SIX

They talk on and on and we sit and listen because there's nothing else we can do. Chiu seems enthralled, as if all his own theories from all his years of reading have been finally confirmed. Farah is detached. I'm worried about her. She agreed to come here, in the end, but it's obvious she doesn't want to be here. I can tell she's thinking about London, about leaving Benedict to his experiments and disappearing off into the city … *to have fun*. Existence here is terrible, but it might be preferable to what waits for her in the ordinary world, she thinks.

I don't agree with her. I can't stop thinking about her hands, those prehensile growths, unfurling, breaking through the skin. I can't lose her like that. There was a long time when I locked myself in my room and told myself I was OK, I was *safe*, I didn't need anyone. But I know now that I was wrong. I know now what it's like to have someone, to have Farah.

I can't lose that.

Frustration boils inside me. Abi thinks we should use the machine but Benedict stands his ground, claiming that it's too risky. It feels like an old argument, one they've been having for the past two years.

"Doesn't Devon making it back mean anything to you?" Abi says.

"It's data," Benedict says. "Data we should consider. That's all."

"You saw the date on the paper. It's been *six months* in the ordinary world. We don't know how much longer our bodies can survive in this state."

"It's a risk we have to take," Benedict says.

"I don't *want* to take that risk."

"It will be OK," Benedict says. "We're going to change the world. I promise."

I don't understand why Benedict won't just let her go if she wants to. "We'll go," I say. "We'll use the machine. Farah's sick. According to your theory – and Chiu's – she can't be saved while she stays here. So we'll chance the machine, just like Devon did."

Benedict shakes his head regretfully. There's something about him that makes me uncomfortable. His certainty. His unwavering faith. *I've seen it before*, I think. In all the priests and vicars I've encountered in all the churches Mum took us to.

"I wish it were possible," he says. "But I can't allow it.

Not while Farah is ostensibly well. I'm responsible for the safety of *everyone* in this lab."

He picks up a journal from the coffee table and flicks idly through it, indicating that the conversation is over. Abi squeezes her forehead in frustration. Vikram tries to place a reassuring hand on her shoulder, but she shrugs him off.

After a moment she offers us a wan smile. "There's showers in the basement if you'd like? No offence, but it looks like you haven't had a wash or a change of clothes in a while."

Farah's eyes widen. "A shower?"

"They're cold, but…"

"Yes. Please," Farah says quickly. "Very much so."

I hadn't noticed how filthy I was until now. Without bacteria there are no smells and it's easy to forget. But now that Abi mentions it, I realize that my T-shirt and trousers are stiff with Farah's blood and two nights' sleeping in the soil have added a gritty overlay to the gore.

We follow Abi into the stairwell and down to the basement. There's a musty concrete smell, so familiar in this small moment that it would be easy to believe that the ordinary world is still there, just on the other side of the fire door.

"There's a lost-property box as well," Abi says. "I'm sure we can find you some fresh clothes."

I glance at Farah and see the delight in her eyes. "Thank you."

We're about to go through the fire door into the basement when Abi stops us. Her face is grim. "You're wasting your time here," she says darkly. "He'll never let you use the MRI."

"Why not?" I say.

"He doesn't really think Devon is brain-damaged. He knows we could go home. He just doesn't want to go back empty-handed."

"What does that mean, empty-handed?" Farah says.

"We're pretty sure people naturally make it back to the ordinary world once in a while. Not often, but sometimes."

"So?"

"But there are still no stories of this place. *Somebody* would have come back with evidence by now if it were possible. A scientist would have known how to convince people."

"What are you saying?" I say.

"Our best theory is that even if somebody makes it back, their memories are garbled when they return. Bright lights. Rushing tunnels. Religious stories. Think about it. So many of the stories in the ordinary world might come from glimpses of this place. But no detail, nothing coherent. I hate to admit it, but Benedict's right. Devon hasn't told them about this place, which means he has no memory of our time here."

"So?" Chiu says. "At least he's alive. If we go back, at least we'll be alive too."

"You don't understand," Abi answers tightly. "Do you think they grant ethics approvals for this sort of thing? This whole project is entirely unethical and probably illegal. But we figured when we came back with world-changing results nobody would ask too many questions."

"But if you go back with nothing…" I say, realizing what she means.

"Benedict will go to prison for sure," Abi says. "Maybe Vikram too. And the rest of us will be a cautionary tale of ethics gone wrong for every medical student for evermore." Abi glances anxiously up the stairs like she's afraid Benedict has come after her. "Benedict's got too much at stake. As far as he's concerned, there's no point going back unless he's sure we can remember what happened here."

"But *we* can go back," Chiu says. "I don't *want* to remember this place. I just want to see my parents again."

Farah reaches out and places a comforting hand on his shoulder.

"I'm sorry," Abi says. "I know him and he won't let you. Not yet."

"Why not?"

"We think we can change the field protocol in the machine to preserve some of our memories. But there's an element of trial and error and we only get one shot for each of us."

"So he wants to keep us here and use us as guinea pigs?" Farah says.

Abi nods. "I'm afraid so."

"He can't stop me," Chiu says firmly. "I'll go. When he's sleeping."

"Benedict is the only one who knows enough about computers to get the system running," she says. She sighs, her face softening for the first time. "He won't let you near the machine until he has a new protocol to test – then there might be a chance."

"But that might be too late," I say.

"I'm sorry." Abi turns to go. "Try to enjoy your shower."

We rummage in the lost-property boxes, digging through years of forgotten towels, gym outfits and water bottles. In the ordinary world they probably stink, but here, it's fine. Just a dry staleness no different to anything else and far better than our own blood- and mud-caked clothes. Farah finds a turquoise sports top and a pair of black leggings. They're loose, but she uses the belt from her jeans to cinch them tight. I find jogging bottoms and a white T-shirt. Chiu hardly bothers looking. His face is dark and brooding, still reeling from Abi's news. He sifts half-heartedly through one of the boxes, then gives up and disappears upstairs without even bothering to shower.

The water in the shower is so cold it feels like it's burning my skin. I get the peculiar sense that it might be cold enough to propel me back to the ordinary world and

I close my eyes and plunge my head into the water again and again. But it doesn't work. When I open my eyes, the world is just as real and immovable as ever.

I'm towelling off my hair afterwards, still only half dressed, when the door opens a crack and Farah slips inside. The sports top she's wearing is about three sizes too large for her, but it sets off small explosions in my brain when I see her. She walks purposefully across the changing room, reaches her arms around my neck without a word and kisses me. I stumble back, causing one of the locker doors to slam shut. She laughs, then kisses me again, and this time I kiss her back.

After a few moments she pulls away just a little, her face still very close to mine.

She says, "Hi."

"Um … hi."

She kisses me again, and I feel the weight of her pressing against me. There's an urgency in the way she kisses me. Even when we stop, we stay like that, holding tightly on to each other, breathing each other's fresh, soapy, shower gel smell. I never held anyone like this before, I never knew how it felt or what I was missing.

"Let's get out of here," she breathes. "Somewhere we can be alone."

"We're alone here?" I reply, hopefully.

"I mean … somewhere else." She grins. "Let's go to the Ritz!"

I stiffen. "We need to persuade Benedict to let you use the MRI and go home."

She sighs and pushes away from me. The coolness of her absence makes me ache and I want to reach out to her again. But we can't avoid this conversation.

"Talk about a mood killer," she says.

"I'm serious," I reply. "We don't have time to wait around for him to come up with a new protocol. We need to make him understand."

"Or..." Farah says, her eyes flashing. "We don't. Let's go to the Shard! Let's go to the very top and give God the finger."

"No."

"I'm not going back to the ordinary world," Farah says, darkly.

"You're not serious—"

"I'm done with this bullshit. We got Chiu here, that's what he wanted. This lot will look out for him, they might even get him home eventually. But I'm not waiting around here to die and I'm not going back so I can wait around to die either."

"But we're going on a date, remember? A real one. At the cinema. Or out for dinner."

"Real?" Farah snorts. "Real for me is tests and scans and needles and operations. You wouldn't care much for me in that state. Why don't we just *live* while we can."

"But we're so close," I say.

Farah shifts, takes another step back. I sense her closing off. *This is how she survived*, I think. *This is how she got through all that crap.* She looked like she was out there giving the teachers grief because she wanted to but she was hiding just as much as I was.

"With or without you, Kyle," she says. "It's your choice."

"Farah, please," I say, sickly. "I don't want to lose you."

She bites her lip. "You don't get it, do you? You *are* going to lose me, Kyle. It's inevitable."

"What do you mean?" I say, my voice small, almost nothing. "It's the good kind of cancer, remember? You're going to be OK."

"It doesn't matter," Farah says. "You heard Abi. Even if by some miracle I get better… I'm not going to remember you, am I? And you're not going to remember me. Either way … if we go back, we lose each other. We lose all this."

THIRTY-SEVEN

Either way, if we go back, we lose each other.

I must have known at some level; I just didn't want to face it. We aren't the first to be here and yet nobody in the ordinary world knows about this place. Even if some people make it back, the most that's left are garbled memories, fragments, the unspoken fear that fuels our horror stories. I think about Father Michael's pamphlets, the religious stories and all the ecstatic visionaries in history. Perhaps those people were here, perhaps their wild convictions, their rushing glimpses, are all that's left of their memories of this place.

It's not enough, I think. I'm not like Chiu. Everything Chiu loves and cares for is at home, he doesn't need to remember this place. For me, it's the opposite. Everything I care for is here. Farah, of course, but not just Farah. Also, those parts of myself I've found since I came here. *If I forget everything I ever was, does that mean I'm still me?*

Maybe Farah's right: we should stay here.

But if we stay, she might die.

Marcus is working in the hallway when we get back: delicately resetting the charges that they used to stun us when we first arrived. He's stacked their weapons neatly by the door to the sleep lab and now that I can look at them more closely, I see that they've been stolen from the stock cupboards of a nearby sports outlet. Hockey goalie equipment. Golf clubs. Something that looks a bit like a home-made mediaeval flail, crafted from the bar of a dumb-bell, a length of chain and a string of weights that have been padlocked together.

"You probably should know about our system," Marcus says. "In case anything happens."

We follow him back into the common room. Vikram and Benedict haven't moved since we left. Benedict scrawls in his notebook, ignoring us entirely. Vikram looks up from his journal and watches with an air of faint amusement as Marcus talks us through the systems.

"Do you see this area here, marked with tape?" Marcus says, pointing to the floor.

"Sure," I say.

"That's the kill zone. In the unlikely event that somebody gets past the airlock we'll fall back to this room here. They'll probably want us sitting down – less of a threat, right?" He sits on the sofa next to Vikram to demonstrate, then leaps up and heads over to the taped-off area near the window. "And they'll probably stand here, in this taped-off area."

"Then what happens?" Farah says.

"We have a codeword."

"Make us a cup of tea would you, Marcus," Vikram calls obligingly.

"*That's* my signal," Marcus says. He walks briskly towards the kitchenette. "I go to the kettle – innocent enough, right? We figure nobody will be able to resist the prospect of a cup of tea in this place. But" – he stands by the switches – "if you see me go for the *red* switch, instead of the *blue* one, you'll want to get behind the sofa sharpish."

"Why?" Farah asks.

"Home-made claymores." Marcus nods proudly towards the kill zone. He seems to be enjoying this much more than he ought to. "Three of them, pointing straight up, but angled towards the window."

"You'll probably blow the legs off everyone in the room," Vikram remarks.

"Not so," Marcus insists. "I was in the ROTC at university; I know what I'm talking about."

"How did you make explosives work?" I ask.

"Basic exothermic oxidation reaction," Marcus replies. "Anybody with an A-level in chemistry and an army surplus store can make them work."

Vikram laughs. "He nearly blew his balls off before he remembered the principles of a timer fuse though."

Marcus looks hurt. "Timer fuses are tricky. I have it wired up to the electrics now so there's no need for a timer."

He grins at us, like a child eagerly presenting his homework. I fidget uncomfortably. *There are more people out there*, I think. A whole city filled with people caught in this state. A lawless, hopeless world.

A shiver runs through me and a sudden memory of Jonah. *We are the Founding Fathers, Kyle.* And Ose glaring at me in the semi-dark of the service station. *Imagine what a man like Jonah could do if he had weapons.*

"Wait," Chiu says. "What's the codeword again?"

"'Make us a cup of tea, please,'" Marcus replies.

Chiu frowns. "But Benedict said that earlier … when we came in."

Marcus smiles broadly, shaking his head. "Ah! No, not at all. *He* said: 'Make us a *pot* of tea, please.' It's different."

Farah looks incredulous. "The difference between making us tea and blowing us all up are the words *pot* and *cup*? What if you mix them up?"

Marcus laughs, before he realizes that she's serious. "That's impossible. You'd *never* make a *cup* of tea when there's a group, would you?"

*

Not long after, Benedict joins us, his attention still absorbed by his notebook. "Make us a pot of tea, would you please, Marcus," he says absently.

Farah flinches and my eyes flick to Marcus as he clicks the blue switch without a second thought.

Vikram puts down his journal and gives me an inquisitive look. "Tell me, Kyle, what brought you to this place?"

"I have epilepsy," I say. "I think I must be having a seizure." A meaningful look passes between Vikram and Benedict.

"Eduardo had epilepsy, too," Vikram replies. "People with epilepsy look different in this world, don't you think?" Benedict nods. Vikram continues: "You're more ... *here* than the rest of us. More comfortable in this place. Have you noticed?"

"No," I say.

"Yes," Farah says.

"Is anything familiar about this place to you?" Vikram asks.

"Maybe ... impressions, feelings. I can't explain it."

The air feels charged. Even Abi appears interested for a moment. Mugs clink as Marcus narrowly avoids dropping them. "Ow! *Hot!*" he hisses to himself.

"What is it?" I say.

"What does it feel like, coming back after a seizure?" Benedict says.

"Like dying and coming out the other side."

Benedict raises his eyebrows. My words surprise me as much as they do him, but as soon as I say them I know they're right.

"Most people only come here to die, maybe a few have made it back. But we have a theory that people with epilepsy are different. They come and go from this place whenever they have a seizure."

"Of all of the people we studied, the only ones who had some form of memory of this place were those with epilepsy," Abi says.

"Memory?" My heart knocks in my chest.

Benedict seems almost amused by my excitement. "Memory is a strong word, Kyle. We're talking glimpses, fleeting visions. Things you might dismiss as dreams unless you had good reason not to. Tell me, did you know about this place before you came here?"

"No," I say, shaking my head. All the same, those snatches I saw … the man in my aura, the familiar, rushing sensations. *There is something*, I think. "But it might be different with the machine, right? I might remember more."

"Perhaps. With the right protocol in place. That's what we're working towards."

"But we don't have time to wait," I say. "Farah is sick."

"Yes, yes," Benedict says calmly. "We'll monitor her, I promise."

"But we could *try*? If I got back and I could remember, I could contact your colleagues and let them know the experiment is a success after all?" I catch a flicker of interest from Benedict. I press harder. "We've got to get the message back about this place, right? About what you've discovered."

Abi's eyes catch mine and then quickly dart away. "Benedict? It's possible," she says, hopeful. "It does seem that people with epilepsy are more prone to retaining memories. It is a chance we never had before."

Benedict nods, and for a moment I think we've got him. "It could be important, I agree." He gives me a regretful look. "But that's exactly why we need to be extra cautious. We have new evidence, new lines of investigation. We mustn't squander them."

Vikram heaves a deep sigh: a signal that, for him at least, the conversation is over. He reaches behind the sofa and produces a pair of bongo drums from a pile of plastic bags and bubble wrap. He taps a short beat, adjusts the tension and taps again.

"Marcus," he says. "It's time."

Marcus grins and unearths a guitar from the far corner of the room. He strums a few experimental, soft chords and then they begin to play.

It's a slow, melancholy piece. The bongos beat a rough, syncopated rhythm, like somebody stumbling, walking beyond the point of exhaustion, while the guitar seems to dance around them, darting ahead and doubling back, skipping excitedly away but always in step. I was never much into music in the ordinary world, but here it paints pictures in my brain that feel vast and lonely.

I think of Jonah's gang, making music in the service station.

"Well, this is what we do, isn't it?" Benedict says, making a gesture that takes in the cluttered room and our small group. "We huddle together and make music to keep away the darkness. It's what we did there, it's what we do here. Everything else is window dressing."

A chord tightens inside me, Jonah dancing, Levi playing his accordion. Benedict rummages in his jacket pocket and pulls out a pack of crumpled cigarettes. He lights one, inhales and breathes out in a deep, contented sigh. He offers the pack around. Vikram takes one, pops it in his mouth without breaking his rhythm, Benedict lights it for him. He holds out the pack to me and I shake my head.

"Are you sure?" Benedict says. "There's no evidence that they cause cancer in this world."

"There's no evidence that they don't," Abi counters.

Benedict waves her away. He breathes another cloud of white smoke into the air above our heads. Farah wraps her arms around my arm and rests her head on my shoulder. Chiu curls up into a tight ball, watching Vikram with rapt attention.

After a while, Benedict leans forward.

"Consciousness?" he says, as if I'd asked a question. "They call it 'the Hard Problem'. It's such a fascinating question, don't you think?" He crosses his legs and his trousers ride up to reveal threadbare socks. "Here we are, we intrepid explorers, already possessing knowledge that no other scientist or human in the world possesses. We make astronauts look like children playing in their sandpit, don't we?" His eyes are shining and I can see at once that Abi is right. There's no way he'll give up on his great discovery, it's worth more to him than his own life; more to him than any of our lives. "We are travellers in the Undiscovered Country. Did you ever consider that?"

We are the Founding Fathers, Kyle.

"But what happens if we dig a little deeper? If this world exists behind our ordinary world, maybe there's another world behind this one?"

"I just want to get back to the one I'm familiar with," I say.

"Really?" Benedict seems disappointed. "I want what every scientist wants: to get closer to the truth."

"What truth?"

"Layers upon layers, I think. Like strata in the earth and beneath it all, what do you think we'll find…? Bedrock? God, perhaps?"

"I don't believe in God," I say.

There's silence and the music dances through alien landscapes around us.

"I don't think it's as simple as that," Benedict says. "God is just a word. A word to describe a person or a force. I wish I knew which."

"Why does it matter?" Chiu says.

Benedict turns to regard him. "Because if it's a person, it can *want*."

"What could God possibly want?" I say, laughing slightly.

Benedict's eyes flash. Abi shifts uncomfortably.

"I have a theory about that," Benedict says. "I think It wants the same as me." He waits, holding back a knowing smile. "Let's for a moment assume that It, in some form or another, exists. If so, It exists for ever. And It can no more imagine the finite than we can imagine the infinite. Don't you think it would be curious to understand what death is like? Don't you think it's possible that It would create an experiment to find out?"

"You mean us?" I say.

"Exactly." Benedict smiles. "The only creatures born with an understanding of their own finite nature."

"You think It made us to know that we'll die? To see what we'll do?"

Benedict nods.

I snort, bitterly. "That sounds about right."

"It's just a theory," Abi says. "You don't really have any evidence."

For a moment I'm afraid they're going to fall into

another of their debates, but they're interrupted by a shrill buzzer – a rough, grating sound like an old-fashioned doorbell.

"What's that?" I say.

Vikram and Marcus stop playing and Marcus leaps over the sofa to inspect the television. "*Oh crap!*" he gasps.

"Four of them," Benedict says, joining him.

Suddenly Marcus, Vikram and Abi are in motion. They rush to their store of weapons and start pulling on their gear. Golf clubs. Cricket bats. Face masks.

"Ohshitohshitohshit," Abi is saying.

The rest of us stare at the screen. I squint at the black and white image; the angle is too tight and the light too poor to make out anything other than the slow prowl of suspicious movements. *Four?* I feel an unreasonable shudder of relief. With Tongue dead, there was only Jonah, Levi and Ose, so this must be some other gang. Perhaps the people who attacked this place before? Dangerous, but not Jonah.

"Ready?" Vikram breathes.

"We're ready," Marcus says, pulling his hockey mask down.

"Go," Benedict replies.

He flicks a switch and, on the screen, I see the edge of the second set of fire doors swing and latch firmly into place. Slow, suspicious movements turn into swift, angry, caged reaction. Like kicking over an ants' nest. Then, a moment too late, I see the grainy image of a man turn and I realize that I'm wrong.

It's Jonah.

"Wait, no," I start. "You can't—"

But everything is happening too fast. Benedict flicks a second switch and the screen is whited out and there's a loud *crack! crack!* of the stun grenades in the airlock. Then Abi, Vikram and Marcus bundle in and the door snaps shut behind them.

Shouts echo, faintly, through the wall.

Marcus: "Get down! Get DOWN!"

A heavy thump that I hope is Marcus hitting somebody, hopefully Jonah. I glance anxiously at Farah. She's pale, terrified. It's impossible to see anything through the smoke except flashes of movement and shadow. In a fair fight Jonah would kill Marcus in a second, but like this...? Maybe, just maybe—

The smoke clears and I spot something new: somebody I don't recognize. He's slight, no taller than me, probably no older than me either. A slim, black smudge on the screen but it feels like an electric shock running through me.

Why is he so familiar?

Vikram's hockey stick is braced against his throat. The boy struggles, twists and tries to unbalance him. He puts up a better fight than I did. Then he reaches up, almost lazily, and slaps Vikram in the side of the neck. It seems too much of a glancing blow to hurt but Vikram falls back clutching his throat.

There's something in the boy's hand. A knife? Vikram leans against the wall, his eyes wide and terrified. Even on the grainy screen I see the blood pulsing through the gaps in his fingers.

Another shape moves into frame, obscuring him.

Jonah.

He has Marcus by the scruff of his neck, his hunting knife pointing straight up against the underside of his chin. Marcus's eyes swivel in their sockets in a vain and ill-advised effort to catch a glimpse of the knife. Jonah presents him to the camera like a sacrifice.

Open up or else, his grin says.

"Don't open it," Farah says quickly.

Benedict's hand hovers over the switch. "I have to."

There's a snap of metal as he flicks the switch and a hollow *clunk* as the electromagnets give way and release the corridor. Noise bursts into the lab. Abi staggers in, swearing and shouting as Levi pushes her ahead of him. Vikram follows, his mouth open, struggling to breathe, his hands clamped to his neck.

A tray of Petri dishes clatters noisily to the floor. An office chair is knocked over. We stand rigid in the doorway, feeling like the world dropped out from beneath our feet. Benedict's hand pulls my shoulder and I follow him back to the common room.

The sofas.

The taped-off area.

Marcus's trap.

I glance at Farah, Chiu and Benedict as we find our spots. Farah is closest to the switch. If they stand in the right place, she could—

Levi pushes Abi roughly on to the sofa next to us. She's bleeding from a gash across her cheek, but Levi's nose is broken and gushes blood and both eyes are beginning to blacken already. *Good for her,* I think.

Vikram crashes on to the sofa and rolls on to his back, still clutching his throat.

"You stabbed him! You stabbed him!" Marcus shouts hysterically. Jonah steps forward and slaps him and he sits down with a shocked expression on his face.

Ose comes in next. He's got a cut on his head and a sullen look. Maybe Vikram managed to knock him out. Maybe he doesn't like this part. Fighting and killing people, that's Jonah's style, not Ose's. For Ose, it's just the price of admission.

Behind Ose comes the new guy. Gaunt and lean, dressed in black T-shirt and black jeans, with a khaki-green rucksack. My stomach twists when I see him. I can't explain it, but I know he's the reason I wouldn't go down that road, the reason I made us take such a long detour. He's the person I sensed lurking in the shadows, waiting for us.

He's just a kid, but he's all wrong.

"You're trespassing," Benedict says, trying to keep his voice from trembling.

"I'm sorry," Jonah says, lifting his hands in a calming gesture that's undermined by the vicious-looking hunting knife he's still holding. "You jumped us, we didn't mean for anything... Oh, *god*! Is he OK?"

"You stabbed him!" Abi says, accusingly.

"We were defending ourselves," Jonah says, his voice pleading.

It's an act, I think. It's not even a good act. But the others don't know that. I spot a rapid exchange of looks between Benedict and the others. Jonah pauses, seems to notice the knife in his hand and makes a point of placing it carefully on the coffee table, backing away with his hands up and his eyes fixed on Benedict.

"I'm ... I'm sorry... My name's Jonah."

All I see is violence and malice, a knife pressed against an old man's chest, but Benedict nods slightly in return. A calmness is coming to the room, the adrenaline of battle ebbing away. Only Vikram, breathing tightly next to me, to remind us what just happened.

"You're trespassing," Benedict says again, more softly. "You need to leave."

"Look, it's OK," Jonah says. "It's OK, really. I'm Jonah. This is Levi. Kevin. Ose."

Silence.

A flicker of impatience on Jonah's face. He's done his piece and now he's expecting a response. He catches my eye and I know at once that he's here for me. He'd kill the others in a second but maybe he's trying to save himself the trouble. Or maybe, now he's here, he's figuring there might be other things of value he can lay claim to.

He waits, requiring an answer.

"I'm Dr Benedict Brownstein," Benedict says, carefully. "This is my lab."

"I'm sorry," Jonah says again. "We didn't mean for…" He turns to me and flashes me a look that's filled with hurt. "We've been looking for *him*."

Benedict glances at me, then back to Jonah. "What's he to you?"

"We took the three of them in," Jonah says. "Tried to help them. But … he murdered one of my friends and left. I don't know why."

"It's a lie," Farah says.

Benedict looks troubled. "Kyle?"

"I…" My voice trails off. I see Tongue's questioning eyes, his hand reaching up and covering my own. I don't need to say anything else; Benedict sees it in my face.

"It's not true," Farah insists. "He's twisting it."

It doesn't matter. Benedict wants this over with. He wants to go back to his books and his theories. All he needs is an excuse to make everything OK.

"What do you intend to do now you've found him?" Benedict asks.

Jonah feigns a nervous laugh. The act is slipping now, he's getting bored of it anyway. "Well … we have a situation, don't we? I lost a good friend and I have a score to settle."

Benedict looks down and stares thoughtfully at his hands. I can see him calculating, trading my life against the inevitable injury and death, the threat to his work.

"I don't have any quarrel with you," Jonah goes on. "Let me take the boy and we'll get out your way. No foul, no harm. Forgive and forget and all that."

Farah gives me a stark look, one that tells me she's ready to launch herself at whoever's closest the minute I give her the nod.

Jonah stands half in and half out of Marcus's kill zone, one leg straggling the taped line on the floor. Levi is next to him, fully in. But Ose and the new guy are safe. Marcus is sitting on the very edge of his seat, waiting for Benedict to tell him what to do.

They're scientists, I think. *What would be the rational choice?*

"I'd need your guarantee you wouldn't harm him," Benedict says, unconvincingly.

I don't know why I'm important to Jonah, but if he cares so much maybe I have something to trade for everyone else's lives after all. It doesn't matter either way, I can't let Benedict try to fight Jonah, even if he wanted to.

"It's OK," I say. "I'll go with them. I'm sorry, Jonah. I didn't mean to—"

Jonah's voice softens. "It's all right, lad. We'll get through this."

Benedict and Abi both give me questioning stares.

"Kyle?" Benedict says. "Are you sure?"

I nod, weakly.

"We need a moment to think about this," Benedict says to Jonah.

But he doesn't say it with any conviction. His decision is made, this part is just about making sure he can justify it to the others afterwards. The new kid moves closer, menacing. The long, thin kitchen knife that he used to stab Vikram glints in his hand. He's a step away from Marcus's line now. If they set off their trap, he'd probably be caught in it, maybe injured, maybe enough that we could get the better of him.

But in the same moment, Jonah steps forward to get a closer look at Vikram. Vikram lets out a small, terrified whimper in response. He tries to squirm away but Jonah grabs his hand and prises his fingers roughly away from his throat.

"Be careful," Abi cries.

Woodlice pour from the wound in a tiny, silent, panicky swarm. Woodlice. Ants. Spiders. A millipede wriggles from under Vikram's skin and drops on to the floor. Jonah seems mildly disgusted. He brushes a few stray woodlice from his hand.

"Yeah, you'll want to keep pressure on that," he says.

He heads over to the equipment. He's a long way out of the kill zone now. "What is this place? A lab, right? That'll explain all the fancy equipment." Jonah squints into the microscope. "They were some pretty impressive pyrotechnics back there. Who's the explosives wizard?"

"Be careful with that," Marcus says.

Jonah flashes him a murderous look. All the pretence has gone now, the old Jonah is back. Cold, predatory. Benedict sees it as well.

"Last chance," Jonah warns.

Benedict sighs regretfully. "OK. You win. Take the boy and go."

I hold my breath, panic squeezing me. I know it's the right decision, the only decision Benedict could have made. But I'm terrified.

Jonah smiles. "You didn't answer my question though." He moves back to the window and peels away a corner of the cardboard so he can peek outside. "Who's the explosives wizard?"

Benedict tenses. "You came for Kyle."

"Price just went up," Jonah replies.

Benedict takes a breath. He knows he's beaten but he's willing to do anything to protect his experiment. "Fine," he says, dryly. "Let's talk terms."

"Terms?"

Benedict's nerves begin to get the better of him, his

voice trembles. "I don't know about you, but I always like to drink tea when I discuss terms."

Jonah looks confused. "What?"

"Marcus, be a good chap and make us all a nice cup of tea, would you?"

THIRTY-EIGHT

The noise is devastating: like being torn apart, like somebody smashed my head with a hammer. It's so sudden it doesn't occur to me to move, let alone duck behind the sofa like I was told to. I close my eyes and for a moment everything is black and I think I must be dead.

Then I can see again, except I can't understand why Jonah is still standing there, with Kevin, Levi and Ose standing next to him. Kevin has a knife in his hand, but a different knife to the one before. Smaller. Blunt looking.

Then Abi shrieks, *"Marcus!"*

I turn and Marcus is leaning back against the counter, a dumbfounded expression on his face. The hole in his chest looks like a crater on the moon and as I watch, its edges turn white and dry and start to crumble away. They fall in clumps of calcified dust. His mouth opens like he's trying to speak, but then his jaw cracks and his eyes turn white and he stumbles forward and falls.

I turn back to Jonah and realize that the thing in Kevin's hand isn't a knife; it's a gun and I can smell the gunpowder now, sharp and spicy, like bonfire night.

"Oh, I forgot to mention," Jonah says. "Our new member has a trick or two."

He eyes the crudely thumbtacked wires that lead from the switch to the floor panel with an air of contempt. We sit in silence, waiting to see what he's going to do next. My ears are ringing. Next to me, Vikram groans. There's no blood anymore, just woodlice that are pushing their way between his fingers, rolling down his neck and getting caught in his shirt collar and the lapels of his jacket. He struggles and chokes and a few waterlogged ants escape his mouth. Abi leans in close, soothing him, stroking his hair with a tenderness I wouldn't have expected between them.

"He won't last much longer," she breathes.

"Enough, Jonah," I say, standing up. "Let's go; it's me you want."

A satisfied grin spreads across Jonah's face. "Oh, ho. Squeaky gets brave all of a sudden!" He gives me an admonishing look. "You know, if you'd been brave five minutes ago, Kyle, your new friend here might not have had to die."

"Let's just go," I say. "You don't care about them. No one else has to die."

Jonah shrugs. "That *was* my original intention, Kyle, honest it was. But you've all gone and piqued my curiosity now." He turns to Abi. "A bunch of scientists like this, I bet you got some kick-ass skills, haven't you? And then there's this *machine* I keep hearing about." He looks at me. "That's what you're here for, right? That's what was so important you made me chase you halfway across London?"

"It's a specialized MRI," Abi says. "It can help you get back; it can save you."

"Show me," Jonah says.

"Vikram needs to go first," Abi says.

Jonah smiles. "Then it's a party. Let's go see what this thing can do."

Abi shudders with relief and starts to haul Vikram to his feet. Farah moves quickly to help her, taking Vikram's other arm and looping it over her neck.

Jonah nods at Chiu. "Levi, stay here with the little one. The rest of you may as well come along for the show."

"Benedict?" Abi says, a question edged with anger and blame.

Benedict stands. "Of course."

Kevin gives me a smug, satisfied look as we follow Jonah back out into the corridor. Anger and hatred glisten inside him and I feel what I felt when I was in the street. That terrible, terrible blackness. It's like a vision, an insight. I see it all too clearly. Jonah and his followers in control of this place. Organized. Ready to enslave or murder anybody unfortunate enough to find themselves here. *There are worse things than dying*, I think.

We come to another set of double fire doors, these ones framed with thick bands of black and yellow tape, with a sign over the top of them that reads: HIGH MAGNETIC FIELD — AUTHORIZED PERSONNEL ONLY.

The sight of the MRI brings back unpleasant memories. It stands alone and severe in the centre of the room, something between an industrial tumble dryer and a giant plastic doughnut. White casing, grey panels, a kind of mechanized stretcher that feeds you in head first like it's feeding you into the fire at a crematorium. It's the noise I hate most. Loud and alien, like bones being ground up by steel teeth. I had lots of trips to the MRI in the run-up to my operation and in that jaw-grinding noise it's not hard to convince yourself there's something else… A voice. A sound like lots of people talking at once. Hell.

Farah and Abi lower Vikram on to the bed, his hand still clamped to his neck and the woodlice forcing their way out where they can. He coughs, leans awkwardly to one side and spits three more woodlice and a millipede on to the ground in a pool of saliva. Ants explore the back of his hand.

I wish there were blood, I think. *My god, I wish there were blood*. But the blood, when people are dying, is short-lived and is quickly replaced by something else. Another rule, I note, with no sense of pleasure.

Benedict is at the console, typing rapidly.

"How does this gizmo work then?" Jonah says, stooping to peer into the mechanism.

"Thoughts are cytoelectrical impulses exchanged between neurons," Benedict explains as he types. "But qualia, the self-narrative *I*, is a standing wave composed of these impulses that extends across the whole brain."

Jonah flashes me a playful wink. *He doesn't care*, I think. There's a punchline coming, I can feel it. This is just the build-up.

Vikram convulses, coughing uncontrollably, gasping for breath.

"What's taking so long?" Abi snaps at Benedict.

"Nearly there," Benedict says. "I'm updating the field alignments."

Abi looks confused. "Use the same ones as Devon."

"We may as well try the new ones—" Benedict begins.

Abi exhales a disbelieving gust that's half laugh. "He's *dying*, Benedict! This isn't the time to try out a new protocol."

"It's what he'd want me to do," Benedict insists, still typing.

Vikram vomits a stream of yellowish fluid.

"Hold on, Vik," Abi whispers, her voice cracking. "You're OK, you're going to be OK."

"What's this with the field alignments?" Jonah asks, coolly.

"We're still working on the protocol required to preserve our memories," Benedict answers, without looking up. "There's no point in us coming here unless we can take news of our research back with us, is there?"

My breath catches. Benedict doesn't know what he's done. To Benedict this is science, self-evidently the right thing, but there's a dangerous look in Jonah's eyes.

"He'll remember this place in the ordinary world, will he?" he says.

"We hope," Benedict answers. "It would be a tremendous discovery."

"We can help you too," Abi says. "Get you back. I don't know how long you've been here but it's less time in the ordinary world. Do you have a family?"

"What makes you think I want to go back?" Jonah says.

He smiles at me, like we're sharing a secret joke. I see the anticipation in his look. Oh, no, I think, no, no, *no*... It's the way he looked at the man he murdered, the way he looked at me the first time we met. I feel like I'm in a nightmare, the kind where you want to scream but you can't, where all you can do is watch the horror unfold in front of you.

"You want to come back and study this place, I suppose?" Jonah enquires.

"Of course."

"So you can carve it up and buy it and sell it and *own* it, I suppose?"

Benedict looks up, confused. "I'm sorry?"

Jonah shakes his head slowly. "We can't have that."

He takes the gun calmly from Kevin's outstretched hand and turns and fires into Vikram's chest. Three thunderous, world-ending cracks.

CRACK! CRACK! CRACK!

Vikram's body jerks with each impact and the woodlice and the ants and spiders become instantly more frantic and boil from the wounds as his body dissolves into them, *becoming* them. Abi staggers backwards, her hand to her mouth.

"NO!" Farah screams.

She runs at Jonah and he slaps her aside with the back of his hand, knocking her down. He takes aim at the machine now.

"This is *my* place, do you understand?" he shouts at nobody in particular. "I *own* this place. God has a plan for me, in *this* world. And nobody else gets to muscle in on it."

He goes to pull the trigger.

Except he doesn't make it, because my little fruit knife has found my hand and I've darted forward and plunged it into the small of his back. I pull it out and stab again. And again. And again. I imagine it slicing through kidney and spleen. There's no resistance. Just the dry *thud, thud, thud* as my clenched fist hits his shirt.

THUD. THUD. THUD, THUD.

Jonah twists, turns away from me and then elbows me

in the face. I feel my nose pop and two of my front teeth hit the back of my throat. It feels as if the world has fallen in on me. The ground clouts me from behind and suddenly Jonah is glaring wide-eyed at me and I know he's going to kill me for sure this time.

"You *ungrateful* swine!" he howls, clutching his side and trying to peer around to see what the damage is. "Look what you've *done.*"

A sick, singing blackness rings in my head. In the ordinary world I'd have passed out by now, but there's no passing out in this world.

"I'll *kill* you," Jonah slurs.

He starts towards me but his legs give way and suddenly he's on the floor with me. He tries to stand, staring at me in genuine disbelief and confusion. He sees, in the same moment that I do, that the fingers on his hand and the fingers clawing their way out of the wound in his side have become tangled together. He tries to pull his hand away but the fingers stretch like hot toffee and more sprout from his hand and his side like they're trying to hold on to each other.

He's dying!

The realization hits me as it hits him. He twists again, scrabbling on the floor for his knife. Kevin steps past him now. He picks up the gun from the ground and he points it at me. I'm still gasping and choking on my own blood and a part of me is checking my hands and expecting to see insects or dust or more fingers.

A cold feeling swells inside me. I know now why I was so scared I couldn't even walk down the same road this kid was living on. Because there's something wrong with him, something *missing*. He's empty inside and it goes down and down and down like a hole. And where other people have *something*, with him it's *nothing* and all he wants is to kill and kill and kill. I feel it inside me. How long he'd been waiting in his bedroom before Jonah found him, waiting with his sniper rifle set up and ready for the next unfortunate to pass by.

Years. Decades.

He raises the gun and points it at my face.

In the same moment, Farah hits him, hard, in the shoulder with a fire extinguisher. It's so heavy she can hardly lift it. The blow is only glancing, but it's enough. He goes down and she drops the fire extinguisher and nearly takes me out in the process. She doesn't pause. She hauls me to my feet.

"Come *on*!" she screams.

She doesn't need to tell me twice. I scramble to my feet and we bolt through the door and down the corridor.

I can't see what's happening behind us, but I *know*. Somehow, I know. I *see* Kevin with something other than my eyes. *Blindsight*. I see him the way I felt him on the street that first time, the same way I got us out when we were lost in the side roads, the same way I win my games of Uno.

He's pulling himself to his feet. He's scanning the floor for his gun.

"Let's get Chiu and get out of here," Farah gasps.

I shake my head. "No time."

I push through the fire door at the end of the corridor that leads into the stairwell.

Farah pulls back. "We can't leave Chiu—"

I shove her on to the stairs just in time as Kevin fires through the little glass window. The glass shatters and the noise echoes around the stairwell and a cloud of plaster dust and splinters erupt from the wall near my head. I glance back and I feel the lightning strike of his pain, which tells me that Farah probably broke his collarbone.

She's up and running now and I'm right behind her, round the dog-leg stairwell and out into the corridor on the next floor.

Kevin doesn't run. He limps at an odd angle down the length of the corridor, his mind tightly coiled in pain and fury. He glances up, his gun ready, in case we're waiting to jump him at the top of the stairs.

Farah and I run, hand in hand, down the length of the corridor. We only have a second or less before Kevin appears behind us and gets a clear shot at us.

We dart round the corner and stop. I have to stop. I gasp and choke. My nose is broken and blood drools from where Jonah hit me.

Kevin is in the corridor. He knows we're close.

"That wasn't nice," he complains loudly, his voice petulant and childlike. "That *hurt*."

We listen to his footsteps coming closer. We're trapped. Farah makes to run, but I know that if we run, he'll hear us. We wouldn't get as far as the next stairwell before he caught up to us.

He pauses outside one of the labs, presses his body against the door.

"Coming, ready or not!" he calls in a sing-song voice.

He bursts in, swinging the door open and raising his gun in one swift motion.

Nothing.

He used to practise this at home with a dart gun. When that stopped being enough of a thrill, he went to the wasteland behind his house with an air rifle and took potshots at the stray cats he found there. He liked it best when he wounded them, when they lay panting for breath and trying to bite him as they died.

He knows he has us. He's just making the fun last longer.

"I'm going to shoot you in the stomach," he calls. Anticipation trembles in his voice. "It's supposed to take a really long time to die if you're shot in the stomach."

Another door. In and step around, gun raised. Like a movie.

He's dreamed of doing this for real for as long as he can remember.

My head feels like a thunderstorm. My nose throbs and my breath scorches my throat. But it's Kevin's mind pressing against my own that hurts the most. All that bitterness and hatred. In the ordinary world he lies dying in the woods behind his house. *Shot myself!* he thinks. The thought comes back again and again, torments him. *Stupid, stupid, stupid—*

But it's OK now, he thinks. *This place is better. Especially now Jonah has found him.*

Suddenly Kevin has a new idea. He slips his rucksack off his back and stoops to look inside. The backpack smells of excitement, control, payback. He finds what he's looking for. Weighs it briefly in his hand and tosses it in our direction.

The object rattles to the ground next to us. I know what it is, even though I've only seen grenades in movies.

It bounces against the wall and spins a couple of times as it comes to rest. I feel it. A flash and a taste of death inside my head – the explosives and above the explosives a slower-burning material. The fuse. I see it sparking and sizzling in my mind, I feel Kevin's own mind on it as well.

He's learned that you have to imagine the burn or it won't go off. In the first years after he died he spent many happy hours in his flat figuring out how to make the grenades explode.

Except this time, it doesn't come because I feel it too.

The idea of the grenade passes from him to me and I reach forward with my mind in just the right way, like squeezing a candle between my thumb and forefinger…

I smother the idea of the grenade.

I feel Kevin's fury as he realizes what I'm doing. I feel

him bear down on the *idea* of the grenade exploding, pressing with his mind, willing the fuse to burn through.

But I'm stronger than he is and I hold on to the flame tightly. I step forward, scoop up the grenade and fling it back down the corridor towards him.

I catch a glimpse of him, kneeling, his gun ready for me. The grenade is in the air between us when he fires and I … let go…

THIRTY-NINE

I'm knocked back against the wall. Pain layered upon pain. *Dying is only a bad thing if you don't want to do it.* That's what the old lady on the bench told me. And right about now dying feels like it might be an OK option.

Farah is leaning over me, shouting, frantic. I can feel her hands on me, checking to see if I'm falling apart or spitting out woodlice. The world slides back into focus.

"I'm OK," I groan.

"You're shot," she replies.

I look down and see that my arm is drenched with blood and I realize that there's a chunk missing from my biceps where Kevin's bullet must have grazed me.

Farah removes her belt and cinches it tight just below my shoulder. I scream in agony. She checks the wound.

"It's not as bad as it looks," she says.

"Oh, good," I say. "Because it looks bloody awful."

She smiles and presses her face against my cheek, kissing me. Even through the world of pain that I'm half drowning in, it feels good. "I thought you were dead," she whispers. "God, oh god, I thought you were dead."

I cough and she gives me some space. I can see down the length of the corridor for the first time now. I missed it, whatever happened to Kevin, there's only a stain and a few blasted shreds of material in the corridor where he was kneeling.

"How did you do that?" Farah asks.

"I don't know," I say. "I just kind of … felt it."

"Blindsight?"

"I guess."

Farah considers this. "It's a more useful trick than always winning at Uno."

I laugh tiredly and let her haul me to my feet.

"Let's get Chiu and get out of here," Farah says. "I'm done with this place."

I nod, I'm OK with that plan. But there's still Ose and Levi.

And Jonah.

In spite of everything, I know that Jonah is still very much alive and very much not happy with me. I can feel him downstairs, the same blindsight that showed me what Kevin was doing. Not as clearly though: just moments, disconnected freeze-frames.

He heard the explosion. He's coming this way.

"I've got an idea," I say.

It's not much of an idea as ideas go, but it's as good as I can think of right now. I take us back down the staircase on the opposite side so we can avoid Jonah. Pain roars inside my head like a waterfall. I can *see* them all.

Ose in the MRI room. Levi guarding Chiu. Jonah coming up the stairwell.

Abi kneeling over Benedict… Something is wrong with Benedict.

But I have no time to worry about that now.

We have to get Chiu first, I think. Then we can make a break for it.

We stop outside the common room where Levi is still watching Chiu. "Go around through the sleep lab," I whisper to Farah. "Go in with the golf club but stop as soon as Levi sees you. Don't go past the doorway."

"What are you going to do?"

"Just … just don't go past the doorway," I say.

She nods. I can feel Chiu and Levi in the common room. Now that I know what I'm looking for, blindsight is easy.

Levi has heard the explosion and he's standing tensely, listening, caught between his own burning desire to be in the fight and his fear of getting in trouble with Jonah if he doesn't do what he was told. Chiu is on the sofa, inching closer to the red plug socket every time Levi looks away.

I wait. My arm feels like a white-hot boulder that has

been chained to my side. I watch with my mind as Farah moves soft-footedly through the sleep lab, careful not to make a noise as she picks up the golf club.

She steps through the doorway.

Levi sees her. His mind is filled with violence and murder as he moves towards her. But his path takes him right across the square of taped-up floor to Marcus's trap and I'm running in through the other entrance.

Chiu sees me and understands what I'm planning to do and he lunges for the space behind the sofa. Farah is one step too far into the room but if I stop now, Levi will be on her and he'll kill us all. There's no time to think, no time to question myself, no time to be scared. The palm of my hand hits the red switch and I feel a spark and the ignition and I chase the current in my mind until I feel it flare in the floor beneath Levi's feet.

Ears ringing. The pain in my arm, monstrous. The air so thick with dust and plasterboard and the smell of explosives it's hard to breathe.

I'm tired of explosions and gunshots. They're exciting in movies. In real life they *hurt*.

The first thing I see: Chiu staggering to his feet, plasterboard falling out of his hair. He grins and flashes me a thumbs up.

I lurch to my feet and see that Levi isn't dead, but he's not far off. He's slumped in the corner of the room and one arm is hard and calcified, cracked almost in half. He's starting to turn to dry white dust, ready to flake away at the slightest touch.

"*Kyle!*"

It's part shout, part cry, all mixed up with anger and pain. I rush to Farah as she staggers to her feet. She's leaning heavily on the counter and I can see from here that her ankle is smashed. I guess the blast pushed out low and she was too close. I catch her before she falls and my arm screams as she lands against it. I help her on to the sofa and she sits, squeezing her eyes tight shut in pain, lifting her head to the ceiling.

"Dammit," she says through gritted teeth.

"You're OK," I say. "We'll make it work."

She shakes her head. "There's no time. Jonah's coming, isn't he?"

He's staring at the spot where Kevin died, but he's heard the noise and he knows what I've done. The anger he feels towards me sparks inside him like a match head.

"We've got a minute or two," I say.

"Take Chiu and go."

"No way. I'm not leaving you."

I know what she's thinking. She's thinking that I've killed his guns and I've killed his motorbikes and I've damn near killed him, so if Jonah catches up with me, he's going to take me apart one piece at a time.

"I'll be OK," she says. "It's you he wants. I'll convince him to keep me as a hostage."

"I'm not leaving you with him."

She winces in pain. "Come back when he's not expecting it. Kill him."

"*No.*"

I find the golf club among the piled-up chunks of plasterboard and pick it up, clumsily, wiping it off with my hand. It's heavy. My shoulder burns.

He lurches down the stairwell. I've hurt him. The pain where he had to hack off several of the fingers on one hand to save himself burns like phosphorus.

"Kyle," Farah says. "You know I'm right."

She takes my arm and pulls me to her and kisses me. I'm aware of Chiu sitting quietly nearby, feeling awkward in spite of everything.

Farah holds my face close to hers and speaks seriously. "Listen to me. I think you're pretty cool, Kyle, OK? You picked up on that, right? I think … even in the other world I'd think you were pretty cool. So you can't make me lie here and watch him kill you."

"I'm not scared," I say.

"You *ought* to be scared," Farah says. "He's a scary man."

"I *choose* not to be scared," I say.

Farah laughs, kisses me again. "What bloody idiot told you that?"

Tears pour down her face. I try to pull away but she doesn't let go. "*This* is the brave move," she says, gritting her teeth in pain and frustration. "Get away and come back tonight."

I know she's right. It's our best chance. But I don't want to. "You didn't want to use the machine," I say, trying to keep the challenge from my voice. "If I come back and kill him for you, will you go back and let the doctors treat you?"

Farah smiles. "Look, you win, OK? This ankle *really* hurts and I'm warming to the idea of going back to a world where they have painkillers."

A flood of half-formed images flash through my mind, a high-speed flickering daydream of me and Farah back in the ordinary world, studying, getting our A-levels, moving to London…

Except…

"You'll forget me," I say.

She shakes her head. "But *you'll* remember. That's what Benedict said. There's a chance, anyway."

"Benedict said 'impressions' … 'glimpses'."

"Well, you're going to have to do better than that," Farah says. "And then you're going to have to come and find me, OK? And then you're going to have to ask me out."

The idea of it sounds so ridiculous. Farah, back in the ordinary world, with no memory of me or any of this. And me, walking up to her, the awkward kid who she last saw throwing up in maths class, and asking her out?

"I think I'd rather fight Jonah," I say.

Farah laughs through her tears. "You're just going to

have to be brave, aren't you?" She swallows. "Promise me. Promise me you'll do it."

I nod. Serious now.

"I'm going to be awful to you. But you'll try anyway, right?"

"Of course I will. I'll remember and I'll ask you out." The thought hardens inside me. "And I'll keep asking you out until you're sick of it and you say yes just to shut me up."

A smile spreads across her face. "That'll do."

I turn to Chiu who nods solemnly and stands up, ready. I kiss Farah again and then I'm leaving, I'm really leaving. My brain twists and strains against the idea but I know it's the only way. Leave now, come back tonight.

Jonah is at the bottom of the stairs.

I don't have much time. But if I go back out through the sleep lab and the airlock, I'll avoid him. I grab the golf club and Chiu and I head past the crumbled remains of Levi and out into the lab. I catch a glimpse of the sad little beds where, in the ordinary world, Benedict and Abi are the only survivors of their sleep study, then I turn and—

Jonah is there.

A slow smile spreads across his face. "Boo," he says.

I can't breathe. I *felt* him. I *knew* he was coming back along the other corridor, past the MRI room. He *can't* be here.

"How did you—?"

315

Jonah taps his temple. "Same way you got the better of me when you murdered poor old Tongue," he says. He tuts softly. "Did you think you're the only one who's got some tricks, Kyle?"

I hold the golf club out in front of me, fighting hard to keep it steady even though I'm shaking all over. Jonah's face is red and shining with sweat. I've hurt him, I can see that much. Hurt him and come pretty close to killing him. Goddamn, why couldn't I have finished the job? *If anyone deserves to die it's him,* I think. *Not Tongue, not the old lady in the park, not Marcus, or Vikram, not even Levi or Kevin. It's him.*

Jonah steps forward and spots what remains of Levi slumped in the corner. "You ungrateful sod," he growls. "I should've killed you the first time I met you."

"Why didn't you?" I say.

Jonah gives me a cunning look. "I thought I'd take you under my wing, didn't I?"

That's not the whole truth. What does he want from me?

Farah is trying to haul herself to her feet. Chiu is backing away, rigid with fear. Jonah advances another step and I can't help it, I take a step back.

"I can't believe you walked all this way just for revenge," I say. "It's pathetic."

"I didn't come for revenge," Jonah says. "You still don't get it, do you?"

Another step. *He's going to rush me.* I see it in the tightly knitted tendons of his arms and neck, I feel it burning at the back of his mind.

"This is *our* world, Kyle," he says. "Yours and mine. Don't you see? I can make you a *king*! Give you anything you want. We're the only ones who really belong here."

"Nobody belongs here," I say.

"We do. We're going to make an incredible team, Kyle. You and me."

"Team?" I almost laugh. "You're messed up."

"You don't understand what I'm offering you, Kyle. We're on a mission from God."

"I don't want any mission."

Jonah grits his teeth. He's like an animal, all spit and anger and *need*. "I can see I'm not getting through to you."

Another step. But it's OK, I've got the measure of him this time. I don't care how strong he is, or even if Ose is right and all the evil things he's done have made him damn near invincible. I came pretty close to killing him once, I'm going to finish the job this time.

He springs forward.

I swing my golf club.

I time it perfectly.

I know, the minute my arm flexes and my shoulder comes around, that I've got him. The head of the club arcs towards him so fast he doesn't see it coming.

He didn't believe I'd do it.

It's going to cave his bloody skull in, I think.

But it doesn't.

Somehow, the long shaft of the golf club flexes and whiplashes and the heavy steel head pounds into his skull and … *misses*.

It's not possible. I *didn't* miss. It's like he's moved *through* the club, like he shrugged it off. He *chose* to ignore it, just like Ose said. And then he's on me.

"Kyle!" Farah screams.

I'm propelled backwards, the golf club knocked aside. I'm lifted by my shirt until my back slams against the wall and all the air rushes out of me.

I feel the point of Jonah's knife against my chest: a red-hot needle of pain pressing so hard that the skin gives way and the point settles against the slender blade of my sternum.

"It's time to meet your Maker, Kyle," he says. "I hope you're ready."

His weight shifts and I feel him tense as he presses back against my shoulder to brace himself.

He's not going to change his mind this time. He's going to kill me and that's going to be the end of it. Then…

THWACK!

Farah clouts him across the back of his head with the golf club. She hits him so hard she damn near pushes the knife right through me. She has to hop a little to stay on her feet. Jonah falls sideways against the wall. He stares back at her with hatred. Almost falls.

Then he uncoils and lunges forward with his knife.

I catch the moment, a freeze-frame that sears itself into my memory: the knife lost in Farah's stomach. Buried to the handle just under her ribs on the left side.

"*No!*" I shout.

It doesn't look real. It looks like some kind of trick knife with a collapsible blade, a child's toy. But I see Farah's eyes wide open and terrified.

She steps back and sits heavily on the sofa, still watching me, her hand clutched to her stomach. Something black and gelatinous like oil is pushing its way out from between her fingers.

I lunge for Jonah. With all that strength and grief and anger, I could kill him.

But there's no magic, not even in this world, and I'm no stronger than I was a moment ago. Jonah shrugs me off like I'm made of paper. He turns and slams me back against the wall.

Hi, I'm Kyle.

I'm weak.

He doesn't pause this time, not for a second, not for any grand farewell speech. He's done with all that. He brings the knife up to my chest and the point presses against my sternum and there's an instant of pain and then…

A meaty thud, like a friendly punch. Playful.

It doesn't even hurt.

But I can hear Farah screaming like she's a million miles away. I can see that the blade of the knife has gone cleanly into my chest and I can feel it growing inside me, filling me up. I can't breathe. It's like a weight holding my lungs closed, crushing me. There's a buzzing sound in my ears and the creeping purple-blackness at the edges of my vision and the sense of rushing that comes before a seizure.

And I know I'm dying.

FORTY

It's the unfilled space of a seizure that unnerves me the most.

I don't feel it when I hit the ground.

I don't feel it when I crack my skull or scald myself or knock out a tooth.

I don't dream.

Only on returning is there sometimes an impression … a memory. Of rushing, of falling, but mostly of blackness and, for me, noise. My seizures are always noisy.

Dying is a bit like that.

Except this time there is no return.

I die. But thinking doesn't end. Instead, the rushing goes on and on and my head fills with noise. A sound that's somewhere between a building site and a heavy metal band playing at full volume.

For now, I see through a glass, darkly.

Now I know in part; then shall I know even as I am known.

That phrase plays over and over inside my head. So does the memory of Benedict. *"Don't you want to dig a little deeper, Kyle?"*

And Jonah: *"Time to meet your Maker."*

Something is coming. Or rather, I am heading towards something.

And I'm terrified.

The fear is not human, not bounded by cortisol and adrenaline and an elevated heart rate. It's a cosmic fireball consuming everything in its path.

I wonder if this is hell, if this rushing, consuming terror is what "dead" is.

But then other thoughts come. Potent memories.

I remember.

I remember the morning of my seizure.

I remember that Mum had already gone to work when I woke up. I remember making tea and toast like any other morning. I remember sitting at the tiny kitchen table, eating, browsing my phone. I remember the note on the table catching my eye: "Early prayer meeting – see you for dinner. Exciting news!"

The panic is fresh, like I'm there. I watch myself searching through the piles of notes on Mum's table. Leaflets that Father Michael has printed on his inkjet, his badly drawn depictions of an X-rated hell. *What am I looking for?* The bible is not there, of course, she'll have taken that with her. Her notebook where she jots down her own interpretations and ideas about God is also gone. But there's something else … something that I've seen on this table and tried not to think about. Something that *should* be there and the fact that it's not is bad … bad … *bad*.

Then the memory clicks and it feels like falling off a cliff.

The forms!

The same kinds of forms Grandad had shown me in the garage. Forms with big official titles and OFFICIAL USE ONLY boxes:

ID1: Verify Identity – Citizen.

TR1: Transfer of Whole of registered title(s).

AP1: Notification of Change of Register.

I watch myself bolt into the garage and check the gap between the electricity cupboard and the wall. The deeds are gone. She found them. Then she got fresh versions of the forms she needed.

She was going to give the house to Father Michael.

Everything falls sharply into place. Mum's sense of anticipation that had been building for weeks. That terrible visit. After all those years of faith-dating, Mum had finally decided to settle down with God's Scholars.

I should have confronted her when I found the forms

weeks ago but I was too scared and too weak and I didn't want to face the truth and now it was too late.

"*I need you to step up, Kyle.*"

Well, sorry, Grandad, I kind of screwed that one up like you thought I would.

Just a signature in front of a witness, that's all it takes to give someone a house.

And Lacy would make a perfect witness.

"*Don't be fooled by our present circumstances, Kyle. I have big plans. I'm on a mission from God and your mother is going to help me.*"

As I die, I watch myself pacing around the house, trying to decide what to do. I need to go after Mum and stop her. But I'm too frightened to go outside.

I have to go. Even if I have a seizure, even if I have a panic attack.

I have to make her see sense.

I jam my phone into my back pocket and stare out of the window at the terrifying whiteness of the monochrome sky.

I don't believe I'm going to leave until the door has closed behind me.

I'm terrified. The world yawns open around me and I'm sure I'm going to pass out right then and there on my doorstep.

I watch this memory of myself, the me who doesn't know how badly wrong everything is going to go, and I feel proud. Because that version of me was doing something he really didn't want to do. He was terrified, but he did it anyway. It surprises me because I thought I'd only found those parts of me in the Stillness, but it turns out I'd already found them in the ordinary world as well.

Good to know.

Except here I am: dead.

About to meet my Maker.

I feel It all around me now. I taste burnt pennies in my mouth and it occurs to me, in a kind of dream-like whirl, that my auras were nothing but the feeling of God's breath bearing down on the back of my neck.

I'm not too keen on the idea of meeting God, if I'm honest. The timing sucks, because if I'm going to be judged, I have to admit I've killed more than my average number of people this week.

Maybe judged is the wrong word. I feel It now ... not judging me, *studying* me.

For now I see through a glass, darkly.

Now I know in part; then shall I know even as I am known.

I understand, now, what this place is. The ordinary world is on the wrong side of the glass and what we think we know is only a tiny part of the story. Now I'm on the right side of the glass and I know a hell of a lot more, but It gets to see me more clearly in return.

A question plays in my mind:

What are you?

But I'm not sure if *I'm* asking *It* or if *It* is asking *me*. Maybe I'm asking myself.

What are you?

Come to think of it, I actually don't care, I think.

The thing about being closer to the truth is that you get to see a lot of things more clearly than you did before.

Farah was right. I'm brave. I always was. Even if I have to go back to the version of me who wouldn't leave his bedroom, even if I forget every memory I ever had of this world, even if I forget Farah. I know now that I have the *capacity* to become this person again. A person who defends his friends. A person who faced Jonah, who fought back.

This is me; this is who I am.

Most people come to the Stillness to die. But not people with epilepsy. We come here the way some people go on a day trip to the seaside. We die like everybody else, but not in the Stillness. Not like this.

Jonah knew that.

FORTY-ONE

You know it's going to be a bad day when you wake and feel pavement against your face.

My first thought: *Oh, no, not again.*

Then, context: Hi, I'm Kyle. I'm seventeen. I have epilepsy. This happens to me a lot.

I'm lying face down, twisted like a fifty-storey splat, the pavement wet and cold and gritty beneath me—

Wait… Not pavement.

Carpet.

There's something vaguely medical about the long Formica worktops, the equipment in moulded white plastic boxes. I think, for a second, I've passed out in the clinic again.

Then I become aware of voices. Angry, impatient, mocking.

Context rushes back. I sit up and it feels like my body is returning from a million miles and a thousand lifetimes away. My shirt is torn and drenched in blood, I remember now that it's from where Jonah stabbed me in the chest.

Farah is on the sofa. She lies at a lopsided angle, her hand still clamped to her stomach. Jonah is standing over her, his legs astride hers. He's trying to pull her hand away from her side and she's struggling and moaning and trying to twist away from him. Chiu is crouched on the sofa nursing a bloodied nose. He must have gone for Jonah and Jonah knocked him away.

I stand.

I bend forward and pick up the golf club. Everything happens very slowly.

Farah leans forward and bites Jonah's forearm and he yelps and slaps her before returning his focus to getting her to move her hand.

"Let me look at it," he growls.

The wet sound of his hand against her cheek resonates in my head and constricts round my throat. I take an unsteady step forward. I can hardly stand.

But I do.

I shouldn't be able to sneak up on him like this. He knows I'm coming back. Maybe he doesn't expect it so soon. Maybe he thought after I met my Maker I'd see things his way. Maybe I've still got more tricks than even Jonah realizes.

I swing.

The momentum of the golf club almost pulls the rubber handle out of my grasp. But my aim is good and the heavy metal head springs round hungrily and connects with the side of Jonah's cheek. There's a heavy, bellyflop kind of sound and Jonah reels sideways and staggers to one knee. He turns, his eyes wide with fury and surprise and hatred.

I don't hesitate. I bring the club down into the centre of his forehead.

His mouth moves silently. He tries to close his eyes but the side of his face where I hit him doesn't move anymore and so one eye stays open, staring wildly at nothing, while the other eye does a kind of slow, grotesque wink.

Then the skull starts to crack and there's something crawling out ... a million somethings ... falling over each other, clambering out of each other, black and hateful. The skin sinks into the space left as they pour from his body and as quickly as they hit the air, they too split open and fade into the writhing mess. He begins to break: first his arm, then his chest. He falls backwards, cracking as more shapes pour from the remains.

Then he's gone.

Ashes to ashes, dust to dust.

Farah stares at me with wide eyes. Her fear is not normal fear. It's the same fear as my seizures: the inhuman, uncompromising fear of death.

"Let me see," I say.

She shakes her head.

"I'll cut it out," I say. "Whatever it is, I'll cut it out."

I take out my knife so she knows I'm serious. Tendons stand out on Farah's arm and neck from the strain of holding inside whatever it is that's trying to burst out. I catch a glimpse of it: black, bulbous, malignant. The fingers of her hand are being forced apart; I count six of them … maybe eight.

She's not going to live much longer. Not in this world.

"Come on," I say.

"I'm scared," she says.

"It'll be OK."

"I'm scared of losing you."

I shake my head. "I'm coming back for you, don't worry."

"Let's stay," Farah says. "Jonah's dead. I'll be OK. I'll be—"

She hisses with pain. I can see the fear overwhelming her, her old stubbornness coming back. *My god*, I think. *She's not going to move. All this, and she's going to stay here and I'm going to have to watch her die.*

"Come on," I urge her.

She shakes her head.

"Do you remember when I asked you out at the swimming pool all that time ago?" I say. She frowns, wondering why I'm on this now of all times. "Don't you think it was weird that I did it? Even though we'd hardly ever spoken to each other?"

"You were kind of a weird kid," Farah says.

"Sure. But … I knew, Farah. Don't you see? I didn't know how I knew, but I knew." I smile, delirious with the realization of it. "I didn't understand it until right now, but it was blindsight even then. Something made me ask you out even though I didn't know you at all. The point is, it was either a premonition, or a memory, or both. But I did it once, so I can do it again, OK?"

She smiles, lets her head fall back, nods weakly. I breathe a sigh of relief. I scoop her up. She's heavy and I'm not strong. Chiu rushes to my side and slides himself under one arm.

We stagger and I'm afraid we're going to drop her. We make our way down the corridor, Farah clinging tightly to Chiu with her right hand, her left hand pressed between us, holding the thing inside her.

We're so relieved when we see the MRI undamaged that we accidentally walk Farah's broken ankle into the door frame. She screams and I feel her nails dig into the back of my neck.

We half drop her on to the MRI table and she curls on to her side with her legs drawn up. The hand that's gripping her stomach is sprouting tendrils that look like roots reaching out in timelapse in search of water.

I look around, expecting to see Benedict, but he's not at the console. Panic strikes me. Something happened.

Something bad. And he's the only one who can operate the machine.

I see him and it's worse than I thought: he's on the floor, Abi kneeling over him.

I stare disbelievingly. "What happened?"

"That man … Jonah," Abi says. "He attacked him. It was … it wasn't human."

I see it now, Jonah sitting over the unconscious Benedict and pounding and pounding on him. *He didn't want to risk me leaving*, I think. He could have destroyed the machine but he knew that getting rid of Benedict was just as good and would keep his options open. Or maybe he preferred hurting a person to a machine.

"Is he … going to be OK?"

Abi pauses like she's checking him again. In the ordinary world he'd be dead, but here it's impossible to tell. "He's not changing," she says.

"I need to get Farah back," I say. "She's dying."

Abi gives a slight shake of her head. "He won't wake up."

The world rocks beneath me. I press my hands to my face. I want to scream but there's no air inside me. *We were so close!* Tears scald my eyes. We should have made it. We *deserved* to make it.

I want to crawl out of my own skin. I want to die again so I can go back to whatever it was and tear It apart for making us like this: just real enough to love but not real enough to last. Finite and fragile and exactly as It wanted us to be.

"Let me try," a voice says behind me.

I turn and for the first time I notice Ose standing like a shadow over by the far wall. I reach for my knife but he doesn't move towards me. His face is thoughtful, sad. He knows that I killed his friends – Tongue, Levi and Jonah – and yet he watches me calmly, almost kindly.

I flash my knife in his direction. "Don't move."

"Please," he says, holding his hands up. "I can help."

"Why?" I say. "You didn't want to help before?"

"I have enough blood on my hands. I did whatever it took to save my own skin. I think it's time I saved somebody else's for once."

I glance at Farah and she nods weakly. Ose goes to the console and starts typing. "It was all ready to go," he says. "It shouldn't be too hard."

The MRI makes its familiar humming noise as it cycles up. The bench gives a mechanical jerk as the servos kick in. Ose glances up at Farah. She's trembling, doing her best to stay still. She twists and catches my shirt with her free hand and pulls me towards her.

"Come and find me," she says. "Ask me and keep asking."

I nod. "Until you're sick of me."

Ose hits a key and Farah's body slides away from me, into the machine.

"How come you know how to make it work?" Chiu says.

"Microchips are not as complex as people think," Ose responds. "Once you have a sense of them, once you can *imagine* how they work…" He gives us an oddly self-satisfied smile. "Jonah always did underestimate me."

The bed slides and the discordant, rasping sound of the machine grows louder. I swear I don't look away, but suddenly Farah is not there, the machine is empty.

"Did it work?" I turn to stare at Ose and Abi.

Abi looks blank. "It got Devon back. We think."

"Chiu?" I say. "We don't know if the machine is really—"

"I'm going," Chiu says, without hesitation. "I'm done with this place. Anywhere has to be better than this." He looks at Ose. "Fire her up."

Not a moment's doubt, I think. *Brave, brave Chiu.*

Ose types and the bed slides back out and Chiu hops on. He gives me a broad, guileless grin like he's about to go on a fairground ride and has not a care in the world. "Hey, you come visit me too," he says.

"Of course I will."

"I won't remember you and I'll probably think you're a bit weird."

"I won't take it personally."

"Tell me … tell me about my leaf collection. Then I'll know you're for real."

"You collect *leaves*?" I say. "And you call *me* weird?"

Chiu looks like he might regret telling me. "No one knows."

He lies down and the machine does its thing, spinning its magnets and pulling and pushing at the cytoelectric rhythms of his brain in this world and maybe a dozen other worlds and a moment later he's gone.

His absence feels like I've been punched in the stomach.

"What about you?" I say to Abi. "This is your chance."

"I can't leave him," Abi responds.

"Your turn," Ose says.

I shake my head. "I'm staying too." I turn to Abi. "Benedict was working on the protocol, right – to help people remember? So if he recovers he might be able to finish his calculations. Figure out how to get me back without losing my memory."

"That could take years," Abi says.

"But it won't be years in the ordinary world."

"Probably not."

"Then it doesn't matter. I'll wait."

"No," Ose says firmly. "You have to go, Kyle. Now."

I look at him. I can see from the fear in his face that he knows something that I don't.

"What is it?" I say.

"Jonah's coming back. He won't let you leave."

I shake my head, disbelieving.

"I killed him," I say.

"Jonah has epilepsy just like you. He can't die in this

world either. Why do you think he took such a shine to you in the first place?"

Realization spreads through me like pins and needles. My legs feel like the blood has emptied out of them and I resist the urge to sit down.

Jonah has epilepsy.

Of course. How else would he know so much about this place?

I feel it now, the place where Jonah is still falling and falling but not falling. The place where he is not dead and not alive.

I feel him caught in rushing lucidity and raging terror.

How many times has Jonah made this journey?

How many times has he faced It?

I wonder how Jonah faces that feeling, whether he squares up to It just like he claims to, or if It is enough, finally, to bring him to his knees.

"I killed him once," I say. "I'll kill him again."

"No." Ose shakes his head firmly. "There is a time to fight and a time to run. This is your time to run, Kyle."

FORTY-TWO

I stare at the sliding bed where Farah lay only a few moments ago.

"If I go now, I might not remember," I say.

"If you stay, he will burn the machine just to watch your face."

"He'll know you helped me. He'll hurt you."

"I made my choices a long time ago," Ose replies. He smiles thinly. "But if you get on with it, I might still have time to get away."

I look around one more time, desperate. "What if I don't remember—"

"Go and get your girl," Ose says.

The thought solidifies inside me. *Go and get my girl? Sure, why not.*

"OK," I say, at last.

I lie back on the mechanical stretcher, my heart

tightening. I always hated these things. The bed jerks into action and I feel myself sliding towards the arched plastic casing of the main coil.

Jonah stands face to face with God. It's not the first time.

"Hold still," Ose murmurs.

The noise is getting louder and I can feel my thoughts falling over themselves.

I'm scared. Scared of not being in control, scared of not being *here*.

As someone with epilepsy, I always bring back a little of the Stillness whenever I have a seizure. The sound, the sense of movement, the rushing. I've lived this and dozens of other horrors that I only half remember.

If I make it, what am I going back to?

I'm brave. I always was. Even if I have to go back to the version of me who wouldn't leave his bedroom, even if I forget every memory I ever had of this world, I know now that I have the capacity to become this person again.

But I hope I remember. I promised Farah I would, and I need to go back and find her. I need to hold the idea of her, my love for her, clear and simple, in my mind.

Maybe we'll be lucky. Maybe the protocol Benedict keyed in for Vikram will work after all.

I hope I remember. I hope … I hope…

The noise fills my world and my thoughts begin to fall apart.

I think that I must be asleep because why else would I be lying with my eyes closed like this.

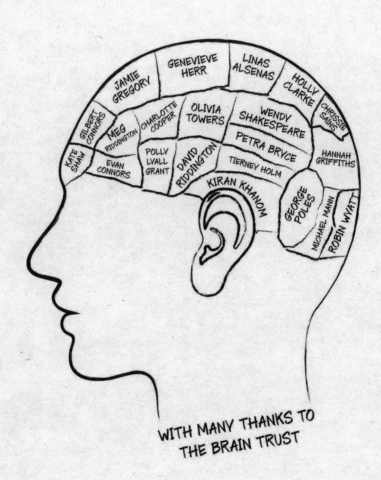

WITH MANY THANKS TO
THE BRAIN TRUST

A. Connors started his career as a physicist, building part of the Large Hadron Collider in CERN. He has also sold encyclopaedias in Chicago, worked for an investment bank, taught physics in Sudan, fitted emergency Wi-Fi in the refugee camps in Greece, and now works as an engineering manager in the Google Research team. He lives in Hertfordshire with his partner, two sons and a dog named Rosie.

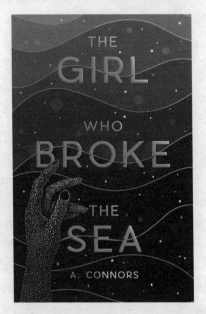

LILY'S EMOTIONAL PROBLEMS RUN DEEP – THREE MILES DEEP.

After she gets kicked out of school for her
destructive behaviour, Lily agrees to an unusual fresh
start: going with her mum to live at Deephaven, an
experimental deep-sea mining rig and research
station located at the bottom of the ocean.
Lily instantly regrets her decision: claustrophobic
and isolated, it's hardly her idea of home.

Turns out, Deephaven has problems of its own.
The head scientist, they quickly learn, has disappeared
– just as he was on the brink of a shocking discovery.
In the darkness of the deep, something is
stirring … something dangerous.
And it's calling out to Lily.